MOUNTAIN HOME

Books by Misty M. Beller

Hearts of Montana

Hope's Highest Mountain

Love's Mountain Quest

Faith's Mountain Home

HEARTS
— OF —
MONTANA
BOOK THREE

MOUNTAIN HOME

MISTY M.
BELLER

BETHANYHOUSE

a division of Baker Publishing Group
Minneapolis, Minnesota

© 2020 by Misty M. Beller

Published by Bethany House Publishers
11400 Hampshire Avenue South
Bloomington, Minnesota 55438
www.bethanyhouse.com

Bethany House Publishers is a division of
Baker Publishing Group, Grand Rapids, Michigan

Printed in the United States of America

Library of Congress Cataloging-in-Publication Data
Names: Beller, Misty M., author.
Title: Faith's mountain home / Misty M. Beller.
Description: Minneapolis, Minnesota : Bethany House Publishers, 2021. | Series: Hearts of Montana ; 3
Identifiers: LCCN 2020035713 | ISBN 9780764238116 (casebound) | ISBN 9780764233487 (trade paperback) | ISBN 9781493421725 (ebook)
Subjects: GSAFD: Christian fiction. | Love stories. | Western stories.
Classification: LCC PS3602.E45755 F35 2021 | DDC 813/.6—dc23
LC record available at https://lccn.loc.gov/2020035713

Scripture quotations are from the King James Version of the Bible.

This is a work of fiction. Names, characters, incidents, and dialogues are products of the author's imagination and are not to be construed as real. Any resemblance to actual events or persons, living or dead, is entirely coincidental.

Cover design by Kirk DouPonce, DogEared Design

Author is represented by Books & Such Literary Agency.

20 21 22 23 24 25 26   7 6 5 4 3 2 1

To my line editor, Jen Veilleux.
Your detail, your ability to strengthen any story line,
your kindness, and, above all, your patience
have blessed me beyond measure. I'm so grateful
to work with you!

For the LORD seeth not as man seeth; for man looketh on the outward appearance, but the LORD looketh on the heart.

1 Samuel 16:7b

ONE

LATE SEPTEMBER 1867
SETTLER'S FORT, MONTANA TERRITORY

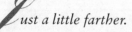*ust a little farther.*

Laura Hannon dared another step on the rock ledge that wrapped around the mountain. The flat space was just wide enough for a person to walk, as long as she stayed close to the stone mountainside on her right. The sheer drop on her left stole her midsection every time she allowed herself to look over the edge, so she kept her focus on the path in front of her. Of course, it would be impossible not to occasionally lift her gaze to take in the magnificent view of the mountain cliffs surrounding her.

This was why she'd come out here, after all. To escape into the beauty of the landscape. To remember that her problems were but a tiny dot compared to the vastness of the mountains God created. And yet, He cared about each one and loved her enough to help her through anything she might face. She paused to soak in that thought as she inhaled a deep breath of the cool, invigorating air.

Then she stepped forward again. Her boot slipped, skidding toward the edge of the cliff. Bits of loose stone skittered out from under her foot, tumbling off into empty air. With a squeal she scrambled to the right, throwing her weight toward the rock wall, away from the edge. She landed hard on her right foot, sending a jolt of pain through the ankle that had always been weak, ever since she broke it as a young child.

As she struggled to settle her trembling and still her racing heartbeat, she repositioned her feet onto solid stone. The right ankle held, only a little pain still throbbing through the joint.

Barely daring to breathe, she eased upright, pulling away from the cliff wall just enough to stand straight.

She took a deep breath, then eased the air back out. She was fine. She'd not fallen, and if she was careful, she could explore a bit farther before turning back.

Turning her face so the brisk wind fanned the loose tendrils away from her cheeks, she soaked in the crisp autumn air. This freedom was what she needed. Out in the beauty of these mountains, she could sense God's spirit. Feel the peace she couldn't seem to grasp anywhere else.

Even in the cooling temperature of late afternoon, perspiration beaded on her face. But the natural views and physical exertion were exactly what she needed to clear her head. To restore some semblance of peace to her raw nerves. She'd thought hiding herself away as an assistant in the doctor's clinic these last three months would soothe the lingering effects from the kidnapping.

At first, the peaceful atmosphere around the Bradleys' home and clinic had provided some healing. But lately, the walls had seemed to close in on her. Especially since every day, she helped care for one of the men who'd taken part in her kidnapping. Aaron hadn't been one of those scoundrels who'd hurt her. In fact, he'd actually tried to help her escape once during that awful ordeal, and he'd paid far worse for his part than she'd ever meant him to when she shot him. An accident that shattered his left thighbone and possibly rendered him unable to walk for the rest of his life.

She still battled the churning in her middle when she thought about the effect of that one single mishap. If she'd only taken a half second longer to focus her aim . . . if only Aaron hadn't dived for Rex to stop him from shooting her. She might have hit the man she'd intended to shoot—the one who'd been aiming his gun at her.

"God, help me move forward somehow," she whispered into mountain air.

After another moment relishing the breeze, she turned back to the path she'd been following. She inched her way along the ledge, circling the cliff's side as she stepped over crumbled leaves and mountain goat droppings. How wonderful to be one of the wild creatures who so easily perched on the side of this precipice, with a majestic view of treetops and distant peaks spread out as far as the eye could see.

Nothing but God's creation. This was a view she could take in for the rest of her life, forgetting about the town hidden below—and the man whose presence served as a constant reminder of what she so desperately wanted to leave behind.

A bird twittered in the distance, pulling her from her reverie, drawing her focus back to the path. Pressing close to the cliff on her right, she took tiny steps around the curving stone. Now that she'd finally broken loose from her obligations for an afternoon, the urge to do something daring grew stronger and stronger inside her.

The mountain goat trail climbed upward, through the crevice between a boulder on her left and the sheer mountain face on her right. Down onto another ledge, she stepped around a jagged stone protruding onto the path.

A black hole appeared in the cliff face beside her, stopping her midstride. A cave? She'd seen a few caves on her journey west from Missouri, and something about their mystery beckoned to her every time. What people or animals had taken refuge within? Outlaws? Bears? Mountain lions?

The opening sat low, only as high as her waist. Maybe this was only a deep indentation in the rock, not a true cave. She lifted her satchel strap over her head and bent low to peer inside. Darkness met her view, so black she couldn't see anything within. She reached out, expecting to brush cold stone. Her fingers touched only empty air.

She stretched her arm farther in. Still nothing. Maybe this was a cave. The ones she'd seen before all had tall openings and shallow insides, so she could see all the way in without entering. This opening seemed more like it led to a deep, dark den.

She jerked her hand back as her pulse leapt faster. It was still too early for bears to hibernate, but a mountain lion or any other manner of beast could be inside. Maybe she should move on.

But . . . her curiosity warred within her. She could at least light a match and peek inside. She wouldn't go far until she knew the place was empty.

Opening the possibles bag she tended to carry with her when she went out by herself, she fumbled past the pistol, the knife fastened in its sheath, and the leather-wrapped food. Finally, her fingers brushed the long, thin matchbox. Too bad she hadn't packed a candle. She'd only brought the matches in case she needed to light a campfire. After the last time she'd ventured out for a walk and ended up kidnapped for a week, she'd never be caught unprepared again.

It took a few tries to strike a small flame, and she held the light forward into the dark hole. The tiny glow illuminated the thick black, flickering off the rock wall on both sides for only a short distance before the wall on the left seemed to fall away.

Still bent low, she grabbed her satchel and inched forward into the darkness, extending the match in front of her. The opening was even deeper than she'd expected, and she shuffled several steps inside.

As though the spark of her match sprang twice its size, the dim, flickering light finally grew around her, opening up a cavern that stole her breath.

This massive room contained a ceiling that rose to at least twice her height. She stood and took in the expanse around her. To her right, the rock stretched beside her in a solid wall. But to her left, the cavern extended twice the width of her bedchamber back at the doctor's clinic. This entire place was probably the size of the cabin where she'd lived her first eighteen years.

Larger, even. She hadn't yet seen the back wall.

Stepping forward, she peered into the murky depths that her tiny match tried to illuminate. The heat at her fingers grew intense, drawing her focus back to the matchstick. She'd have to either drop the stub or blow it out.

She sank to her haunches, then rested the burning stump on the stone floor and reached into her bag for the matchbox. The flame from the first had almost burned out before she finally found a second match to light.

The new flame blazed to life, and she quickly rose and stepped farther into the cavern. To examine everything, she'd need a candle—or better still, a lantern. But at least she could see how far this cavern went before she used up all her matches. Maybe later she could come back with a better light. Exploring this cave was exactly the adventure her spirit craved.

As she advanced farther, something skittered across the floor. She lowered the light just in time to see a mouse scuttle over the stone, only an arm's length away. She barely held in her shriek, suppressing it quickly into a gasp. There was no telling what other animals might be in here. Too much sound could bring on an attack.

A scan with the light didn't show any more creatures. Nothing alive anyway. Plenty of dead insects littered the stone floor, along with leaves and who knew what else. She pressed the satchel and matchbox to her chest as she worked to gather the remnants of her courage.

A little farther ahead, strange spiky rocks came into view, some hanging from the high ceiling with tips pointing downward, others rising up from the floor to point upward. In one place, the upper and lower spikes met in a narrow column, no thicker in the middle than her thumb.

With her next step, the floor dropped out from under her, and she barely caught herself as the stone sloped downhill. She held the match low to better see the ground. The descent steepened in only that one place, dropping about the height of a porch step.

She eased forward carefully, then reached in her case for another match. She'd only brought five with her, so she wouldn't be able to stay much longer. But she still couldn't see the end of the cavern. The flame ate away at the match quickly, and she scrambled to ready a new stick for lighting.

"Miss Hannon?"

She spun at the sound of a masculine voice behind her. At the same moment, the flame reached her fingers, singeing her skin with its fiery touch. She flung the match, dropping her satchel as she scrambled. Her feet tangled beneath her, and the box of matches slipped from her fingers. She struggled to keep her balance. The uneven stone caught her boot, but her body was already twisted in its effort to stay upright.

With a cry, she fell forward onto her knees, the stubborn boot of her right foot stuck in a dip in the uneven stone floor. Her hands caught her from falling even more, and she braced herself on hands and knees for a suspended heartbeat. She had to get up, had to know who stood at the entrance of the cave. A man who knew her name.

Her mind flashed back to the last time she'd been discovered. The fierce anger on Bill's face when he spotted her trying to hide in the bushes. The rage in his eyes as he'd stalked forward. She'd been desperate to get away, grabbing little Samuel's hand and clambering down the bank toward the stream. But her skirt had caught on a tree, slowing her down just enough for Bill's meaty hand to grip her. The pain in his clutch radiated through her arm and up her shoulder. The ropes they'd tied her in had cut into her wrists, leaving scars that still ached with memory.

But it wasn't her arm or wrists that hurt now. She blinked, fighting her best to return to the present.

Her knees. Her ankle. Had she injured anything else?

"Miss Hannon?"

She jerked her head up at the voice drawing nearer. Who had found her? And why?

"Are you injured?"

The voice sounded familiar but . . . it wasn't Bill. Bill was gone. Dead. Hanged for shooting the sheriff. She struggled to orient herself to the present.

The silhouette of a man appeared in the cave opening. Recognition washed over her.

"Nate Long?" Her pounding heart didn't know whether to speed up or slow down at his presence. Why was the brother of one of her patients following her into the mountains, a good half-hour's hike from town?

14

Besides, this man wasn't *just* the brother of a patient. He'd also been a member of Bill's gang.

Only . . . Nate hadn't been there when she and Samuel were kidnapped. He hadn't been one of the men planning to hurt her. When he'd discovered the crime, he spoke out against Bill and Rex's horrible plans—even tried to free her and then had been tied up right along with them.

Still, he'd ridden with those vile men for years and taken part in their lawless robberies.

Since the band had been captured and Nate freed to make restitution, he'd seemed like a changed man. In truth, she sometimes had trouble believing he could have committed the crimes he'd been accused of. He'd spent countless hours at his brother's side, taking over her role as nurse when he could and doing his best to keep up Aaron's flagging spirits.

But why was Nate *here*? Had he followed her? For what purpose?

The match she'd dropped flickered out, blanketing the cave in darkness, save for the light filtering in from the small opening. Pinned between a cavern and a criminal, her heart hammered enough to nearly force its way out of her chest.

"Are you hurt?" Nate had paused just inside the cave. He probably couldn't see more than thick blackness inside, what with his eyes not yet adjusted from the light outside.

The question brought to life the ache in her legs, the pain in her right ankle. Pushing her weight more on her hands, she eased that foot out of the dip in the rock that had snagged it, and the action sent a knife of agony through the joint.

She did her best to quash the groan in her throat as her limb seemed to light on fire.

"You *are* hurt. Miss Hannon, what can I do to help?" Nate's tone echoed with worry, and he shuffled forward. Laura could see the outline of his hands waving in front of him against the light behind him.

"What are you doing here?" Hopefully he would only hear the determined demand in her voice, not the edge of fear she was trying to suppress. Being alone with a man this far from town brought back too many vicious memories of that last time. Panic climbed up her chest, but she forced herself to stay calm.

Pushing down the pain in her leg, she shifted her hand over the floor until she brushed the fabric of her satchel, then quietly rooted around inside and found her pistol. Over these past quiet months at the doctor's office, she'd come to think of Nate very differently than before—almost to trust him—but she couldn't be too careful. Not in this remote place with no other person near enough to hear a scream.

"I'm sorry, I didn't mean to frighten you. I was leaving work at the mine, and I had just reached the base of the mountain when I saw you slip on the rock ledge. I was coming up to make sure you weren't injured, then saw you duck into this cave. Where are you hurt? Have you any more light?" His voice rang so earnest, so concerned. The tension in her nerves eased.

Yet she couldn't seem to still the galloping in her chest.

"I'm not hurt." Her leg screamed that the words were false, but she couldn't let him know she'd been weakened.

Couldn't put herself at a disadvantage. "My matches spilled. Go back outside, and I'll be there as soon as I gather them."

"Are you sure?" His voice hesitated, sounding concerned. "Can I carry something for you?"

"I have it." With the pistol and satchel in one hand, she scooped up the matches and their case, then shoved them in her bag. Nate might not mean harm, but she would only feel safe when they were around other people. And it didn't seem he would leave until she proved she could manage on her own.

She straightened her skirts and shifted her feet to stand, but moving the right boot sent a shot of pain through that ankle. Gritting her teeth, she raised up, keeping her balance mostly on her left side.

With her first step, she bit back a cry. The ankle didn't buckle, but she had to lock her jaw against the pain coursing through her.

"Miss Hannon?" Nate's tone came out tentative. "I won't hurt you, I promise. I only want to make sure you're safe. Let me help."

She shifted her leg to attempt to walk up the incline toward the entrance. Her right leg protested, so she dropped her hands to the floor and tried to walk on all fours, at least until she made it through the cave opening. With the revolver and satchel in one hand, the position proved extremely awkward, but she was able to move forward. Good thing the darkness hid her posterior raised up in the air. No need to add insult to injury.

She made it to where Nate stood, but she may as well

continue all the way outside before facing him, since she'd have to duck under the low cave opening anyway. He stepped aside to allow her to pass.

The bright sunlight pierced her eyes, forcing a squint as she waddled out of the entrance and used the cliff wall to help her stand. While Nate emerged behind her, she slung the satchel strap over her head and moved the revolver to her shooting hand. She kept the gun down by her side, almost hidden in her skirt. No need to draw attention to the weapon, but she'd have it ready if she needed to defend herself.

After ducking out of the cave, Nate straightened and turned to her. Black dirt smudged his face, the edges of his hairline curling a darker brown with dried sweat. He must be telling the truth about having just come from his work in the mine. Evening lit the western sky, so the timing would be right.

His gaze slid down the length of her, snagging on the gun at her side, then returned to her face. "Please don't be afraid. Is your foot injured?"

"Only a slight twist of my ankle. I'll take it slow going back, so you've no need to worry about me."

His brows lowered. "Are you sure?" The earnest concern in his green eyes made her hesitate. But only for a heartbeat.

Even if he could be trusted, she needed to be independent. If life had taught her nothing else these past few years, she'd learned that lesson all too well. She gave a decisive nod. "I'm certain." If she had to crawl all the way back to town, she'd manage.

He motioned to the path beyond her, that thin ribbon of flat rock she'd followed to reach this place. "Go ahead, then."

She wouldn't be able to walk without a strong limp, and there was no sense in calling attention to her injury. "I'll come behind you." She raised her chin and leaned against the rock wall to allow him space to pass. Then she waved the same direction he had.

The breath he blew out made his frustration clear, but he straightened and marched forward. Their clothing almost brushed as he slid past her on the narrow ledge, and she caught the scent of a long, hard workday. And maybe a hint of damp mustiness from the mine.

He strode about ten steps down, then stopped and looked back at her. "I can't leave you stranded here."

Of course he couldn't. Nate had always seemed the kind of man who couldn't resist being responsible for those around him. Especially those weaker.

She would have to show him she could walk.

Lord, make my ankle strong. Please.

With one hand on the cliff beside her to help bear her weight, she gripped the pistol in her other and took a tentative step forward. Using the rock wall for support, she managed to traipse along the flat stone path, one painful step at a time.

When they reached the place where the stone ledge ended and the grassy downhill slope began, her screaming ankle forced her to pause. Nate had stayed just in front of her, casting anxious looks back at her, and he stopped now, too.

Without the cliff wall for support, the distance between this mountain and the town—what had been only a half-hour's brisk walk— now stretched interminably. She'd never arrive at the clinic before dark at the pace she'd managed these past minutes. And without support to keep some of the weight off her ankle . . .

Nate moved to her side. "Hold on to my shoulder."

Maybe she should resist, but the pain shooting up her leg had numbed her better judgment. Without a word, she raised her right arm, and he slipped into place beside her. He stood almost a head taller than she did, so he had to bend in order to wrap his arm around her waist.

The warmth of his closeness should have put her on edge, but something about his manner eased her fear as they took their first tentative steps.

Slowly, they progressed over the rocks she'd clambered up so easily before. It seemed to take at least half an hour just to get back to firm soil. They certainly wouldn't reach the clinic before nightfall.

A root of fear poked through her pain. Would it be dangerous to be out with him after dark? She pressed the thought down. It couldn't be any more dangerous than in daylight. And Nate hadn't done anything to give her the slightest alarm since they'd left the cave. In fact, he was going through a great deal of trouble to help her. She focused on breathing steadily, doing everything she could to calm her irrational thoughts.

Her arm ached from clinging to his shoulder. Which wouldn't be so bad if her ankle didn't feel as though someone pounded it with an iron mallet during each step.

"Let's stop a minute so you can rest." Nate motioned to a fallen tree.

"I don't need to rest. Ingrid and the doctor will worry if

I'm not back by dark." Ingrid had assumed the role of older sister these past few months Laura had lived with them and worked in the clinic.

He helped her take another agonizing step. "If I go to them for help, will you wait here?"

The thought stiffened her spine. As much love and gratitude as she'd developed for Ingrid and Doc Micah, she couldn't always be turning to them for help. In those first weeks after the kidnapping, she'd let herself rest under the shadow of the Bradleys' protection and nurturing care, but she'd let that condition continue far too long. She had to stand on her own two feet now—very literally, in this case.

She shook her head. "Let's keep going."

He didn't speak again for a long while, just kept his steady presence there to support her. The longer she gripped his shoulder and leaned against him, the easier it was to imagine what it would be like to have someone to lean on any time she needed it.

Ingrid and the doctor had been gifts from God, but sometimes their nurturing felt a little . . . smothering. If only she had someone who was there beside her when she needed them, yet not overbearing. A partner.

Just the way her brother Will had been.

A fresh pain stabbed at her, but this time nearer her heart. Her brother would never be there to walk alongside her again. No one could ever take his place, but the gentle touch of the man now bearing part of her weight made this one situation better at least.

But thoughts like that would only get her into trouble.

TWO

Nate Long needed to say something to distract himself. To distract them both—Miss Hannon from her pain and him from the way having this woman pressed against him was bringing his whole body to life.

He scrambled to think of a topic, and finally settled on what he'd wanted to ask her before he stupidly scared her into injuring herself. "I never knew that cave was there. I only got a glimpse before your match went out, but the inside looked larger than I expected."

Miss Hannon's breathing came in rough inhales and exhales, a testament to the pain she was clearly trying to hide. She may not be able to talk through her suffering. If not, he would have to fill in the gaps—that is, if he could get his head straight.

"This was the first"—she winced as her injured limb snagged on a stick "—time I've been up here."

"So you were just discovering the cave when I came by? It's only a few minutes' walk from the mine. I'd heard there were chokecherry bushes nearby, so I thought I'd get a snack and a closer look at the mountain before heading to the clinic. Then I saw you and was only going to say hello until you slipped. I was afraid you might need help." He was rambling, but at least he'd filled the air with words. Anything to take her mind off her pain.

She didn't respond, so he reached for something more to add. "Could you tell what those things hanging inside the cave were? I only caught a quick look."

"Some kind of . . . rock formation . . . I think." She spoke between breaths as she limped forward.

"I'd like to come back with a lantern and see more. Is there only that one cavern?" When he'd find time to come back, he had no notion. He worked every hour they'd allow him to at the mine, and whatever waking hours remained, he tried to spend with Aaron. His brother had no one else to keep his spirits up.

"Don't know." Miss Hannon gulped in a breath. "Didn't see . . . the end."

They'd reached the well-worn wagon path from the mine to Settler's Fort, and he turned them toward the town. "I wonder if there are many caves in this area. Natural ones, I mean. Not made by miners." He spent more than enough time in those dank spaces where blasting powder had blown away the inside of the mountain. Seeing all the natural layers of rock and mineral was interesting, but hours of chipping through stone could weary a man's body.

At least it is honest work, though. That thought was one he'd never grow tired of.

A distant sound pricked his ears. "Stop for a minute." He slowed his pace but kept his arm around her waist. A nicely curved waist, but he pushed that thought aside as he strained to hear the distant sound.

Behind them, the jingle of a harness was joined by the grinding of wagon wheels and the many creaks of a wooden buckboard. They both turned to look, and soon enough, a pair of tired bays came into view, pulling one of the mine wagons. A man in a wide-brimmed hat appeared behind the horses, perched atop the bench.

"I'm sure Hiram will give us a ride. Does that suit you?" He glanced at the woman beside him. Her pretty face had flushed red from exertion. But she was breathing a little easier now that they'd stopped for a minute.

Her eyes lifted to his, and those wide brown orbs struck him in the chest, just like they always did when she looked at him. He'd never been immune to her beauty, not since that first time he saw her all those months ago. He could still feel the fury coursing through his veins when he realized what his jug-headed companions had done—kidnapping an innocent woman and boy just to cover up their robbery gone horribly wrong.

That long-familiar knot pulled tight in his gut. He might never be free of the awful feeling that came when he thought of those past choices. God had forgiven him, but truly putting the past behind him was a whole other matter.

Thank the Lord the good people in Settler's Fort had extended him grace along with the sentence he'd been handed for his crimes. As soon as he earned enough to finish paying back the people their gang had wronged, he'd truly be free to start a new life.

"Ho there." Hiram Mathers reined in the team beside them. The man didn't even raise an eye at the way Nate had his arm wrapped around the pretty lady, but he felt he should explain quickly.

"Glad you came along. Miss Hannon here has an injured leg." He nodded down to her right boot. "I was trying to help her back to town to the doctor's clinic, but it'd be a sight easier if you have room up there for her to ride." As far as he could tell, the wagon bed was mostly empty. Hiram must be on his way back to town from delivering supplies to the mine.

The man removed his hat and wiped a grimy sleeve across his damp brow, leaving a smear of dirt on his forehead. "'Course. You wanna sit up here or in the back?" Hiram wasn't long on social graces, but the man seemed a decent sort.

The bench seat was raised up on springs but wouldn't give Miss Hannon much room to stretch out her injured leg. Nate was pretty sure the ankle was sprained but not broken, since she was able to move the limb. Keeping it raised while she rested would be what she needed most.

"The back is fine. Thank you." Nate helped her hobble around the wagon, then let her balance herself while he lifted off the rear gate. "Can you climb up?"

She turned and braced her hands on the wagon bed to hoist herself up, but sheer exhaustion weighed her features as she paused to summon strength. He moved forward to help. "I'll lift you up."

She didn't object as he reached a hand under her legs and one behind her back, then eased her up into the wagon. She was lighter than he'd have thought, and she didn't look at him as she arranged her skirts.

"Thank you." Her mumble was barely loud enough for him to hear.

He nodded in response, then stepped away from the wagon.

She finally raised her eyes to him. "Aren't you going to ride?"

He glanced up at Hiram, who had turned to watch them from his perch.

"I guess I might as well." In truth, his body was beyond weary from the day's hard work underground. "We're heading to the same place, after all."

Miss Hannon shifted her skirts again to clear a place for him, and he slid into the spot, hanging his legs off the back.

"You folks hang on," Hiram called from above, then turned away from them. "Move on, gals. We're almost done fer the day."

The ride into town was a noisy, bumpy affair, what with the jostling, creaking, and jangling of the wagon. But at least Nate didn't have to struggle to keep a one-sided conversation. He'd have liked to turn and watch Miss Hannon, but that would be impolite for certain. Even with his and Aaron's spotty upbringing being passed from one unwilling family member to another, he'd been taught not to stare. Had it pounded into him by way of a stick against his backside, in fact.

A few fellow miners raised friendly hands to wave as Hiram drove through the town's main street toward the clinic. Nate nodded in greeting, as well, and at last the man reined in the team in front of the building that had become far too familiar these past months.

The clinic door opened as Nate jumped to the ground and turned to help Miss Hannon. The doctor's wife stepped onto the porch and paused to study them. She gasped when her gaze landed on the woman gingerly lowering her injured leg off the back of the wagon. "Laura, what happened?"

"It's only a sprain." Miss Hannon's voice dragged with exhaustion. "Naught to worry over."

She reached up to hold on to his shoulder, and he slipped his arm around her waist. Having her tucked beside him like this now felt perfectly natural. As though they'd walked together like this for years.

"Shall I get the walking sticks?" Mrs. Bradley moved down the stairs as she spoke.

"No." Miss Hannon waved off the suggestion.

The lady sure could be stubborn.

With the doctor's wife at Miss Hannon's other side, they worked their way up the stairs. On the porch, Nate glanced back at Hiram, still watching them from his bench. The man hadn't offered to climb down from his perch to help, but maybe he'd sat up there so long his legs no longer worked. Still, without his timely arrival, Miss Hannon would have endured a great deal more pain.

Nate nodded to the man. "'Preciate it, Hiram. See you tomorrow."

With a parting wave, the driver snapped his reins and called to the team, "Move on, gals."

Mrs. Bradley pushed open the door and stepped in first, still holding Miss Hannon's other arm. "Micah will be home any minute. He went to check on a patient on the other side of town. Let's take you straight to your room." She motioned down the hall, probably for Nate's sake. "It's that middle door on the left."

The center hallway spanned the depth of the house, with several doors along either side. He knew well that the first door on the right opened to an examination room. That was where the doctor had ushered Aaron when they'd arrived in town, his brother in agony with a shattered thighbone, another bullet in his shoulder, and almost lifeless from so much lost blood.

On the left side of the hall, he was pretty sure that the first door opened to a storage room of sorts. And the next door was where his brother would be, the chamber he'd been holed up in for three months now as his leg healed. Lord willing, he'd soon be set free.

The doctor's wife led them to the door down the hall from Aaron's. As she pushed it open, a quick glance inside showed a flowery quilt on the bed. Nate paused. Maybe he shouldn't go in there.

Miss Hannon looked up at him, and her face formed a weak smile. "I can make it from here. Thank you, N—Mr. Long. For everything."

For a split second, it sounded like she'd been about to call him by his given name. Part of him longed to hear it in her sweet voice. *Mr. Long* sounded so foreign to him. No one had ever called him or Aaron by such a formal address. And it wasn't as if they'd known their father, who might have been called such. Not the deadbeat who hadn't had enough respect for their mother to marry her after getting her with child.

So no, he'd really rather not hear Miss Hannon call him something the slacker who sired him might have been named.

He pulled his arm from around her waist and moved it to her elbow. "Call me Nate." *Please*.

She nodded. "Thank you, Nate." Then she turned and limped toward the bed, Mrs. Bradley helping her with each step.

As much as he wanted to linger nearby, he should leave her to Mrs. Bradley's capable care. Miss Hannon surely wouldn't be able to rest with a strange man hovering around her.

A strange man. That was most likely the way she saw him, but before he could start to feel too sorry for himself, he turned away. Aaron was waiting for him, as he was every evening. Nate's time would best be spent trying to bolster his brother's low spirits.

He turned toward the closed door. If only Aaron would keep the room open, he could be more a part of the goings-on in the house and clinic. Mrs. Bradley had offered that option so many times. Those in the clinic surely saw the depths of his brother's moods even more than Nate did, since they were with him throughout the day as they brought food and emptied the chamber pot.

He tapped Aaron's door. "It's me." He reached for the handle and pushed. No snore sounded from inside, so he was probably awake. Aaron had always been a snorer, but with the extra weight he'd gained from lying abed these past months, the sound was growing stronger.

Aaron's bedcover lay flat, the pillow fluffed in readiness. Nate's gaze moved to the chair by the window. His brother reclined against the overstuffed cushion, his casted leg stretched across the footstool.

Nate stepped into the room and settled on the edge of the bed, taking in the downturn of his brother's mouth and the pallor of his skin. "How you feelin' today?"

"Ready to get this confounded cast off."

Nate let a smile tip his mouth. The same question, same response they went through every evening when he came by after work. "Ready to skin a bobcat?"

Aaron snorted. "Any time now."

Now he sent his brother a full-on grin. Each time, he tried to come up with something different to ask for that second question. Something that would bring back pleasant memories from their younger days. *Ready to ride a horse? Ready to go carp fishing? Ready to sleep under the stars?* He had to keep Aaron focused on the good times they'd have once his leg healed and he wasn't locked indoors.

But Aaron's expression lifted only for a second, falling again as his eyes turned hard and his mouth sealed.

Nate leaned forward, propping his forearms on his knees. "I talked to McMillan about starting to train me on the big powder." The blasters earned half again as much as regular laborers. He could cut a fourth off the time it would take him to pay off their debt.

Of course, it wasn't only his debt he was working off. The whole gang had taken part in the robberies, but since Rex had been shot dead when they were apprehended and Bill had been hanged for killing the sheriff in Settler's Fort, he and Aaron were left to make restitution to the many folks and businesses they'd picked off. Until Aaron was back on his feet, the work was up to Nate.

But he'd take the long, backbreaking days as long as his brother was safe and they could both have clean consciences when they lay down to sleep each night.

"That's good. When do you start?" The flatness in his brother's tone stole any eagerness out of the words.

Nate made sure his own voice held enough enthusiasm for the both of them. "As soon as they finish the stretch they're working on now in the new shaft. Then one of the blasters should have time to train me. Another couple days, probably."

"Hmm . . ." His brother didn't seem inclined to ask questions, so Nate brought out the other interesting tidbit he had to share.

"When I was leaving the mine tonight, I found a bit of excitement." As he unrolled his tale about the cave, he caught a glimmer of interest in Aaron's eyes.

But as soon as he spoke Miss Hannon's name, his brother's expression darkened. Even though it seemed like the two had formed an uneasy truce, Aaron still hadn't forgiven her for firing the bullet that wrecked his leg. No matter that she'd been aiming for another man—Rex, the one pointing his pistol at her.

They still weren't sure if Aaron's leg would heal enough for him to walk again, and his brother struggled to keep from sinking into melancholy during the endless days of pain and uncertainty.

"So now Mrs. Bradley's helping her get settled in her room." As he finished his tale, Nate leaned back, propping his hands on the bed behind him for support.

Aaron's frown deepened. "I guess now she'll get a taste of what it's like to be locked up day after day."

Nate raised his brows. "They don't keep your door locked."

"Might as well. Can't go anywhere."

"How about if I move your chair out to the porch?" The sun had set, but the fresh air would be good for Aaron.

"Too much trouble."

Nate worked to keep the frustration from his voice. "I don't mind."

Aaron gave him a pointed look. "Too much trouble *for me*. Leg hurts enough as it is."

Nate leaned forward again, letting Aaron see the earnestness on his face. "Then what can I do to help? I know it's hard sitting here day after day. What can I do to make it better for you?"

A flash of grief crossed Aaron's face, and Nate felt the crushing weight of it in his own chest. "I just want to walk again. If I can't . . ."

He broke off the sentence, but Nate knew what he feared. The thighbone had been broken in so many pieces, even a skilled doctor like Micah Bradley couldn't promise the limb would work effectively when Aaron was finally freed from his cast. At least Aaron didn't complain about the wound in his shoulder anymore. That bullet hadn't struck bone, only flesh.

And also hadn't been inflicted by Miss Hannon.

Nate gripped his knee as he willed his brother to hear him. "You will walk again, Aaron. We have to believe it. Keep praying God will mend the bone. He wants the best for us, the Bible says it."

Aaron's mouth sealed shut again. Since that day right after they'd been brought to Settler's Fort, when Nate had knelt beside Reverend Vendor in the little church at the edge of town and given his heart to the God he'd longed to know all his life, he'd been talking to Aaron about faith and how much it had opened up his life.

Aaron had never spoken a word against Nate's change of heart, but his silence when Nate talked of faith made his spirit ache. Surely Aaron would come to believe soon. Since the day they were born, twenty-eight years before, they'd done everything together. Watched out for each other when they were passed from one family member to another after their mother died, then later when their foolish choices forced them to stay two mountain peaks ahead of whatever lawman chased them at the time.

Now, it could only be a matter of time before Aaron chose to step into faith with him. The peace of knowing he was forgiven from their crimes—both the big ones and those that seemed insignificant at the time—was the biggest blessing God could bestow.

Unmerited grace.

Aaron turned lifeless eyes toward the window. "You better get to your camp. It's full dark out." Then he nodded toward the bedside table. "There's a biscuit in that top drawer."

Nate reached out and pulled the handle. A faint yeasty aroma greeted his nose, tightening the pinch in his belly. "Thanks." He'd wait until he was on the road before he indulged. Since he put every pinch of his gold-dust wages toward their debt, he was doing his best to live without any personal expenses. He slept under a buckskin canopy in the woods and ate the meat and berries he could forage, along with whatever Aaron saved him from the daily meals here in the clinic.

From the looks of the slight paunch of Aaron's belly, his brother wasn't setting aside as much as he could. But eating probably helped pass the forever-long hours, so he couldn't begrudge Aaron the food. Couldn't ever seem to begrudge him anything, really.

The tie that bound them as twins was the one constant in the uncertainty they'd survived through. But as the elder brother by ten minutes, Nate felt the greater responsibility to keep them both alive and well.

He'd not done so well at that when Aaron had been shot, but maybe it was simply God's way of getting their attention. Of bringing them onto the straight and narrow. Now Nate just needed to help guide his brother all the way onto that right path.

He rose and squeezed his brother's shoulder. "Want me to help you back to the bed before I go?"

Aaron shrugged, and probably didn't mean the motion

to shake Nate's hand off his shoulder, but Nate removed it anyway. "Nah. Doc said he'd be back a little after dark to do it."

If only Aaron would let him help more. But he seemed to prefer for Doc Bradley to do the physical lifting when he needed it, such as moving him from bed to chair or using the chamber pot.

He supposed a man should be allowed his pride.

With a final farewell, Nate stepped from the door. He paused in the hall to let his brother's melancholy mood slide off him. The murmur of female voices drew his notice down to Miss Hannon's chamber.

He'd like to know for sure she was settled in, that her injury wasn't worse than a sprain. But he should leave her to rest in peace.

Peace. A feeling he craved every day. Even now that he'd found forgiveness, the full measure of peace still seemed just beyond his grasp.

What more would it take to find that elusive goal?

THREE

$\mathcal{L}$aura kept the walking sticks nearby as she limped around the examination room, damp cloth in hand. Doc Micah had been taking patients all morning, and even though he cleaned up after himself, the place needed a thorough scrubbing at least every day or two. At least Doc Micah didn't make as much mess as Dr. Stanley had, but the older physician had left Settler's Fort at the end of summer when his health began to decline. She couldn't blame him for wanting to spend the rest of his days nearer his children and grandchildren.

But now all the doctoring fell on Doc Micah's shoulders, and Laura did her best to help wherever she could. It was the least she could do in return for the room and board, as well as the safety, that the doc and Ingrid gave her. But since she'd been forced to stay in bed the day before with her injured leg propped up, she'd not been able to do this task that normally fell to her. Ingrid would have taken it on gladly, had she been in her usual condition.

Laura couldn't help a grin.

She and Doc Micah had a baby coming. What joy would fill the Bradleys' home and clinic. An infant would add a fair amount of work to Ingrid's life, making Laura's help all the more needed both in the clinic and with household duties. Was helping the sick and injured the purpose she'd been looking for? The fresh start—the new life—she'd craved? Maybe. Unfortunately, God hadn't sent a host of angels to fill the sky as He'd done with the shepherds at the birth of Jesus.

Make my path clear, Lord.

"Miss Hannon?" Doc Micah called from the hallway.

"Yes?" She laid the cloth on the work counter, then propped the walking sticks under her arms.

"Would you be able to come in here and sit while you assist me?" He appeared in the doorway, but seeing her already hobbling toward the door caused the strong lines of his face to tighten with concern. "I'm not sure you should be up and about so much. I'll do the cleaning when I finish with Aaron."

"My leg is much better." Laura waved him off. Thankfully, this didn't seem to be a full sprain. Already the swelling had gone down. With poor Ingrid usually either in bed or emptying the contents of her stomach into a washbasin, the doctor would have his hands full for the coming weeks.

Laura straightened and pressed on a smile through the pain. She had to carry as much load as she could. If not, Doc Micah would likely shoulder all the work, whether it was too much for one man to manage or not.

"I'm preparing to cut the cast from Mr. Long's leg. If you can sit nearby and be ready to assist as needed, I'd appreciate it. You should be able to stay seated the whole time." His gaze weighed heavily on her, judging whether this job would be too uncomfortable for her to take part in.

Likely his worry was not mainly about her ankle, but whether the sight of the wound would turn her stomach. Nay, the challenge in this role would be whether she could force away her guilt over the fact that she'd been the one to inflict the awful shattering of bone, the mangling of flesh, the loss of so much lifeblood that he'd taken weeks to regain proper coloring. Even now, Aaron maintained a pallor that proved he wasn't well, neither in body nor soul.

Though her insides churned, she forced in a steadying breath and nodded, avoiding the doctor's eyes. "Certainly."

"Come along if you're sure, then." He waited for her to swing past on the walking sticks, then fell into step behind. The devices were cumbersome and pressed hard into the tender flesh under her arms. Ingrid had said this was the exact pair she'd used when her leg bone had been crushed in a wagon accident on her journey to Settler's Fort.

Apparently, that injury was when she'd first met the doctor, and the story Ingrid told of that journey seemed almost too fantastic to be believable. But the love between the pair that had grown out of the adventure drifted like a sweet mist through their home.

Laura held in a sigh. If only she could find a man who looked at her—who treasured her—the way Doctor Micah Bradley regarded his wife. If she could be married to such a man, working alongside him toward a common goal, would she then find the meaning in life she so desperately wanted?

But she hadn't found that elusive man, and she refused to put her life on hold until she did—*if* she did. She had to pursue meaningful work on her own. Had she found her purpose here at the clinic? Some days it felt that way, but other times . . .

"Here she is." The doctor's voice filled the small bedchamber as they entered. "Now we can get started."

Aaron sat on the bed, his casted leg extending in front of him. A clean blanket had been placed under the limb, probably to catch stray plaster and other bits that fell away as they removed the cast. The other tools lay in a neat array at the foot of the bed, including a saw that looked as though it could slice through bone as easily as plaster. Laura cringed at the thought.

A quick glance at Aaron's face showed his jaw was a hard line, and his skin held an even paler hue than usual. He had to be nervous. Removing the cast would show them how well the bone was healing. Whether the leg would heal well enough to bear his weight, or if he'd forever be confined to a chair and walking sticks.

Dear God, let the bone have healed. Please.

If she'd forever maimed this man and altered the course of his life with her single quick reaction, could she ever forgive herself? Would Aaron ever forgive her?

Being around Aaron these last months had been hard enough, but at least she'd been able to help care for him. Small acts of penance, but something still.

Yet, if he could never walk again . . . how could she make that up to him? What if he ended up like Robbie? *Oh God.*

An image flared in her mind of the stump that had replaced her brother's leg, then his lifeless body after he chose to end it all. She had to keep Aaron from spiraling like her little brother had. No matter what she had to do.

As the doctor bent over Aaron's leg, she sat on the opposite side of the bed, within easy reach of the tools. From there, she could catch the cast when it fell away.

"Should he take something for the pain first?" The bone had caused Aaron no shortage of agony through the healing process, although not as much lately. But removing the plaster holding the limb secure might introduce fresh discomfort.

"It will itch a great deal as the blood flow is renewed, but I'd like to see how much pain he has before we mask it." The doctor took up the saw with the fierce teeth, and her stomach clenched. He positioned the tool at the bottom of the cast near Aaron's foot. "We'll start down here and work our way up."

The tension mounted with each minute the doctor sawed. Each steady *critch critch* scraped across her raw nerves. It seemed like an hour passed as the saw broke through the thick plaster at the foot, then worked its way along the leg toward the critical place at Aaron's thigh.

Only once did she glance up at their patient. The sheen of sweat glimmering on his brow had formed a trickle down one temple. His eyes were closed, as though he couldn't bear to see what lay beneath the hard encasement. A burn crept behind her own eyes.

She didn't blame him. As much as she, too, wanted to know whether his leg would heal, maybe not knowing would be better. Perhaps living in hopeful ignorance was better than the murder of hope if the bone had not healed.

After all, when a section of bone the width of two of her fingers was shattered in hundreds of fragments, how could they think the body would grow that much new bone? How could it reattach strongly enough to bridge the gap?

God made the human body to heal itself from so many illnesses and injuries, but surely a devastation of this magnitude would require nothing short of a divine touch to restore the leg to its former use—or even make it passably functional.

And it was all her fault. Hot tears pressed behind her eyes.

As Doc Micah sawed through the last section of plaster, a layer of sweat formed across his own brow. She reached over and grasped the cast at the knee, holding it still to better allow the doctor to work.

The saw broke through the final layer with a jolt, and a deep groan slipped from Aaron. Laura had to grab at the cast with her other hand to keep both sides from falling out of her grasp. The thing was heavy.

The doctor took a deep breath, then released it, and she could feel the weight of his anticipation was as thick as her own. The result of Aaron's healing would have little bearing on the doctor's skill. How much could a physician truly do to repair a shattered limb, anyway? Yet, the welfare of his patients weighed heavily on him. He spent himself fully to give them the best quality of life possible.

Heart thumping in her chest, Laura helped lift the leg as the doctor spread the cast down the limb and over Aaron's foot. The thin layer of cloth that remained had protected his skin from the rough plaster and also covered the damaged area, so she couldn't tell for sure whether the thighbone looked straight. The limb definitely looked smaller than before, but that was to be expected with no use of the muscle these past two months.

The doctor glanced up at her. "You may go now. Thank you." He would need to remove the last layer and reveal skin to assess the bone, and maybe that would be improper for her to see.

But then he'd also need to have Aaron try to stand, to determine whether the leg could bear weight. He'd need her there to help with that. A glance at Aaron's face was almost her undoing. With his jaw set like that, he looked so much like his brother.

She pulled her gaze back to the doctor and gave him her most competent look. "I'll turn away while you inspect the bone, but I'll stay to help when he stands."

The doctor hesitated only a moment, then nodded and focused on the leg again. The doctor was a reasonable and practical man, two traits she could respect, especially if they allowed her to be here to find out the news firsthand about the damage she'd caused. No matter how many times Doc Micah or Ingrid told her she wasn't at fault for Aaron's injury, she couldn't stop the need to do what she could to help his recovery.

She turned away from them, staring at the simple bureau positioned by the side wall. Instead of listening to the quiet rustling sounds coming from the pair behind her and the shaky breaths coming from Aaron, she focused on the drawers. Three, with simple round wooden knobs. The center drawer sat slightly askew, its corners not in perfect alignment with those above and below.

Did Aaron use them for anything? When he'd been part of the group that kidnapped her and little Samuel, Aaron had carried a bedroll and saddle packs. He'd also had a saddle and horse, and the hideout they'd taken her to had been stuffed with crates and piles of stolen goods.

She'd heard Lanton, the mercantile owner who was acting as Settler's Fort's lawman until a new sheriff could be found, had wired all the other towns in the surrounding areas to get a list of items stolen over the years. Everything possible had been recovered and given back to the original owners. Had the personal possessions of the gang members been sold to help pay back what they owed in restitution? Probably. Joanna, little Samuel's mother and Laura's first friend in Settler's Fort, had said Nate would be working for a long time to pay back that debt.

"Does that hurt?"

The doctor's words pulled her from her wandering thoughts. Remembering those days always brought a crushing tightness to her chest and a churning in her middle. But focusing again on the life-changing event happening behind her was hardly helpful.

Aaron grunted, probably in response to the doctor's question. Had he nodded or shaken his head no? She had to fight to keep from turning to look at his face.

"All right. Let's see you stand." The doctor's voice held

no hint of what he'd learned so far. "Miss Hannon, you can come around if you'd like."

She spun to face them. The doctor lifted Aaron's injured leg from the bed, then helped him turn and lower the foot to the floor.

After scrambling up, she fit the walking sticks under her arms and limped around the foot of the bed so she could stand on Aaron's other side.

The doctor stood and moved to Aaron's left arm. "Now, we're going to ease up very slowly." He put extra emphasis on the last two words. "Keep all your weight on your good leg first. Once you're standing, we'll slowly shift some of the weight to both legs."

She laid her walking sticks against the bed and prepared her hands to grab Aaron's arm if he needed help balancing. She was on his good side, so balance should be all he needed.

Aaron's face turned to a mask of concentration as he braced both fists on the bed and pushed himself up. His body hovered halfway up at the point where he'd need to remove his hands. The doctor grabbed an elbow on his side, and Laura did the same. Though Aaron's arm wasn't the solid block of iron it had once been, his upper arm still possessed a fair amount of strength. The muscles flexed in her hands as he straightened to full standing.

After he stood for a moment, balancing, the doctor spoke again. "Now, shift a little weight onto your left side and tell me how it feels."

She couldn't breathe as she studied Aaron's face for signs of pain as he did what Doc Micah said. The outline of his jawbone showed clearly under his skin, and the tendons strained as he grimaced. His arm trembled under her touch. From concentration or pain?

"Does that hurt?" The doctor's voice was sharp, as though Aaron wasn't following orders.

A grunt was the man's only response.

Then his body jerked. It happened so fast, Laura couldn't do anything but grip Aaron's arm, pulling upward with all her might as he tumbled forward and sideways, away from her.

Onto his injured leg.

The doctor cried out—or maybe that was Aaron—and Micah struggled to keep their patient from tumbling all the way to the floor. Tendons in the doctor's neck stood out like cords as he heaved Aaron up, then helped him ease back down on the bed.

Aaron sat with his head dropped, his legs tangled in front of him, and hopelessness sagging his entire frame.

FOUR

"We don't know anything for sure yet, Aaron."

Laura forced herself to breathe as Doc Micah used the magic he wielded so well to encourage his patients—a mixture of sincerity, honesty, and hope. "The leg didn't like that much weight, but maybe it could hold less. We'll start small and work up to it." The doctor crouched in front of Aaron to make eye contact. "I'd like to have you do a few exercises with the leg before we make any decisions regarding the next treatment. Are you willing?" He waited, his gaze steady as he regarded Aaron.

"As you wish." The flat tone made it clear none of this was what *Aaron* wished, but the doctor didn't wait for him to change his answer.

After straightening Aaron's legs, Doc Micah had him try to lift the foot on his injured left side. Aaron couldn't even raise the heel off the floor.

The doctor lifted the foot partway. "When I let go, try to lower the leg slowly."

But when he took his hands away, the limb dropped like

an apple shaken from a tree. Only the doctor's hands waiting underneath kept the foot from banging on the wood floor.

The leg hadn't healed. That fact appeared achingly clear to them all. Had any new bone grown at all?

"I'll be a cripple forever, won't I." The words weren't spoken as a question, but a desperate plea. A clear longing for the doctor to declare him wrong.

"Well . . ." Doc Micah drew out the word. "There is one other option. I've read of surgeons who've successfully inserted a metal bar, attaching it to both ends of the bone in a place where it's healthy. I've never done such, but we could try the operation if you're willing."

The weight pressing on her chest kept breath from moving through her lungs. An operation that required not only cutting through muscle and tissue to reach the bone, but also inserting a foreign object? The doctor hadn't sounded nervous about the possibility at all, but such a surgery sounded dangerous. She flicked her gaze between the pair, waiting for Aaron's response.

Aaron raised his chin. "Will it let me walk again?"

The doctor hesitated. "If the body accepts the piece, then yes, the bone should be strong enough to support you. You'll most likely have a strong limp, but you should be able to regain most movement in time." He paused, but the furrow of his brow showed he had more to say. "The surgery isn't without risk. There's always the chance your body will reject the metal piece. In rare cases, an infection of sorts sets in, and the limb has to be amputated."

Aaron raised his eyes to the doctor, and Micah leveled

a strong look on him as he spoke again. "That's only happened once that I've heard of, but you must understand it's a possibility, however remote."

"Try it." Aaron spoke without pause. Not even a hair's breadth of delay after the doctor finished his warning.

Concern flickered across Micah's face. "Are you certain?"

Aaron shrugged, an action that spoke more of belligerence than lack of concern. "I can't walk now. The surgery sounds like my only option. And if it doesn't work, maybe your God will be merciful and put me out of my misery."

Pain seared through Laura's chest. *Dear God, no.* Tears rushed to her eyes, blurring her vision so Aaron's form shifted before her.

Just like Robbie. The baby brother she'd raised from the day he turned four. The one whose face she'd scrubbed and wounds she'd tended. The one she'd allowed to curl onto the cot beside her, his little body trembling when their father raged in his drunken stupors.

"I can't do this anymore, Laur. I have nothing left." He'd turned those tortured green eyes to her as he sat on the edge of the bed, the stark absence of his missing leg glaring, even though he'd pulled a blanket over his lower half.

If only she'd listened to him. Heard what he wasn't saying. She'd been the only one he had left. The only one who could have saved him. How could she have missed his heart's cry? His desperate plea for help?

"You can do it, Robbie. I have faith in you." Such paltry encouragement she'd offered. No wonder he'd given up. She'd not been what he needed. She'd not been enough.

The pain threatened to double her over even now, a year later. Though her throat tightened to where she could hardly breathe, she forced herself to push the excruciating memories aside.

This was Aaron sitting on the bed. A different man entirely. He'd not lost his leg. The doctor had offered a possibility. He offered hope. Something that could restore him closer to the man he'd once been.

This time the story would have a better ending.

"Let's get you back in the bed." Doc Micah raised Aaron's injured leg as the man worked himself back toward the pillows. "I'll talk to your brother tonight and plan when we should do the surgery."

"Tomorrow." Aaron spoke with authority, but that same belligerence from before still threaded through his voice.

The doctor's brow furrowed. "We should wait a couple days for the skin to adjust to being without the cast."

"Friday then." Aaron nodded, as though it was all settled.

But if Robbie had been given another choice than to lose his leg, he would have gripped it with such a tenacious hold that no man could have kept him from the chance. She could help make this happen for Aaron.

"I can be here in Nate's stead." The words tumbled out before she realized they'd been more than a thought. "Friday, I mean. For the surgery. If he can't get off work." She took a step closer. "I'll care for him as his brother would."

Doc Micah straightened and studied her a moment, then nodded. "Friday it is, then. We'll start just after the noon meal."

This surgery would likely take much of the afternoon, and she'd be there for every agonizing minute. No matter what was required of her, she'd manage. She'd do everything possible to help repair the damage she'd caused.

Nate did his best to push away his weariness that evening as he mounted the steps onto the clinic's porch. He had to be at his best for this visit. Today the doctor had planned to remove Aaron's cast, and his brother would either be finally happy . . . or his melancholy might have sunk to a new low.

At the front door, he paused to prepare himself. Inhaling a steadying breath, then breathing out his trepidation and exhaustion with the spent air. Together, with God, they would face whatever they had to.

He pushed open the door and stepped inside, then closed it behind him as his eyes adjusted to the dim light.

"Mr. Long." The soft voice came from his right, and he turned to see Miss Hannon standing in the doorway of the examination room. She had a walking stick propped under her right arm, but she held a broom with both hands. Something in her manner made it seem her words were more than a simple greeting. She must know what happened with Aaron.

"Miss Hannon." His gut fisted as he took a step toward her, studying her face for any hint of news. "How is my brother?"

She hesitated. Was it bad news and she wasn't sure how to tell him? His pulse hammered in his neck. "Tell me. Please."

"The leg didn't heal as we'd hoped. But the doctor offered a surgery that your brother is eager to try."

The words flew out so quickly, his mind wouldn't process them at first. Then her meaning sank through. *The leg didn't heal.* A weight pressed on his chest, pushing out his breath, leaving nothing behind but those words circling over and over in his mind.

Dear God, please don't let it be. His leg has to heal.

As hard as these last two months had been for Aaron, a lifetime of being confined to a chair would be torture.

A hand on his arm pulled him from his whirling thoughts. Miss Hannon had stepped nearer, and now stared up at him with concern. "The doctor thinks the surgery will help him walk again. He said it's been performed successfully many times in the States."

Nate narrowed his eyes, struggling to understand what he'd missed. "What is the surgery?"

As she explained how the doctor would attach a metal plate to the healthy parts of Aaron's bone, his gut churned. But earnest hope shone in her eyes, lighting her face. She clearly thought this would be the best option for Aaron.

But his own reservations made him pause. "Isn't it dangerous? Putting a piece of metal in his body? What if it hurts him more than it helps?" What if it raised Aaron's hopes only to dash them so bitterly that it stole the last of his will to carry on?

"The doctor will explain the risk. There is some, but there's a much greater chance it will work." She hesitated, and the apprehension on her face made him desperate to know what she was holding back.

"Please, Miss Hannon. Tell me."

"I believe your brother needs this hope. Without the surgery, there's little chance the bone will heal on its own. He's already made his choice to have it done. Having your support will be so much more important to him than you might know."

He scrubbed a hand through his hair, turning so he didn't have to face her luminous gaze. "Of course I'll support him." He'd always done that for his brother. So much more than she even knew. "When does the doctor want to do it?"

"Aaron requested Friday. The doctor plans to begin after the noon meal."

He nodded, as though the action could force his thoughts into order. "All right." This was quicker than he'd prefer, but if it was best for Aaron, he'd do whatever he could to help.

Anything to make things better for his brother—anything legal, at least. He'd spent too many years on the wrong side of the law to go back there.

"You're an outlaw, Long. That'll never change."

Rex's words from months before tried to make him doubt, but he pushed them away. God had changed him. Washed away his former crimes and given him a fresh start.

Now they would make new lives for themselves. Good lives. If only Aaron could find the fresh start he so desperately needed.

◈

Nate plunged his hands into the icy water of the creek on his way to the clinic Friday evening.

Waiting until the superintendent finally released him had been torture, but he'd done his best to focus his mental strain on praying for his brother. How soon would they know whether the surgery was successful? He'd forgotten to ask the doctor that question, and now it seemed one of the most important. How much longer must they endure the unknown?

He scrubbed the grime from his face and hands and forced his thoughts on something more pleasant. His memory instantly conjured Miss Hannon, especially the feel of his arm around her as he helped her back to the clinic after he'd found her in the cave.

When she looked at him, her gaze had sunk deep inside him. It wasn't an innocence her eyes held, more a depth of knowing that could only come from living through pain and struggles. They made him want to know more. They made him want to be someone she would trust enough to share her history with.

With all the distractions a few nights before, he'd forgotten to ask how her leg fared. How could he have neglected such an important question? She was up and moving, which must be a good sign. But was she supposed to be so active? Hopefully she wasn't taxing the limb and slowing its healing. She'd been through enough already.

Striding through the outskirts of town now, he gained on a group of miners who'd left before he did. Danvers and Sloane split off from the cluster at the café. Barlow, one of the blasters, raised a hand in farewell when he paused at the door to the boardinghouse. "See you in the dark, Long. Maybe we can have you start on the big powder tomorrow."

Nate returned the wave. "I'll be ready."

He might have to rent a room soon, too, as cold as the nights were becoming. He'd planned to have a cabin framed out by the time the first snow hit, but between working most of his daylight hours at the mine, and spending almost every other spare moment with Aaron, he'd not done more than lay a square of logs for the base. But if at all possible, he wanted to avoid renting a room this winter. The money would be much better spent paying down the mountain of debt laid to his account.

The clinic loomed in front of him, and a figure stood on the porch, leaning over the side rail. Mrs. Bradley, if he wasn't mistaken, and she appeared to be looking at something on the ground. Rather intently.

As he neared, her body heaved, and she leaned farther. Realization flashed through him. She must be casting up her accounts. He surged forward. Perhaps she needed help, although what he could do, he had no idea.

Just when he reached the porch steps, the front door opened and Miss Hannon stepped out. Relief coursed through him. She'd know what to do.

She gave him a quick glance but then shifted her attention to Mrs. Bradley, who'd straightened now and clung to the rail. "Ingrid, oh dear. Come in and lie down." She stopped beside the doctor's wife and rubbed a hand over her back. Miss Hannon spoke again, but her murmured words were too quiet for Nate to catch, even though he'd now mounted the porch steps.

A moment later, Mrs. Bradley turned and shuffled toward the door. She gave him a weak smile as she passed, but her face was as pale as a sheet of paper. "Mr. Long. My apologies." Even her voice lacked strength.

He nodded to her, even though she'd already turned away from him to go inside. "I hope you feel better soon, ma'am."

As the door shut behind her, Miss Hannon released a long sigh from where she still stood by the rail. He turned to her. "Is there anything I can do to help?"

She shook her head. "She's in the fam—" Her words cut short and her mouth clamped tight as she blushed. "I mean . . ."

Ah. One of the aunts he and Aaron had lived with had cast up her accounts daily when she was in the family way.

He nodded. "I guess that's good." The doctor must be thrilled to have a child on the way. Their first, as far as he knew. Then he realized how his words must have sounded. "I mean . . ." Heat stung his ears. "I didn't mean . . ."

But she was chuckling. "It's a happy occasion. I just hate she's so miserable through this part."

Again he nodded. Better to change topics before he shoved his boot deeper in his mouth. "How's my brother?"

Weariness cloaked her expression. "Well. Sleeping now." She pushed off from the rail and strode toward the door. "He's probably still feeling the effects of the chloroform we used in the surgery, as well as the laudanum for pain."

She reached to open the door, but he grabbed her arm before she could. "Wait."

Pausing, she turned to look at him, her brows raised.

"I . . . How did it go?" He desperately needed to know. But even more, he wasn't quite ready to enter the dim interior of the clinic. Needed one more moment before he faced his brother.

Her face softened, as though she understood his reticence. "The doctor said he cleared out more bone fragments that had fallen away since the first surgery. There was still healthy bone to attach the metal to. Everything he hoped for, I think.

"We'll keep the incision clean, and your brother will need to stay in bed for a couple weeks while the wound heals. After that, he should be able to move to a chair, and then he could start using walking sticks. The doctor even knows someone who could make a rolling chair. It might not work so well outside, but he can move around in the clinic and come onto the porch."

Nate soaked in each word, the knot in his belly uncoiling a little more with each detail. Did he dare hope? After weeks of disappointing news, he'd prepared himself for the worst.

But he'd been praying. Maybe God was answering his prayers the way he'd been asking. He well knew the Lord didn't always respond with a yes to every petition. But maybe in this case He had.

"That's good. Really good." He still wasn't quite ready to enter. To leave the cool breeze blowing fresh air through his hair, still damp from the creek. To face the pallor and melancholy on his brother's face.

He nodded toward her walking stick. "How's your leg?"

"Better." Her pretty cheeks pinkened in the fading light. "I've been without it most of the day. I'm only using it now because I've been on my feet a lot."

"You've had a busy day." He brushed her arm, but the moment his skin touched her sleeve, he regretted the action. What in the world had made him do it?

He propped his hands at his waist to keep them from acting of their own accord again. "Make sure you rest enough to let it heal."

She dipped her chin in a way that she probably didn't realize made her even more endearing. "I'm well. Don't trouble yourself."

"I was thinking about going back to the cave," he blurted out. "With a lantern and supplies this time, to see how big that cavern is. Maybe there are offshoots that go in farther. Would you like to come if you feel up to it?" Why that came out, he couldn't have said, but his entire body strained as he waited for her answer.

"I would." Was that excitement lighting her eyes? Probably only wishful thinking on his part.

He nodded, trying to steady his reactions. "Maybe Sunday after the service." But could he really spare so many hours on his only day off? Sunday usually meant extended time with Aaron, and he'd also hoped to cut down more trees for his cabin. "Or maybe next Sunday. I should spend the hours after church this week with Aaron. That will also give your injury more time to heal." There. A compromise to ease his conscience about his brother.

The prospect of a few hours in Miss Hannon's company felt like a light in a murky, fog-filled night. And when she sent him a tentative smile, that light brightened into the hope that maybe things really were about to get better.

Just maybe.

FIVE

Nate inched over the rock ledge around the mountain, straining to see the footing in front of him. He'd thought the early morning moon would be bright enough that he wouldn't need to light the lantern on his way to the cave, but the last thing he wanted to do was step on a loose rock and tumble sideways.

He could almost feel the haunting sensation of empty air underneath him, his hands clawing for a rock or tree or anything to catch his fall. Sharp boulders striking his body, slamming into him with blow after blow as he rolled downward, maybe finally ending his pain when his head struck, pulling him into blissful oblivion. How long would he lay out here before someone discovered him?

His fellow workers would miss him, but would anyone actually come look for him? Or would they think the worst? That he'd left town, abandoning both his commitments and his brother in a single selfish act?

Pain pressed his chest. How long would it take before he'd

proven himself reliable, before people began to trust him and the changes he'd made? Believe in this new man God was growing him into being?

His foot hit a bump in the rock, and he stepped up onto the higher stone. If he remembered correctly, the cave should be not far ahead. If he was going to bring Miss Hannon here, especially with her still recovering from her injury, he needed to get a better understanding of the place. Make sure he had the right supplies.

He'd not been able to sleep much anyway, what with the cold pressing through his blankets and his mind whirling with worries about his brother. He might as well put the energy to better use with a quick stop in the cave before he made his way to the mine.

As he rounded a jut in the cliff beside him, the cave opening yawned wide just ahead. Within seconds, he had his lantern lit. He adjusted the rope over his shoulder as he started into the blackness. It seemed like he should need more, but this had been all he could think to bring.

After ducking through the opening, he straightened and raised the lantern to get a good look around. The hollow place was massive, even larger than he'd thought last time in that quick glimpse. Its shape didn't stretch wide, but extended as far back as he could see, and all kinds of rock pieces hung like stone icicles.

He stepped forward, letting his gaze wander from one to the next, examining the odd shapes and varied thickness. Some extended all the way to the cave floor, narrow in the middle and wide again at the base. He was so intrigued by them that he almost missed the drop in the floor and stumbled as he fought to keep his balance. This must be where Miss Hannon had twisted her ankle. He'd do well to take more care.

Moving slowly enough to take in his surroundings, he inched his way farther. The cavern maintained a consistent width as it moved deeper through the core of the mountain, almost as though planned by an engineer and dug out by a team of workers. But the beautiful formations throughout couldn't be manmade, nor the elaborate striations in the rocks along the side.

A dark circle appeared in the wall on his right, a shaft possibly. The opening rose above his shoulder, so it might be a good size. Perhaps he and Miss Hannon could investigate that when they returned. Would she be recovered enough by this Sunday? He didn't want to explore more without her, not since he'd already offered the invitation. But he wasn't sure he could quell the curiosity inside him another full week.

Yet he would if he had to. The last thing he wanted for her was another injury.

◈━━◗ ◖━━◈

"Good morning." Laura made her voice as pleasant as possible as she spoke into the barely cracked doorway. If she kept her voice bright enough, perhaps some of her good cheer would rub off on this grumpy patient.

Aaron didn't answer, so she elbowed the door open and stepped inside. "I hope you're hungry. I made fresh biscuits this morning." That seemed to be one of his favorites. He always finished them, even when he left some of his porridge untouched. Salt pork was the other food he never failed to finish, although his room often smelled for several hours after she served it. Maybe he smeared the grease on his shirt.

A light snore drifted from the man in the bed. She stepped nearer, listening to see how steady his breathing was. Sometimes he lay still groggy when she came in with breakfast, and he was always still grumpy, but she'd spoken loudly enough to wake a deaf dog. Could he be feigning sleep so he didn't have to face her?

"Mr. Long, it's time to wake up. You'll want to eat while the food's hot."

The snoring continued. He lay with his mouth parted, the muscles of his face sagging with a relaxation he wouldn't be able to pretend. Her belly clenched. She'd seen that look before, the same oblivious stupor her father showed after spending hours with his whiskey bottles.

But that couldn't be the case here. Aaron had no way to obtain the wretched poison.

She set the tray on the bedside table, then turned to shake his shoulder. "Aaron, wake up."

The snoring continued.

She gripped his shoulder harder and shook enough for his head to wag back and forth. He was out cold.

Maybe the laudanum she'd given him last night had caused this lethargy. She'd never seen the effect last this long, but perhaps combined with his pain and his body's struggle to heal, this stupor was the result.

Just to be certain, she pressed a hand to his forehead. Not overly warm. She moved her fingers to his cheek. The same.

Breathing out her tension, she straightened and studied him. Sleep must be what he needed most. Perhaps this was his body's way of forcing rest so it could recover. Maybe this healing would cure his sour mood, too.

Having Aaron in better spirits would be a blessing for them all.

But as she studied the relaxed skin of his face, she replayed the events of last night. He'd complained of pain, and she'd checked with Doc Micah to see if they could do something about it. Then she'd administered exactly the amount the doctor had prescribed. And they kept the bottle locked in a drawer in the storage room. Aaron would have no way to get extra, even if he were able to walk.

Still, she'd have to mention this lethargy to Doc Micah. She'd seen the effects of addiction on a man fighting through pain and despair. She wouldn't lose Aaron the way she'd lost Robbie.

No matter what.

⸻◈⸻

Laura peered through the crack between curtains in the examination room, her stomach doing a nervous flip at the sight of Nate riding down the street. She must have lost her senses. Truly. What was she thinking leaving town alone with this man who'd been part of the group who'd kidnapped her?

He sat a horse well, his broad shoulders back in a confident, comfortable position. But then, he'd spent many years riding horseback on the trail, running from lawmen and the good people he'd helped rob of their hard-earned goods.

The sobering thought crashed in to churn her nerves.

Yet, she knew this man, not just his sordid past, but also the changes he'd made. In every interaction they'd had over these past few months, he'd showed himself earnest in his efforts to make amends. To live an honest life. She was fairly certain she could trust him while they explored the cave together.

She packed her pistol just in case, though.

Besides, exploring the cavern would be a good deal safer with a partner. An extra set of hands and eyes and ears.

She turned away from the window and moved toward the door. He didn't need to come inside for her. That would feel too much like he'd come courting.

Even the thought sent a rush of heat up her neck and started that nervous flipping in her middle again. She'd never been courted in her life, not with her father's drunkenness hanging like a shroud in their home. She'd had her hands full with her brothers anyway. Then Will's sickness . . . then the war . . . the last few pieces of her former life she'd tried desperately to cling to had shattered.

Now was hardly the time to dwell on the past. She'd begun a new life and was about to set out on a grand adventure.

With a man.

She needed to be careful to keep their relationship from going beyond friendship. Especially when she still didn't know for sure where her place was in this town. Adding in the attentions of a man would only muddy things further.

And was Nate even a man whose attentions she would want? A cohort of the men who'd submitted her to so much fear and pain?

But Nate had been opposed to the kidnapping as soon as he'd met up with the group in the woods. He'd fought to free them. Put his own life in peril. But still . . .

With her hand on the front doorknob, she grabbed the satchel she'd packed and slung it over her shoulder. This excursion simply served as an opportunity to search the cave. To put the weight of past struggles behind her and enjoy the afternoon.

She inhaled a strengthening breath, then pulled open the door and stepped out. She no longer limped, and her ankle was barely tender with each step.

When Nate turned from tying the horses and noticed her, his countenance brightened, and he offered a shy smile. "Ready?"

She nodded and couldn't help returning his grin. The man had a face far too handsome for his good. The way his smile pulled slightly crooked, forming a dimple on one side, would melt any woman's heart.

And those eyes.

She glanced toward the horses to regain her composure, yet her mind held on to the image of how his eyes darkened to forest green in the bright afternoon sun.

"I hope this mare suits you." Nate reached for her satchel as he spoke, and she handed it over. "Sam at the livery said she's plenty dependable. He called her Nugget, I think."

She moved to the horse's head while Nate tied her pack

behind her saddle. "Hello there, pretty." The mare shone a dark sorrel, the color of rich garden dirt fertilized to the peak of readiness for planting.

Laura soaked in the savory scent of horse, an aroma that swept her back to some of her favorite memories. She and Will had spent every hour they could steal away roaming the pastures and woods. They'd only had the one mare, an aged farm horse who plodded along wherever they directed her, and of course they'd never wasted time with a saddle.

Those bright moments with Will had been among her best. She could still see his cheeky grin. His wind-ruffled hair. Her brother. Her confidant. Her only friend through every dark day after their mother died and their pa took to the bottle.

"Do you think she'll suit?" The gentle rumble of Nate's voice sounded nearby.

She pulled back from the mare. At some point, she'd rested her forehead on the animal's wide blaze. Maybe that touch had drawn Will's memory so vividly. She struggled to recover herself. To push back the emotions that still swarmed in her weakest moments.

Nate still waited for an answer, so she nodded and worked to clear the tears from her voice. "She'll do fine."

His strong hand rested on her elbow, his warmth soaking through her woolen sleeve. "Can I do something? Help with something? Is it your ankle?" He must have heard the emotion in her voice, witnessed another of her moments of weakness.

She sniffed and fought for normal composure. "I was just thinking of my older brother, Will. He and I used to ride together whenever we could. I . . . miss him." A fresh burn of tears surged up to her eyes. If they didn't get riding soon, she'd not be able to stop herself from blubbering.

Squaring her shoulders, she nodded. "I'm well. Ready when you are." There. Her tone sounded normal. If she looked at him he'd see her reddened eyes, so she shifted sideways beside the horse, toward the saddle, forcing him to step back out of her way.

"All right, then." His voice sounded both concerned and amused, if that combination were possible.

Within moments, they skirted toward the edge of the town. Nate had suggested the roundabout way, which would give them both a better view of the surrounding mountains and also keep them from riding straight through the center of Settler's Fort. Both served as valid reasons for the direction they now rode.

Her conscience twinged. She should have told Ingrid exactly what they were doing. She'd only mentioned to her friend she wanted to get out for a walk after church, and Ingrid had looked worried at the words, probably because of Laura's ankle injury. But the limb was recovered enough. She'd been careful not to limp for days now.

Keeping quiet about the true nature of their excursion proved easier since the doctor and Ingrid had planned to picnic with Joanna and Isaac. They'd invited her, of course, but Nate's previous offer to explore the cave had overridden all her desire to relax with their friends.

She would have liked to spend extra time with Joanna, who'd been her first friend here in Settler's Fort, and was still one of her dearest, although they didn't see each other often since her marriage had moved her more than an hour's ride outside of town. But being the fifth person in a party of couples might make Laura wish for something she shouldn't at this point. Not with her life so unsettled.

In truth, whether or not to explore the cave with Nate today was her decision, and hers alone. Perhaps she should have told Ingrid where she was going for safety's sake, but Ingrid wasn't her mother or her guardian. She was answerable to God alone.

Am I doing something wrong, Lord?

"Wanna run?" Nate's voice broke through her thoughts, but the words flashed her back to another time. Another grinning boy on horseback. Although that time she'd been sitting behind him, clinging around Will's waist as he kicked the old mare into a canter. Both of them would lean low as their mount stretched out, and Laura's hair would fly behind her, the wind cooling her neck. She could breathe the freedom even now.

Those times slipping away with her older brother had been some of her best memories. Her happiest. When little Robbie would be taking one of his afternoon naps and Pa was nursing a jug of something, Will knew she needed the few minutes of no responsibility.

Maybe a childhood of sneaking away for stolen pleasures was why she'd hidden her plans to explore a cave with Nate from Ingrid today. Her fun with Will had always been innocent. She prayed today's adventure proved to be just as harmless.

She glanced over at Nate. And possibly even more thrilling.

SIX

*D*o we need to take things slow?"

Nate's voice and challenging stare jarred Laura back to the present. She hadn't answered his question, only stared like a person who'd lost her wits.

She couldn't help a grin, the kind Will had always been able to pull from her. "Not on my account." She nudged her mare and the horse broke into a jolting trot.

Nate pulled alongside, and she kicked Nugget a little harder. Finally the horse began to canter, and Laura settled into the rocking gait. Other than the kidnapping, she'd not had much chance to ride since she left the farm, but this mare kept an easy rhythm as comfortable and familiar as breathing.

She inhaled the fresh air. The crisp scent of autumn in the mountain country brought all her senses to life. This jaunt might possibly be even better than those long-ago rides.

When they reached the stony ground where the land rose toward the rocky crag of the mountain, Laura eased back on her reins, and Nate slowed his horse beside her. As the animals settled to a walk, she let out a long breath. "I needed that."

He gave her another one-dimple, crooked smile. Maybe he needed these moments of freedom as much as she did after all his backbreaking work in the mine.

The horses breathed easier by the time they reached the base of the cliff. Laura dismounted and unfastened the satchel from behind her saddle.

"I brought two lanterns and plenty of rope. I think that's all we'll need." Nate stepped up beside her, his arms laden with supplies. "Shall we hobble the horses so they can graze while we explore?"

Laura gave a nod.

They made quick work of the job, then climbed up to the rocky ledge. Nate motioned for her to lead the way around the mountain, and she stepped forward boldly. Not too boldly, though. She already had a weak ankle; she didn't need any other injuries to waylay her.

When they reached the cave opening, the hole yawned black against the bright daylight. Even after they lit both lanterns, part of her hesitated to duck low and step inside. Where had her thirst for adventure fled to?

"I'll go in first." Nate studied her as though he could read her mind.

"No, I want to." She didn't need to be babied. She'd already been in the space and knew there was nothing to fear.

Bending low, she held the lantern out and followed its light through the dark hole. Once through the archway, she straightened and lifted the light higher to scan the interior. The hanging rock formations and narrow columns were there, as she'd first seen them in the light of her match, but she'd forgotten how numerous they were.

As she shifted the lantern so she could see from one side of the cavern to the other, her gaze caught on something. Was that a darker-colored rock at the base of the wall on the far left? It almost looked like fur. An animal?

Nate had just ducked into the cave and now straightened, the motion of his lantern sending the shadows jumping and dancing. She reached for his arm and grasped it, stilling him with her touch.

"Look." She kept her voice low and pointed to the spot. "What is that?" Had a bear already come to hibernate? The nights had turned cold enough to indicate that winter would soon be upon them.

He took a step nearer, raising his lantern as he peered at the spot. She dropped her hand from his arm but moved in close behind him.

The creature against the wall shifted. Just barely, but she was almost positive it hadn't been a shadow flickering from the light. "It's alive." Her chest tightened so much the words barely came out loud enough for him to hear.

Nate slipped the coil of rope from his shoulder and dropped it to the floor, then glanced back at her. "Stay here. I'll see if it's dangerous." She couldn't see more than shadows in his eyes, but the strength of his frame beside her bespoke protection. Even against a raging grizzly, this man would do everything he could to keep her safe.

Still, the last thing they needed was for him to be mauled by a bear. "Do you need my pistol?" She reached for the satchel hanging at her side. The small gun may only infuriate a grizzly. She'd heard stories of these beasts being shot five or six times with a rifle without dying.

He nudged aside his jacket and pulled out his own pistol. "I have this, but I won't get close enough to stir up whatever that is, especially if it's dangerous."

As he turned toward the creature, she forced herself to take in steady breaths. Nate crept forward, the lantern in one hand, pistol in the other. His boots scuffed a little on the stone floor, especially as he moved down the slope where she'd twisted her ankle. When the rock leveled out again, he stilled. Every part of him seemed trained on whatever lay tucked at the base of the wall. From what she could tell, the creature had a dark, curly coat, almost the color and texture of a buffalo, but smaller and long, like a bear's carcass.

In an instant, Nate's bearing changed. He straightened, raised his handgun to level the barrel at the animal, and cocked the action. He sent a glance around him, as though he expected something else to jump out, but then returned his full focus to the animal.

"Show yourself." His voice came out low and hard. Lethal.

The sound sent a chill down her arms despite the thickness of her woolen coat.

Then his words sank through her. Did he think it was a man? With new eyes, she studied the figure. Yes, that may well be a man stretched out under a buffalo skin.

As quietly as she could manage, she reached into her

satchel and felt around until her hand brushed her pistol. She pulled out the gun and scanned the cavern, peering as far into the shadowy depths as she could. While Nate focused on whatever threat hid under the fur, she would protect them from anything that lurked outside the light.

She took a few steps closer to him.

"Don't, Laura. There's a man under there." Nate never took his eyes off the figure, but his voice still held that hard edge. She'd never heard that tone from him, and it made him seem more the seasoned criminal and less the man she'd come to know these past months. And the sound of her given name in that tone sent a swirl of confused emotions through her chest.

But he was only trying to protect her.

She held her ground and didn't move any closer. Still, she raised her lantern higher and kept her focus on searching the cavern.

Nate stepped toward the stranger hiding under the pelt, and she couldn't help but split her attention between the pair and her efforts to scan the rest of the room for any new threats.

"Show yourself now, or I'll send a bullet through you."

She pressed her mouth shut to hold in a gasp. Would he really shoot a stranger when they didn't even know if the man presented a threat? But if the person wouldn't show himself, he must have some nefarious motive. Right?

How did Nate even know for sure this was a human and not a sleeping bear?

She crept forward, keeping quiet enough that Nate shouldn't hear her move. He might notice the flickering of her lantern light on the walls around them, but his focus seemed intent on the figure he was moving toward. Only three or four strides separated him from his target now. The thing still hadn't moved much. Maybe it was dead or nearly so.

"This is your last warning." His voice still held that hard, icy chill, but he hadn't fired his gun. Maybe he didn't intend to until he knew more.

God, help him. Help us.

Nate closed the last strides between him and the covered figure. Then he planted a boot in the fur. Hard apparently, for the man underneath grunted.

Whoever was under there was alive.

With a swift motion, Nate set the lantern down, then jerked the covering away, stepped back, and aimed. The motion was so swift, the stranger likely wouldn't have gotten the draw on him if he'd tried.

Still, she kept her pistol pointed at the threat from where she stood, back by the incline where she'd twisted her ankle.

As her eyes adjusted to the figure, she sucked in a gasp. Lying on the cave floor was a man. An Indian, from the look of his tawny skin and sharp cheekbones. His gray hair lay in loose strands over his face but didn't conceal his rounded eyes.

There was no fear in his gaze. In fact, she couldn't name exactly what emotion was there. He was simply . . . staring.

Nate seemed to gather himself. "Who are you?" His voice wasn't as hard as before. It sounded to Laura like there was still a bit of lingering surprise in his tone.

The old man didn't answer. Only stared. Was that a look of resignation on his face? He must not have a weapon.

Why hadn't he moved farther into the cavern when he heard them coming? Maybe he was too old or injured. The shadows lining the deep grooves on his face made it hard to tell his age. But the long strands of salt-and-pepper hair showed he'd likely been an elder for a number of years.

At last, the man made a sound. A grunt that changed in pitch just enough that it might be a word. Perhaps in his native tongue, anyway. Not English that she could tell. He shifted, and a grimace crossed his face. He seemed to be working his hands out from under the fur.

She tensed, and she could see Nate readjust the angle of his gun. To be safe, she glanced around the perimeter of the room. No one else seemed to be there. Had the old man's companions left him here to rest? Or was he injured?

The moment he extracted his right arm from under the fur, his situation became all too clear. His buckskin tunic had been sliced open and peeled back, revealing a nasty wound on his forearm. The bright red of raw flesh glared up at her, extending almost from his wrist to elbow.

She was already moving toward him before she realized what she was doing. That injury needed tending right away, or the infection that would overtake him would be his demise. No doubt about it.

"Laura." Nate's sharp bark was a warning, but she only let it slow her for a moment.

She started forward again, although she kept a keen eye on the man. She still gripped her pistol, but kept the barrel pointed at the floor. If he pulled out a knife or some other weapon, she could easily protect herself.

"Laura, stop. We don't know if he's dangerous." A tinge of fear edged Nate's voice, and from the nearing tone, he'd shifted close behind her.

"He's hurt, Nate. Besides, if he wanted to hurt us, he would have tried already."

"We don't know that."

She dropped to her knees beside the older man, and Nate hovered just behind her. He would protect her. She had no doubt of it.

She sent the older fellow a smile to show she meant no harm, then turned her attention to his arm. The flesh appeared raw and exposed, with pale striations of muscle or tendon showing through in some places. She couldn't see any sign of scrapes or lacerations that would give a hint of what had caused this. Maybe a burn?

If so, the water must have been scalding. The arm looked as though the skin and top layers of flesh had simply dissolved. Bile churned in her gut, rising into her throat. She had to look away and inhale a deep breath through her nose to force her gorge back down.

To cover her upheaval, she focused on the man's face. "What happened to you?"

A flash of confusion touched his eyes. Maybe he didn't understand English.

"He bested a wildcat." The voice from behind made her spin. She almost fell over from the shot of pain through her weak ankle, but she pressed a hand to the stone floor to keep herself upright.

A figure stood across the cave, just inside the circle of lamplight but still a dozen strides away. A child, maybe seven or eight years old, her raven hair pulled back from her tawny face.

But it was the regal glare she sent them that was the girl's most striking feature. As though she had the upper hand and barely deigned to appear before such common visitors. "He fought off the cougar with only his hands. Now he rests to prepare for his next victory."

The girl spoke with an accent, but she pronounced each word distinctly. Was she here alone with this man . . . maybe her grandfather?

Laura turned back to the man and offered a respectful smile before sneaking another glance at the arm. "I can tell he is brave." That wasn't a lie. The man *was* incredibly brave to have faced them and their weapons without a flinch.

And the girl needed to know they weren't a threat.

From her glimpse of the wound, she still couldn't reconcile it with an animal attack. There weren't clean lines that would have come from claw marks. Something more must have happened.

She inhaled, but only a faint wisp of body odor drifted to her. Not as much as she would expect from an elderly man who was injured enough to make washing hard, even if he could get to a source of water.

Had the injury just happened, then? A wound this open would fester quickly, especially with the contagion from a mountain lion's claws. Maybe the cat had surprised him during a bathing. There must be more to this story. There had to be.

She turned back to the girl. "I'm not a doctor, but I've

spent the past few months working alongside one. May I see if I can help his injuries?"

The girl still stood across the cavern, and she seemed to be trying to keep a stoic expression. But the way her fingers twitched at her sides spoke of her nervousness. Trying to decide if she could trust them, no doubt.

"I'll only work on his arm. If there's anything you're not comfortable with, I'll stop if you ask me to." She offered a smile. "My name is Laura, and this is Nate." She nodded toward the man standing guard behind her. She glanced up at him, just to make sure he wasn't still pointing his gun on either of these vulnerable strangers.

The weapon hung at his side, although she had no doubt he could raise the pistol, aim, and shoot before she could draw breath to scream. He would probably hit whatever he aimed at, too. Not accidently shoot the man who was coming to his defense, shattering that person's thighbone in so many pieces he might never walk again. Aaron had to walk. He simply had to.

She forced the memories aside. She couldn't let her focus shift from these people who needed help.

The girl stepped toward them, and the shadows flickered across her face as she wove her way around the hanging rock formations. Surely the child feared facing two strangers with guns, but the nearer she came, the braver she looked. At last she reached them, stopping only a pace away from the older man's head.

Her gaze met Laura's with a solidness that many adults couldn't muster. "Help him if you can."

A burn sprang to Laura's eyes, and a knot clogged her throat. She could remember being like this brave girl. Standing up to strangers when her father was too ill from drink to do what his children needed of him, which was more often than not in the early days after Mum had passed. Then again near the end.

She'd learned how to read people. How to judge whether they could be trusted. Women were usually easier to see through than men. And more kind, generally. This girl probably knew that fact well.

Laura smiled at her again. "I'll do everything I can."

SEVEN

*L*aura turned her focus to the wound, keeping an ear tuned to what Nate or the child would do or say.

This injury would require a great deal of attention. Although, as she studied it, there didn't seem to be any pus or signs of festering. Only a few bits of hair and dirt that may have come from the buffalo hide the man had covered himself with. How had the wound stayed so clean?

She turned back to the girl, who'd been glaring at Nate. The child's attention jerked to Laura the moment she turned.

Laura bit back a smile. "Have you cleaned this in water?"

The girl nodded, but a flash of fear passed over her features. "The water burned him. It ate the skin away before we could get him out."

Laura returned her focus to his arm. "Water did this? Boiling water?"

"The hot spring in the cave."

Nate stiffened beside her. "In *this* cave? Where at?"

The child raised her chin as she sent Nate another glare. "In this cave."

Laura had to fight to keep her smile hidden. She could understand why the child didn't trust a man, but this pair was safe with Nate. Should she tell the girl so?

Before she could speak, Nate took the task into his own hands. He dropped to his haunches, rendering his size not so formidable. "I won't hurt you. I want to help, too." The earnestness in his voice would win anyone over. He nodded toward the older man. "Is this your grandfather?"

The child looked wary.

Don't ask personal questions. Talk about something inconsequential. Or share about yourself. She could tell Nate exactly what would break through the girl's barriers, but perhaps it would be best for him to work through this on his own.

"I had a grandfather once." His voice was gentle. "We lived with him for a couple years when I was a boy, after my ma died."

Her heart caught, both at the tenderness in his tone and at the picture he painted. Just like her, he'd lost his mother as a young child. And so had Aaron.

She pushed away the thoughts. She had to stop comparing Aaron's situation to what her younger brother had gone through. Robbie had lost his leg, but Aaron wouldn't. Aaron wouldn't give up the way Robbie had. She would make sure of it.

She forced her focus back on the girl to see the child's reaction to Nate's words. Her posture had softened a little.

Nate nodded toward the older man, who was watching

them with intense regard, not showing whether he understood anything they said or not. "It's good you and your grandfather can help each other. Miss Hannon is good at healing. She'll be able to make your grandfather's arm better. You can help by telling her what you've done for it so far."

Heavens, he was good. She gave the girl another gentle smile. "Can you tell me more about the hot spring?" She could get some burn salve from Doc Micah and bandages to keep the wound clean. She was fairly certain she wouldn't be able to talk this pair into coming to the clinic, but maybe the doctor would come tend the wound up here. He usually spent afternoons making house calls, after all.

The girl gave Nate one more look, her posture not nearly so guarded. Then she knelt by the older man's head and placed a hand on the thick gray strands. "There was a deep gash on his arm there, and he has more on his leg." She spoke with only a slight hesitation now, her manner and voice completely softened from moments before.

She motioned toward the buffalo robe covering the man's lower half. "I put a mineral salve on him like my grandmother used, but he was still bleeding a lot. So, we took him to the hot springs back in the cave to wash. When he put his arm in the water, he screamed. When he pulled his arm out, the skin looked strange." Her voice quavered as she pointed to the raw flesh.

Laura had to fight to keep from resting a hand on the child's shoulder. If only she could ease the girl's fears. But touching her would only worry her more, so she kept her focus on the arm. "Was the water too hot?"

"No, I touched it first. It bubbled and smelled funny, but it wasn't hot enough to burn him."

Laura didn't glance at Nate, but hopefully he was listening. The hot springs she'd seen on her journey from Missouri had also smelled foul, but she'd never heard of the water eating through flesh. Perhaps the salve the girl mentioned had been the problem?

They could sort through that later. For now she needed to tend the man's wounds.

Turning her focus to his face, she reached for the edge of the fur covering. "I need to see the wounds on your leg."

The girl spoke quietly using sounds Laura couldn't decipher, and the fellow nodded in answer, keeping his eyes on Laura. Consenting.

She pulled back the hide to reveal the rest of his body. It took a moment to figure out what all she was seeing. He wore a breechclout and buckskin leggings, the latter mangled at both knees. She quickly averted her eyes. This man was no relation, and she was examining him as if she was a true physician.

But she *did* need to ascertain the extent of his injuries. They had to know what supplies to bring back to dress the wounds.

She forced herself to take in steady breaths, forced her mind to focus on the wounds only, then turned back to the leg. He had several lacerations on both legs, all of which would require cleaning and a healing salve, and should be wrapped to keep them from festering. But none required stitches.

The arm, on the other hand, would need stitches and much

more, but there was no skin left at the edges of the wound to bind together. The injury would have to heal with a salve and bandage, as far as she could tell, but the doctor would know better.

At last, she turned back to face the girl fully. "What's your name?"

The girl's face turned shy, an adorable look that softened her expression in every way. "Bright Sun."

Laura placed her hands on her knees. "Well, Bright Sun. I have a friend who has some things that will help your grandfather, but I need to go get him and his medicines. Will you both stay here until we return?"

The girl darted a glance at her grandfather, then back to Laura with a nod. "We will wait."

Laura looked to the grandfather. "And what's his name?"

"He is called Eagle Soaring in your tongue."

Laura gave the man a smile. "I'm honored to meet you, Eagle Soaring. I'll return as soon as I can with help."

The man grunted. Whether the sound was greeting, or a sign of pain or displeasure, she couldn't have said. No matter what, her mission was clear.

He needed help.

⋰⋱⟨⟩⋰⋱

Nate's mind churned as they left the cave. He let Laura lead the way along the ledge around the cliff, and neither of them spoke until they reached the place where the rock met grass.

He was pretty sure he knew what Laura was thinking, but he asked, just to be certain. "We're going to get Doc Bradley?"

"I have to. That arm is in bad shape. It looks more like a burn than a mountain lion wound, but I've never seen a burn like it. There's so much raw flesh exposed. . . . Great care will need to be taken so it doesn't fester."

The hesitation in her voice made him look over. She met his gaze, a haunted look in her eyes. "He could easily lose the arm, but more likely his life, as weak as he seemed."

Nate's chest ached for little Bright Sun. She'd been so brave. Did she truly understand he and Miss Hannon weren't a threat? "I wonder if they have family or other people nearby. Why are they here alone?"

Laura's brows furrowed. "I don't know. I'm surprised she speaks such good English."

At least that he could answer. "Men from the trapping companies often stay with the tribes for months at a time. Most of the Indians have learned English or French from them. The children are often raised speaking multiple languages."

She nodded, but didn't speak again, and they soon reached the horses. The ride back was quiet, though likely her thoughts were as active as his own. What could he do to help the pair? He wasn't a doctor, and he had no doubt Bradley would do everything he could to dress the wounds. He'd seen time and again that the man inspired confidence with his determination to help his patients.

Did Bright Sun and her grandfather have enough food?

She was thin, but not gaunt. Yet, if the two of them were separated from the rest of their people, she'd not be able to hunt to keep them both fed. He could bring them roasted venison from a deer he'd taken down two nights before. That would see them for a few days. He'd have to hunt again to have enough meat for himself, but he could manage.

Maybe he'd take some of his hides to them, too. Likely the girl already knew how to scrape and tan them, but if not, he could show her. He'd not managed to find time to work the furs, so giving them to someone who could put them to good use would be helpful. And with the nights so cold, the pair would need more than one buffalo robe to keep them warm enough.

They reached the place where he should split off toward his camp, and he raised his hand to signal a halt. Laura looked at him expectantly.

"I'm going to get some food and furs from my camp to take back to them. I'll meet you at the clinic?"

Laura looked up in surprise. "Your camp?"

His breath stalled, but he forced himself to inhale again. He'd not told anyone he wasn't staying in one of the boarding-houses. Not that he was trying to hide anything, but he simply hadn't wanted to raise questions. "I have a tent where I keep my supplies outside of town. That way I don't have to waste my earnings to pay for lodging." He shrugged, doing his best to show the matter was insignificant. The last thing he wanted was to draw any pity.

She tipped her head. "You sleep in a tent? The nights are freezing now."

That fact he knew well. But he shrugged again. "I'll take a room when I need to."

Her mouth pinched, but then she finally seemed to let the matter go as she turned her horse toward town. "Hurry to the clinic when you get what you need."

Nate eased out a breath as he nudged his gelding into a lope. His secret was out, but maybe that was for the best. He had nothing more to hide. And his focus now needed to be on whatever he could do to help the pair back at the cave.

The fact that Laura seemed determined to do the same thing shouldn't add to his eagerness, yet it did.

⊰⊱

Laura had known the doctor wouldn't mind coming to tend the old Indian, but she was still grateful for the tenderness he showed as he bandaged Eagle Soaring's injuries. Doc Micah hadn't blinked when she'd told him the man needed help, although he'd given her an odd look when she told him the fellow was hidden away in a cave in the mountains.

And his look had narrowed even more when she told him Nate had gone to gather blankets and food, and would ride back with them.

Ingrid hadn't come with them, as she'd been in bed when Laura returned for the doctor. Worn out from their afternoon activities, no doubt. The baby was certainly taking a toll on her.

An inkling of worry slipped through Laura's chest as she handed the doctor another bandage to finish wrapping Eagle

Soaring's arm. Was something going wrong with the pregnancy? She'd assumed Ingrid's struggles were simply the normal throes of expectant motherhood. Now wasn't the time to ask the doctor, but she'd find a moment later.

Doc Micah was finishing up his work, so she began packing the supplies into his satchel. He motioned for her to stop. "I can do that. Don't worry yourself."

She immediately set the jar of salve back on the cave floor. They'd worked together in the clinic, but she'd never accompanied him on house calls. He probably liked his bag packed a certain way.

With nothing left to do, she pushed to her feet and turned to Bright Sun. The girl had been standing beside them, keeping watch over everything the doctor did.

Laura offered a smile. "Where are your people? Do you have other family who are looking for you?" Surely these two weren't traveling by themselves.

"Our people will come for us soon." Bright Sun spoke with certainty, yet her words didn't offer enough details.

"Do you know how soon?" She snuck a glance at Nate. "Do you have supplies anywhere?"

The girl's chin rose. "We have what we need."

She should have known better than to ask so many questions. The girl wouldn't acknowledge a need, of course, and Laura's queries would only remind the child she had to be tough.

The doctor straightened after putting the last of the supplies in his bag. Something in his manner made Laura tense as they all turned their focus to him. He shifted his gaze between the older man and the young girl. "The wounds are clean now, but I'm worried they'll get infected. It'd be best if you both come back to the clinic with me."

At the uncertainty that crossed Bright Sun's features, he spoke again. "The clinic is my home in town, where I take care of people who are sick or hurt." He motioned to Eagle Soaring's arm. "Like your grandfather."

The confusion cleared from the girl's face, replaced by a look that seemed to say she was thinking through all the implications of leaving the cave and going to a white man's town. But did she really understand?

Laura smiled again. "What he says is right. We can help your grandfather best if you both come with us."

Bright Sun turned to her grandfather and spoke a string of words. The older man answered, and the slight shake of his head started a twist of disappointment in Laura's middle.

The girl turned back to Laura and jutted her chin in a look filled with such determination that Laura almost smiled. "We stay here. Safe here. I will help him."

Doc Micah looked to Laura, too. His raised brows showed he'd realized the girl answered her, not him. But that was no great surprise. Laura would be less of a threat to the child than a man would be, even one as genuinely caring as Dr. Micah Bradley.

After all, he did have a bit of a mountain-man aura about him. At least until you got to know him.

She turned back to Bright Sun and addressed both her and her grandfather. "Are you certain? We want to help you, and we can do that much better if you come with us. Please."

This time, Eagle Soaring shook his head with firm resolve. He spoke a few words in his own tongue, and Bright Sun translated in a resolute tone. "We stay here."

Doc Micah sighed. "It's important you keep this clean, then, and wrapped at all times. You should check the bandage every day and look for signs of redness or festering."

Bright Sun leaned close to see what he pointed to as he explained more signs to watch for and how to know if the bandage should be changed. The girl nodded each time he looked up at her as he spoke.

At last, he finished, and then glanced around. "That's it, I suppose."

Laura leaned forward to catch Bright Sun's attention. "Could you show me the spring where your grandfather washed? I'd like to see what burned him." She sent a glance to Nate. If she'd read him correctly earlier, his curiosity was more than piqued, as well.

"I'd like to see it, too." Doc Micah rose with his lantern. "Is it nearby?"

The girl nodded, then turned and started across the cavern, in the direction that she'd first appeared earlier.

Laura scooped up one of the other lanterns and strode quickly to catch up with the girl. The child wove around the hanging rock spikes as though she'd maneuvered through this cavern all her life. How long had she and her grandfather been here? They hadn't seen any trace of a fire or other signs of habitation.

Bright Sun reached the cavern wall and didn't slow, looking like she would walk straight into the rock. She ducked at the last minute, disappearing into a black hole that swallowed her completely.

Laura reached the spot, and her lantern filtered into the darkness. A cave, just as Bright Sun had said. Holding the light as far in front of her as she could, Laura stepped inside. The ceiling wasn't as tall as she was, so she had to duck.

Her light flickered off a stone wall ahead, blocking the path at an angle. But there was just enough room for her to step around it.

Taking a breath for courage, she stepped toward the narrow opening, the men close behind her. What they'd find on the other side was anyone's guess.

EIGHT

*L*aura rounded the jutting stone—Nate and Doc Micah shuffling just behind her—then raised her lantern high as the low stone ceiling opened into another high cavern.

This one didn't appear to extend very far ahead, but her light glinted off water running through from right to left. Bright Sun stood at the edge of the little creek.

The girl pointed to the right. "The spring makes a larger pool up here."

As they trekked that direction, the ground sloped uphill. A strong smell had begun to fill the air, like eggs rotting in a burning summer sun. The air grew wet and warm as steam wafted from the creek. Between the stench and the thick blanket of hot vapor, this larger cave was almost suffocating.

At last, Bright Sun halted at a place where the creek widened into a pool. A solid stone wall behind the spring showed that this must be where the cave ended. Laura held the lantern over the water and could see the bubbling at one end. Between the steam and the bubbling, the liquid sure looked hot enough to burn skin, although maybe not to the extent of Eagle Soaring's injury.

Doc Micah crouched near the area that was bubbling and eased his hand out to touch the water. After a quick splash, he inserted his hand farther, then looked up at them. "It's not very hot."

Laura dropped to her haunches, too, and eased her fingers into the liquid. The perfect warmth for a bath, but certainly not hot enough to burn. At least, not here at the surface. She'd have to remove her coat to feel deeper, but she'd wager none of the water was much hotter.

She studied the steam rising from the surface. "Do you think whatever makes it smell causes the steam?"

"Could be. Maybe that's what reacted with the ointment they used on his arm." Doc Micah rose and turned to the girl, who stood back a little, watching them. "Thank you for showing us, Bright Sun. Can you take us back to your grandfather?"

The girl turned without a word and strode back the way they'd come. Laura did her best to take in both sides of the creek as they walked, at least as much as her light showed. A glimmer of daylight appeared on her left to mark the small opening in the stone wall back to the front cavern.

"Have you explored to see how far the creek goes?" Nate's voice paused them all, and Bright Sun looked downriver where he pointed.

"It flows the same distance as that way"—she pointed back upstream to the spring they'd just visited—"then goes back into the rock."

Nate nodded his understanding. "Are there other caves than what we've walked through so far?"

"No." Without another word, the girl ducked into the entryway again.

"I guess that means she's done answering questions." Nate's mutter pulled a chuckle from Laura.

She held the lantern higher in front of her and followed Nate into the small opening, the doctor coming behind. As she stepped around the rock wall jutting out, her left foot caught on a stone at the base, throwing her weight onto her right.

A sharp pain shot up her ankle, and the joint bucked beneath her. A cry escaped as she stumbled forward, trying to keep from going down. A hand grabbed her arm, slowing her fall as she landed on her knees.

"Laura." Nate was in front of her, holding her up so she didn't fall any farther.

She drew in gasping breaths as her heart surged in her chest. Her ankle throbbed. She clung to her lantern, clenching her jaw through the pain. At least her skirt had eased the damage to her knees.

"Are you hurt? Your ankle again?" Nate's voice sounded nearly frantic.

She forced measured breaths. "Not bad. I can stand." She hoped. But this pain felt so much worse than the last time.

He still gripped her arm with one hand, and he placed his other hand in hers, giving her something to hold as she pushed up to her feet. She'd fallen forward into the front cavern, so at least there was more light from the sun shining through the entrance.

If she kept her weight on her good foot, the pain was quite manageable. "There, see?" She infused a bit of cheer in her voice. "Not hurt."

"Let's see if you can walk." Doc Micah spoke with his measured doctor voice as he looked at her with concern.

Keeping her jaw clenched against the pain, she stepped forward. The knives piercing her ankle forced an exaggerated limp, but at least she could move on her own.

She ignored the men's stares and marched forward. She had to at least reach Bright Sun and her grandfather, and then she could sit and visit for a few minutes while her leg recovered. Thank the Lord they'd brought horses so she wouldn't have to walk back.

"Laura, if you walk on that ankle, the damage will be much worse. Here, use us for support." The doctor moved up beside her on the left. "Let me have that lantern."

He took the handle from her and gripped her hand, placing his arm under hers so he could bear some of her weight. As much as she wanted to protest, her ankle ached more with each step. She could force herself to keep going through the pain, but the joint felt like it might buckle again at any moment.

Nate came along her other side—the injured one—and slipped his arm around her waist, dipping his shoulder low so she could cling to it. The same way she had the last time, during that torturous walk back to town. What was it about this cave that made her always come away injured? If she believed in bad luck, she'd say these underground chambers held their fair share of ill will toward her.

As they wove through the rock formations to reach the

pair, the girl's dark eyes never wavered from watching them. They still hadn't learned why these two were alone in the cave, or even how long they'd been here. But Laura's ankle throbbed too much for her to string together the right words and gentle tone she'd need to pull answers from the child.

Just keeping from moaning with each step took more strength than she had to spare at this point.

The doctor stopped them before they reached the pair. "Wait here while I get my bag. Then we'll go."

She was too relieved to argue. The sooner they reached the horses, the sooner she could get off her feet and back to the clinic.

While they waited for the doctor, Laura leaned more of her weight against Nate, letting her head rest against his shoulder. His hand tucked tighter around her waist, holding her secure. Letting this man bear the weight of her pain— even for just a moment—was more relief than she could describe. His head rested atop hers, and she would almost have thought he'd pressed a kiss to her hair.

But he wouldn't do that. Of course not.

All too soon, Doc Micah returned to them, and she had to walk again. Step by painful step, they left the cave behind and scaled the ledge around the cliffside. Part of her never wanted to see that cave again.

But another part kept the image of Bright Sun sitting beside the prone form of her grandfather. What would happen to them? If Eagle Soaring didn't survive his injuries, did the girl have anyone who would come back for her?

No matter how hard Laura had to work for it, she must

make sure the pair had what they needed until Eagle Soaring recovered enough to handle the job himself. She couldn't let them suffer.

Perhaps this was exactly the purpose she'd been searching for. At least for now.

Sitting in bed with her leg propped up all day made Laura feel useless. Especially when Ingrid had to do all the work for both the clinic and the household, even though she was pale as a white bedsheet.

She'd finally pinned Doc Micah to ask if Ingrid's sickness might be a sign of something more serious. He'd scrubbed a hand through his hair and sighed, but said he'd not seen signs of anything that should worry them.

At least she had that relief, but she was pretty certain she heard Ingrid retching at least twice through that first day. Neither Ingrid nor her husband would allow Laura out of bed, and knowing for sure how much her friend suffered would only make her feel worse. Now the second day was almost through, and she should hobble in and sit with Aaron for a while. Maybe they could bond over their common frustration of being bedridden.

But her injury was so much less severe than Aaron's, and he might think she was flaunting the fact that she'd be up and moving in only a few days. The last thing she wanted was to bring his spirits lower.

In truth, everything seemed to dampen his attitude. He

seemed always to be either angry or in deep melancholy. Had he tended to shift toward such deep moods before? She didn't remember him that way during the time she'd been forced to ride along with the gang. Aaron had been quiet, but not mean-spirited or depressed.

Lord, let him return to the man he was before—only a better one this time. Not a thief. A good man who can walk and smile and fulfill the right calling you made him for.

Was that too much to ask? Surely God wanted the same for Aaron, the man He'd created in His own image.

Aaron's spirits were probably even lower today than usual because Nate hadn't come to see him the night before. Had he gone to visit the Indians in the cave instead?

Possibly, although she was surprised he hadn't stopped by the clinic first. The doctor had said he'd collect some food and other supplies Nate could take to the pair, and she'd seen Ingrid carrying a load past her open bedchamber door twice that day. Bright Sun and her grandfather wouldn't be hungry or cold for a while.

Now if only Nate would come get the supplies. Doc Micah had been summoned just after the noon meal for an elderly woman who'd taken fever on the other side of town. He still hadn't returned, or he probably would have gone to the cave himself.

A noise drifted from the hall outside—the front door opening, if she wasn't mistaken. Yes, that was definitely the door being closed, then a familiar pattern of boots thudding. Tentative, as though he wasn't sure he belonged, and walking toward Aaron's bedchamber.

The sounds of men's voices drifted through the wall, but she couldn't make out the words. Only the light rumble of Nate's, then the deeper grunts of his brother. As twins, Nate and Aaron certainly carried a strong family resemblance, but there was also such a difference between them.

Both were quiet and respectful, but Nate had an optimism that fed into everything he did, even into the tone of his voice. She noticed it more now than when she'd first met him. Maybe because she'd spent so much more time with him.

A chuckle drifted through the wall. That had to be Nate, and she could picture how his deep green eyes danced as he laughed. He was surprisingly witty and could pull a smile from her even when she didn't want him to.

Her chest tightened, and something inside her yearned to see those dancing green eyes now. She desperately wanted something to smile about.

NINE

*L*aura eased her legs off the bed and reached for the walking sticks. The throbbing in her ankle had lessened to a dull ache, but a twinge of pain shot up the limb when she pushed upright. Once she hobbled through the first few steps, her body found the same rhythm she'd learned last time. This injury was definitely worse—a second-degree sprain, the doctor said, probably more severe because it happened so soon after the first one—but as long as she didn't put weight on the bad leg, she should be able to get around with help from the walking sticks.

Quiet draped the hallway when she stepped from her room. Hopefully Ingrid was resting, although she might be back in the kitchen. The low vibrato of male voices still hummed from Aaron's chamber, so she limped toward his door, making sure to let the sticks thump loudly enough that they could hear her coming. Just in case they were speaking of private matters.

She tapped on the door, loud enough for them to hear inside but not so loud she'd draw Ingrid to check on them.

"Enter." Nate's voice.

She pushed open the door and peered inside. Both faces looked up at her, Aaron from the chair in the corner, Nate from his seat on the edge of the bed. "I hope I'm not interrupting. I . . ."

What excuse could she give for barging in on their visit? It would be selfish to say she'd been lonely. Maybe this hadn't been such a good idea. She looked to Nate. "I wanted to see if you'd been to see Bright Sun and her grandfather. Ingrid has some supplies set aside to take to them."

His face wore weary lines across his brow and at the corners of his eyes. "I haven't been back, but I plan to go in the morning on my way to the mine. I can take the goods with me tonight."

He hadn't gone the night before? Where had he been then? "I thought since you weren't here last—" She bit off the sentence the moment she realized the way her words would sound. It wasn't any of her business whether he took a night off from his responsibilities. He wasn't required to come check on his brother—or her.

His shoulders sagged a little, and his gaze moved away from her, wandering to his brother. "I had to do some hunting, replenish my meat supply."

She blinked as her mind struggled to form a new picture of him. First she'd learned he lived in a camp outside of town, and now he hunted for his food? Surely wild game wasn't all he ate, but it would certainly ease the weight of his tab at the mercantile. Or would Mr. Lanton not sell to him because of his past crimes? That didn't seem like the reasonable man she'd met. As the acting lawman until the new sheriff arrived, he was the one who'd suggested Nate and Aaron be allowed to work off their debt instead of being imprisoned or hanged for the crimes.

Or maybe Nate didn't earn much at the mine. And with Aaron still recovering, it would be some time before he could earn his part. That was the more likely reason he was so frugal. And she could respect the way Nate cut back expenses everywhere he could. At least the doctor had insisted Nate not pay any of the costs for Aaron's care and board. Aaron was to work that off once he was able.

But if one thing was certain, it was that Nate didn't seem to fear hard work. If only her father had been the same way, the childhood she and her brothers had endured might have been very different. Maybe Will and Robbie would even be still alive today.

"How's your ankle?" Nate's attention had returned to her. "You're up and around already?" He raised his brows, as though he was surprised the doctor had released her.

Part of her wanted to raise her chin and tell him she was perfectly well, thank you. But in truth, her ankle had resumed throbbing, even though she wasn't pressing any weight on the joint. She should probably sit down.

"Are you supposed to be sitting right now?" Nate narrowed his eyes at her.

Fiddlesticks. How did the man read her mind so well? She couldn't stop the heat from flooding her ears. She did raise her chin this time, though. "I've been sitting with my foot propped up for two days now. Using these should be perfectly fine." She tapped the walking sticks.

"Let the woman walk around, Nate. If she *can* do it, why shouldn't she?" Aaron spoke up for the first time.

She sent him a grateful smile, but his lips turned down in the grimace that seemed to be his constant expression these days.

"At least come and sit." Nate shifted over and patted the empty part of the bed.

She hesitated. That didn't seem proper at all, sitting on a bed beside a man. For that matter, neither was being in a bed-chamber with two men, no matter that she would leave the door open. Did it matter that it was also an invalid's room?

Nate seemed to realize what he'd offered. He jumped up, his face turning red. Stepping over to his brother's side—as far away from the bed as he could get—he motioned toward the seat he'd just vacated. "Sit, if you think it's all right. Or not. Whichever you think is best."

She couldn't help a smile at the sheepish look on his face. The offer had certainly been innocent. With the door open, maybe there wouldn't be too much impropriety.

And the last thing she wanted to do was return to her bed.

Doing her best not to show her pain, she hobbled into the room and eased down on the edge of the bed. A silence settled over the room, so she summoned a smile for Aaron. "How are you feeling today? I've missed getting to visit when I bring your meals."

He grunted, then laid his head back against the chair and closed his eyes.

Nate frowned at his brother. He turned to her, a mixture of worry and embarrassment clouding his eyes. "Sorry. His leg is paining him a lot today."

Laura glanced back at the injured man. His eyes looked sunken in, his face pale as it usually was these days. Those were definitely signs of strain.

"It's nigh unbearable." Aaron's growl was almost too rough to make out the words.

Nate refocused his attention on his brother. "I don't suppose there's anything we can give him? Something to ease his hurting?" He turned back to Laura, his eyes so beseeching that her middle tightened.

The doctor had said Aaron could have laudanum once or twice a day if the pain grew severe, especially for the first two weeks after the surgery.

"I'll get something." She pushed up from the bed and balanced on her good foot until she had the sticks positioned under her arms.

"I didn't mean—" Nate straightened. "I can go get whatever you need if you'll direct me." He motioned toward her feet. "You shouldn't be walking. I'm here. Let me help."

She shook her head. The doctor was extremely careful with the laudanum, keeping it in a locked drawer. She and the Bradleys were the only people allowed access. "It's no trouble. I'll return posthaste." She waved toward Aaron. "Visit with your brother."

By the time she'd retrieved the medicine and given Aaron

a dose, her ankle had taken all the exercise it would bear. She said a quiet good night, then hobbled back to her room.

When she reached her door and glanced back, the figure standing in Aaron's doorway gave her pause. Nate was watching her, and the soft expression on his face made her chest ache. He gave her one of those off-kilter grins, and it pulled a smile from somewhere deep inside her.

"Good night, Laura." His voice emerged so gentle, it made her want to linger there, to rest her head against the doorframe and watch him.

She couldn't, though, so she settled for another soft "Good night" and stepped into her chamber. Even as she lay back on her bed, she could still see his face, that gentle expression marking his handsome features. She wouldn't mind lying still for hours if she could hold on to that memory.

Nate heaved the pack higher on his shoulder and pulled his coat tighter as he maneuvered the rock ledge in the scant moonlight. A gust of wind whipped at his hair and slid down his neck, despite the thick buckskin of his coat. This path to the cave was definitely more treacherous in the dark, especially when his eyes were so grainy from lack of sleep.

Between long days at the mine and evenings checking on Aaron, then the work he had to do around his camp at night just to feed himself and keep warm, early mornings were the only time left for him to take supplies to their Indian friends. If only the air didn't nip so icy cold without the sun's warmth. Winter was coming on with a ferocity.

Hopefully the deer meat he'd roasted last night would last him for a couple weeks, and he'd be able to focus on the people who needed him. That and his endless days at the mine. Now that Barlow was training him with the explosions, he was working even longer hours than before.

As he neared the mouth of the cave, he strained to hear any noises. Nothing sounded except the constant blowing of the wind. The air tasted wet and heavy, like snow might come today. He leaned down into the cave opening and called, "Bright Sun? Eagle Soaring? It's Nate. I've brought food and other supplies for you."

He ducked inside and dropped to his knees, fumbling to find the lantern and matches they'd left next to the inside wall. The scent of a campfire pricked his nose. He needed to make sure the pair had enough wood to burn for light.

"It's Nate, I've come to bring you food," he called again, just in case they hadn't heard him the first time. The last thing he needed was an arrow or knife wound because they didn't know it was him.

When the match flared to life, he glanced around the area. Bright Sun stood at the base of the incline—the place where Laura had fallen—staring at him. The child rarely made a sound, either in her movements or her speech.

He offered a smile as he lit the lantern. "I can't stay long, but I brought you food and blankets from the doctor. How's your grandfather?"

"He sleeps now. I take you to him."

Nate stood and hoisted the pack, then followed her. She didn't go to the place the man had lain before but instead turned the opposite direction toward the other chamber that held the hot springs. She moved into the dark opening without pause, but Nate had to gather his nerve before ducking into the low entrance.

The thick scent of rotting eggs pricked his nose as he stepped into the humid cavern. This room was much warmer than the front chamber. By the side wall, in the flickering lantern light, Eagle Soaring lay with the buffalo robe pulled over him. The ashes of a fire sat nearby, as did the pile of furs Nate had brought them.

He dropped his bundle beside those, then knelt at the older man's head. "How are you today, my friend?"

Eagle Soaring poked his good hand out at the top of the fur and reached toward Nate. He wasn't certain what the man intended, but it looked like he might be offering to shake hands. Nate clasped the other man's palm in his. The hold was weak, and the bones felt as though they might shatter if he squeezed too hard.

But Eagle Soaring looked up at him with an expression of gratitude. He spoke a few words Nate couldn't understand, but the man's thanks warmed his eyes and brought a rise of emotions into Nate's throat.

He rested a hand on the buffalo robe where Eagle Soaring's shoulder should be, then turned to Bright Sun. "Do you have enough wood to keep a fire going?" Even if they were warm enough between the heat from the hot springs and the furs, a fire would provide light.

"I will gather more wood this morning." Bright Sun spoke in a quiet yet confident tone.

"Better do it as soon as there's daylight. I think snowfall will start any time now." He released the man's hand and pushed to his feet. He'd be late to the mine if he didn't leave right now. "Is there anything else you need?"

"Nothing." Bright Sun spoke the word quickly, with a definite hint of defiance in her tone.

The older man murmured something, and the girl spoke again, but this time with less venom. "We thank you for your kindness."

Nate bit back a chuckle. "I'll come check on you again soon." Then he scooped up his lantern and strode back toward the cave entrance.

When he stepped into the dawning light, tiny snowflakes drifted down around him. The ice crystals landed on his face, stinging his nose and cheeks with their wet chill. He fished his felt miner's hat from where he'd tucked it inside his waistband. In truth, he hated the thing, but it would keep his head dry.

Faint rays of sunlight struggled to lighten the thick cloud cover in the eastern sky, which meant he'd best double-time it to the mine. He lengthened his stride as he maneuvered the ledge around the cliff. He'd done this so many times now that the steep drop-off on his right no longer clenched his nerves. This must be how the mountain goats felt, scrambling up and over rocks with nary a concern.

Snow fell thicker now, turning into a curtain of white flakes that melted the instant they struck stone. The tread of the mining boots he'd been forced to purchase had worn thin through his months of hard work, and his foot slipped as he jumped down from a rise in the stone.

He gripped a flat part of the boulder to steady himself, then pushed on. His pay would be docked if he arrived after the others, and he couldn't afford to lose that money.

His mind drifted back to the pair in the cave. Bright Sun had better gather wood soon, or she'd find only wet fodder. Then they'd have to suffer the cold until the logs dried enough to light. He should have thought to bring dry tinder. Maybe after work today, he could gather a load and come—

A rock under his boot broke away, and his right foot shot out from under him, slipping off the edge of the ledge. He dived left, throwing his weight nearer the mountain as he scrambled for something to grab onto.

With one leg dangling over the side, he landed hard on the ledge. His shoulder slammed into the vertical rock on his left, and he clutched at the solid ledge underneath him.

No matter what, he had to keep from sliding off the mountain.

TEN

*N*ate's body stilled, and he barely dared to breathe as he clung to the rock beneath him. His shoulder and hip pressed hard into the stone, and his legs splayed wide, one still dangling off the ledge.

A powerful pain burned through his shoulder. *God, let it not be injured.* He'd have a few bruises, no doubt. But he couldn't afford to be less than able-bodied. Not with all the responsibilities he had to fulfill.

Slowly, he rolled himself closer to the mountain beside him, pulling his right leg back up on the ledge. He'd not seen evidence earlier that the stone was loose. But this type of fall came from being too confident. In fact, if he wasn't mistaken, this was the same dip in the rock where Laura had lost her balance and nearly teetered over the edge that first day—the reason he'd followed her up and eventually frightened her in the cave, causing the injury to her ankle. If he didn't know better, he might think this cave was cursed.

But he did know better. Laura's injury, Eagle Soaring's

wounds, even this feather-brained fall were all the results of either choices or accidents. Yet, none of them surprised God, and He could and *would* work all things together for their good. All they had to do was keep working at the tasks He'd given each of them. For Nate, that was the mine. And at this rate, a pay docking seemed to be in his immediate future.

With a groan, he gathered his legs under him and pushed upright. A surge of fire speared his left shoulder, buckling his arm underneath him. He pulled the injured arm into himself, cradling it as he struggled to find a position where the shoulder didn't burn like it was going up in flames.

Not this again. He reached up to feel the back side of his shoulder. The hard knot was there, just as he'd felt the last time the shoulder bone pulled out of its socket. Bill had relieved most of the pain in minutes by working the joint back together—or something like that. They'd been running from a Virginia City posse at the time, so he'd not had the liberty of consulting a doctor. After the initial fire had been quenched, the joint had still ached for weeks.

Holding the injured arm close to him, he gritted his teeth and worked himself up to standing. If he didn't at least show himself at the mine, even as late as he was, they might think the worst and cut him loose altogether. Maybe someone there could work the joint back in place and he could get started on his day's work.

By the time he reached the mine, a wagon was parked outside the opening. Must be a freighter delivering supplies. Hiram's team, if he wasn't mistaken.

Sloane and Danvers were each lifting a box from the rear

of the conveyance and eyed Nate as he stumbled across the clearing toward them. They didn't speak, but words weren't necessary to convey their censure. Most of the men were friendly enough toward him, but a few still kept their distance. It didn't help that he now appeared to be shirking his share of the work.

He followed the men into the mine entrance. "Know which shaft Marson is in?" The superintendent would be best to speak with.

"That way." Sloane motioned with his elbow toward the left opening where the blasters were working.

Nate didn't pause to grab a candle from the stack and attach it to the bracket on his felt hat. This shaft wasn't long, and he could already see the glow ahead where the others were working.

Marson was speaking to Barlow, the lead blaster, but paused when Nate approached. *Let him be reasonable, Lord.* This superintendent usually was. More so than the other brawny man the owners had brought in from the States.

As Nate stopped before him, Marson's gaze landed on Nate's arm, stalled there a moment, then swung back up to his face.

"My apologies for being late, sir. Had a run-in with a rock on my way here. By chance, do we have anyone who knows how to move a shoulder joint back in place? If so, I can get to work straightaway." Maybe he should say he'd get to work either way, but the fire in his shoulder surged hotter with each minute. He wouldn't be worth much without the use of both hands. "If not, I can try to repair the arm myself."

Marson shook his head. "Sloane and Danvers should have the wagon unloaded. Ride back to town with Hiram and have the doc tend you. He'll tell you to lay out for a week, but if you're up to coming back tomorrow, I'll start you with Barlow here. Working with the blasters should let your arm heal, since it's the left you've injured."

Bile churned in Nate's gut. Take the day off? "I'll see if Doc Bradley can get it fixed quick, then I'll come right back."

Again Marson shook his head. "I've seen plenty of these injuries. If you don't let the shoulder heal, you'll be more worthless to me when it happens again." He leveled a look on Nate weighty enough to sink into his bones, even in the dim light of the mine's interior. "I know you'd do it today if you could. But I'm telling you not to come back till tomorrow. At the soonest."

Nate eased out a breath. "Yes, sir." Then he turned and trudged back through the darkness. The sooner he shed the weight of this agony in his shoulder, the better.

The jingle of harness outside was Laura's first warning a new patient might have arrived. She shifted closer to the window in the examination room so she could peek through the curtain for a glimpse, while Doc Micah worked with Judith, Mrs. Bailor's baby, who'd been suffering from fever for three days now. The woman had knocked on the clinic door so early the doctor was still breaking his fast, but of course he'd welcomed in the worried mother and fussing child.

Through the glass, a stout wagon stopped in front of the clinic, the kind freighters used to carry supplies back and forth to Fort Benton. She well knew how hard the bench seats were, for she'd ridden for two weeks on a similar conveyance on her way back to Settler's Fort all those months ago.

The lean man sitting atop the bench looked vaguely familiar and didn't appear to be coming into the clinic but instead sat eyeing the porch. She followed his gaze.

Her heart jolted at the sight of broad shoulders mounting the last step. What was Nate doing here so early in the morning? His workday had surely started by now. Did he come to get the doctor for an accident at the mine?

"Nate's here." She murmured the words barely loud enough for Doc Micah to hear, just so he'd be prepared, then swung on her walking sticks toward the hallway and the front door.

Nate was stepping inside when she reached the corridor. He paused, as if to get his bearings. Her heart did another leap as she caught sight of the odd tilt of his shoulders. "Nate, what is it?"

He spun to face her, and she took in the lines of pain at the corners of his eyes even before she saw the way he clutched his left arm to his body.

Her pulse slammed in her throat. "What happened? Come and sit." With the examination room full, they usually had patients wait in one of the chairs in the hallway. "Or do you need to lie down?"

He was standing now, but maybe he shouldn't be. She could make a bed pallet on the floor. Or maybe Aaron's bed would be large enough for him to rest beside his brother. Aaron would want to know Nate was hurt.

Nate shook his head. "Just slipped on an icy rock. Need the doctor to work my shoulder joint back into place."

She sucked in a hard breath. The last time they'd had a man in with that injury, he'd been in tears when he arrived. And the scream he'd loosed as Doc Micah performed his work had echoed through the house for hours afterward.

"Come and sit." She motioned toward the chair but hovered near his side as he shuffled toward the seat. "Rest while I get the doctor."

Doc Micah was handing a bottle to Mrs. Bailor when Laura poked her head back in the room. He turned to her with raised brows while the mother packed up her child and satchel.

"Nate's here with a shoulder out of joint. Said he slipped on an icy rock."

The doctor nodded. "Have him come in as soon as I wipe this down." Doc Micah was fastidiously clean when it came to his clinic, especially after patients who might carry a malady that was catching. She was more than grateful for that particular trait. The last thing Nate needed was a fever on top of his other struggles.

Laura hobbled with her walking sticks back through the antechamber to the hallway, Mrs. Bailor on her heels. The woman was murmuring soothing words to her child and barely offered Laura a farewell wave as she left the clinic.

She turned her focus to Nate. "Come back to the exam room. The doctor's preparing for you."

The rock-solid set of his mouth showed his pain, but tears didn't run down his face as they had with the other brawny man who'd suffered the same injury. Ingrid had helped the doctor that time, but that wouldn't be the case this time. She'd returned to bed of her own accord after making the morning meal, so she must be feeling worse than usual.

That meant Laura could help, and for that she was grateful. If there was anything she could do to ease Nate's pain, she wanted to be there.

She followed him back to the room where Doc Micah pointed toward the table. "Sit and let's get your coat off."

Again, she stayed back against the wall until she was needed. Better to stay out of the doctor's way until he needed a second pair of hands.

Within less than a minute, the doctor had expertly eased Nate's coat off and was examining his left shoulder. "It's dislocated, but we can get it back in place quickly. The pain'll get worse, but that part will be quick, and you'll feel immediate relief."

Nate nodded. "I've had it before." He spoke through his clenched jaw.

"Should I get him something for the pain?" She didn't usually interrupt the doctor's work, but seeing Nate in so much agony pressed a weight on her own chest.

The doctor looked up and raised his brows at Nate.

He shook his head. "Just do it."

As Doc Micah positioned Nate on the table, he motioned to Laura. "Can you get me a bandage? We'll need to wrap the arm close to his body."

Ah yes. She should have remembered that. She hobbled to the anteroom where they kept oft-needed supplies. Her injured leg was already growing weary, though she did her best not to put weight on the limb. There would be time to rest after Nate was settled.

As she turned to take the bandage back to the examination room, a sharp cry sounded from that chamber. She hurried forward. Had the doctor's poking become too much for Nate? Surely Micah hadn't reset the arm the moment she walked away.

But he was helping Nate sit upright, holding the arm close to his body. Clearly the hard work had been done. "It'll be sore for a week at least, maybe two. How many times has it been dislocated in the past?"

"Just once." Nate's face had lost much of its color, but he no longer held his jaw in a clamp.

She handed the bandage to the doctor, then stepped around the table to Nate's back so she could assist in the wrapping. Nate's shoulders seemed to be shaking a little, probably from the pain, or maybe it was simply his body attempting to recover from so much shock. She laid a hand on his back, the only way she knew to soothe.

His warmth emanated through his shirt, making her want to lean closer. Maybe she shouldn't have touched him at all. She'd only meant the action as a nurse helping a patient. Mostly.

In truth, there didn't seem to be an easy way to draw that line where this man was concerned. How could she soothe him without opening herself to care more about him than

she should? Between his attractiveness and the deeper quali-
ties she'd seen these past months as he visited and cared for
his brother, it was hard not to respect him. Hard not to care
more than she wanted to.

They finally finished wrapping his arm tight, and then
Doc Micah helped Nate pull his coat on his good arm and
button it. She moved back around the examination table to
take her place by the window. Hopefully far enough from
Nate that these unwanted emotions would settle. He gave
her a glimmer of a smile when she turned back to face him.
Probably just a smile of thanks for her help, but the grin was
his off-kilter one that showed his single dimple and always
started a fluttering in her middle.

Thankfully, the doctor claimed his attention. "You need
to take it easy for a week at least. Keep this bandage on. Do
I have your word?"

Nate faced the man, determination cloaking his eyes. "I
promised Marson at the mine I wouldn't come back today,
but I need to return to work tomorrow. I'm not sure how I
can do that with the arm tied up like this."

At least the man was honest. But that didn't make him
right.

She wanted to step forward and tell Nate he didn't have a
choice in the matter. He had to allow the joint time to heal.
But she forced herself to stay back. To let the doctor give
orders. Patients were more likely to obey him anyway.

Doc Micah released a sigh and scrubbed a hand through
his hair. If she wasn't so concerned about Nate, she would
have smiled at the motion he made any time he fought his

own frustration. When he finished with his more difficult patients, Doc Micah's hair would often be sticking up in odd places.

"Nate, it's like this. If you've dislocated your shoulder once, it's more likely to happen again, no matter how good the doctor was who reset the joint. Each time the shoulder dislocates, the joint becomes looser and looser, so another dislocation becomes more likely. If you don't give it time to heal completely, it won't need nearly as hard a blow to separate the bones next time. Unless you want to be in my office again the next time you slip on a rock, I suggest you follow my advice now."

A wisp of sadness slipped across Nate's face. "I wish I could, but I've committed to working. I need to be there. Taking time off isn't an option." His tone was earnest, without a hint of disrespect.

Again the doctor sighed, then he stepped back. "Do your best to be careful then. I suppose while you're here, your brother would welcome a visit. I worry about his spirits."

Nate's jaw flexed again as he met the doctor's gaze. "I do, too. How is his leg recovering?"

"The incision site is healing fine. I want to give it one more week before we see if the leg can bear weight."

Nate nodded as he let out a long breath. "All right, then. I'll go spend a while with him."

With a nod, Doc Micah turned to her. "Now you, Miss Hannon, have spent more than your allotted time on that leg. Off to bed with you. Ring the bell if you need anything. As your doctor, I highly recommend you don't leave that room." The twinkle in his eye softened the command in his tone, but the pain in her ankle grave proof to the wisdom in his words.

She hated being this weak, but maybe a short rest wouldn't hurt anything.

ELEVEN

*N*ate fought to push through his exhaustion. His shoulder ached. In truth, his entire body ached. But the yearning in his spirit was stronger than any of it, and that was why he now traipsed toward the clinic. Sundays were by far his favorite day of the week—between church services when Reverend Vendor was available and the chance to spend unhurried hours around both Laura and his brother. He'd not been able to attend service that morning, but at least he would get to do the other.

He'd gone all week without the two things that had been eating at him: seeing Laura and checking on their Indian friends at the cave. Between his days at the mine and his struggles with his arm, he'd only been able to stop and see his brother for two brief visits. He'd not glimpsed Laura during either of those.

Was her leg injury that much worse this time? Maybe she was simply wearing herself out during the day so she had to rest in the evenings. Or perhaps she was helping in other parts of the house. He'd not seen Mrs. Bradley in several days, either.

Nor had he been able to stop by the cave. With so many people around him in need, he was failing miserably at helping any of them. He could only imagine how the little girl and her grandfather had managed these past days. In fact, his mind had conjured all sorts of struggles they might be facing. Bright Sun was so young to be fully responsible—not just for her own care, but for her injured grandfather, too.

Maybe Nate should insist they come to town to receive proper attention. Would being around so many white strangers be too much for them to handle?

He mounted the steps to the clinic and paused at the door. Should he knock? He didn't usually, but this time he was coming to see Laura more than Aaron. And he needed a word with the doctor, too. Maybe he should just walk in like usual and call out if he didn't see anyone. When he pushed open the door and stepped inside, his eyes took their usual moment to adjust to the dim interior.

"Mr. Long. It's good to see you," Mrs. Bradley's voice called from the far end of the hall. "We missed you at church this morning. Micah was going to check on you and invite you to eat with us. Then we realized none of us knew where you were staying."

Heat flushed his face. "I appreciate the kind intention. I'm afraid I overslept this morning. Didn't make it to the service on account of my laziness." At least he'd been able to spend some long overdue time with his own Bible, although he'd missed singing hymns with the others and hearing the reverend's thoughts on whatever Scripture he chose to speak about.

She loosed a light chuckle. "Laziness is not a quality I'd ever lay to your account. I'm sure oversleeping was God's way of forcing you to rest, especially with your arm injured." She stepped toward the doorway he was fairly certain led to the kitchen. "There's plenty of food left. Come have a plate when you're ready."

"Actually . . ." He spoke quickly before she disappeared through that doorway. "I was going out to check on the Indians in the cave. I came here first to see if anyone wanted to accompany me."

Mrs. Bradley's hand went to her middle. "Micah would want to go, I'm sure, but he was called to visit some patients on the east side of town." She darted a glance toward the wall where Laura's and Aaron's chamber doors both stood closed. "I'm sure Laura would do almost anything to go. She's not been very patient with her injury this time around." The woman's face turned rueful. "Micah hasn't approved her to walk without the sticks yet, but I know for a fact she's doing so anyway."

Laura's door pulled open. "I want to go." The woman herself stepped out, walking sticks under each arm and her coat hanging from one hand. "Ingrid, did you say you have food set aside for them?"

Nate had to bite back a chuckle at the determination on her face. In fact, that was the first time he'd wanted to laugh all week.

Mrs. Bradley strode toward them. "I do, but you're not

going out to climb a mountain, Laura Hannon. Mr. Long can take what I've packed." Then she turned her ire on him with raised brows. "For that matter, you don't need to be traipsing over those rocks again right now, either. I'm fairly certain my husband told you to rest for a week."

He almost stepped back from the glare shooting from her eyes.

Thankfully, Laura stepped forward, reaching to place a calming hand on her friend's arm. "Ingrid, please. It's up to Nate whether he feels capable of going to visit our new friends. I'm sure that if he does, he'll be very careful. I know *I* will be."

The way she made it sound like a casual parlor visit made his mouth twitch, but he kept the smile hidden. Mrs. Bradley clearly didn't find humor in the comment, based on the frown she leveled on Laura.

"You shouldn't walk all the way out there, even with walking sticks. Not only would the distance wear out your ankle, your arms would be raw." Concern wove through her tone, raising the same sensation in his own chest.

Maybe he should tell Laura she couldn't come. As much as he wanted her to be with him, to spend as much time with her as he could, doing so at the cost of her comfort would be selfish.

But before he could open his mouth to say so, she spoke. "Maybe we could take the horses again." She looked to him, the question lingering in her gaze.

His gut plunged. He'd splurged on the cost of renting them from the livery that first time, but Laura would need a mount even more now. Unless he told her she couldn't come. "Of course. If you're sure you're able." He should clamp a hand over his mouth, which clearly hadn't heard his thoughts.

He rushed to say something better as Mrs. Bradley turned her frown on him. "Maybe you should wait a week for your leg to heal, though." That wasn't quite the absolute no he perhaps should have given, but he couldn't bring himself to utter that word when Laura looked at him with such earnest hope in her eyes.

The joy that sprang to her face was worth any cost to rent horses. He'd make sure she didn't overtax herself. In fact, he'd carry her over the rocks himself if it would make the journey easier for her. Although, given his recent record, she might be better off hobbling on her own.

Either way, as he left the women to their preparations and went to rent horses from the livery, his body suddenly didn't ache nearly as much as before. The prospect of a few hours in Laura's company shouldn't lighten his load this much.

But he couldn't seem to help it if it did.

⋖⟜⟩○⟜⟨⋗

Ingrid wasn't happy with her leaving, but Laura couldn't bring herself to worry too much. At least, not enough to let her friend's concerns dim the wonderful freedom of being outside, even as cold as the afternoon was. The icy wind blew across her face and worked its way under the scarf Ingrid had loaned her.

They kept the horses to an easy walk in deference to both their injuries. But that gave her time to learn a little more about this man she was beginning to think of as a friend. She sent a glance at his relaxed, confident profile as his horse kept pace with hers. "What is it you do at the mine, exactly? Are there assigned jobs, or does everyone work at whatever needs doing? I notice you've taken off the bandage the doctor worked so hard to fasten."

A corner of his mouth tipped up at her words, but he kept his focus straight. "I was a grunt laborer for a while, but these past few days I've been training with the blasters." He looked over at her. "I might have suspected them of going easy on my arm, except I'd been promised to move to that role as soon as they had time to train me."

She cocked her head. "Blasters?"

"We handle the big powder. Set the explosions when new rock needs to be cleared." He spoke so matter-of-factly, as though his words held little import.

But a niggle of worry threaded through her. "Isn't the big powder dangerous? I've heard it's unstable." She'd not been around mining before coming to Settler's Fort, and she hadn't yet seen the results of an explosion gone awry, but Ingrid had told her about an episode where a thawing of frozen powder hadn't been handled exactly right. The result had been five men killed on the spot, another with horrible burns on his face, and still another who'd never fully recovered from his injuries, both the physical ones and the scars in his mind. His grave lay among the endless clusters of stones behind the little church building at the edge of town.

What if Nate met with the same fate?

He must have heard the twinge of fear in her voice, or maybe she'd spoken some other sound that drew his attention. When he turned to her, his brows formed a *V* of concern. "It can be dangerous if not handled properly. But Barlow is the lead blaster, and he's been working with the powder for years. He's teaching me every precaution."

Fear welled in her chest—maybe unreasonable, but she didn't think so. "Why would you tempt danger? That type of work might be easier, but is the risk really worth it?"

"It pays a great deal more than working as a grunt." His eyes bore into her for only a moment, then he turned to face forward again as their horses trudged up the rocky incline.

Was his financial state really that dire? Wouldn't Mr. Lanton give him a reasonable amount of time to repay the debt? In truth, she had no idea how much he might have to recompense. She remembered the crates stacked in the cabin where they'd taken her during her kidnapping. But every thought of that day churned bile in her middle, so she'd never let herself dwell on the remaining debt.

And now she didn't want to waste this afternoon of freedom with such memories. She glanced at the beauty around them. The snow earlier that week had melted the same day, and even with the brown dusting of winter grass and leafless trees, the landscape still boasted spots of color and life. The deep green of pine and cedar filled in the gaps between barren limbs. The tweeting of a sparrow was greeted with a resounding answer from a shrike.

A clatter from high on the mountain ahead grabbed her

attention. "Look." She couldn't help but smile at the half-dozen goats skittering over the rock on their way around the steep slope. One tossed its head and kicked up its heels as it ran.

Her sentiments exactly.

Nate's deep chuckle rumbled, filling the space between them. Silence threatened to settle over them again, but he was the one to speak this time. "And what of you, Miss Hannon? Has it always been your desire to care for wounded souls alongside our good doctor? I'm assuming you hale from the States. Is the brother you mentioned still there?"

He spoke with a lightness, but his words clogged in her chest like a massive lead ball. The kind that had been shot from a cannon to decimate her baby brother's leg, and with that loss, destroyed the boy she'd loved as her own.

She had to answer . . . had to say something in response . . . something that wouldn't give away the pain his questions resurrected. *Lord, I cling to you in this. Be my strength as you promised.*

"I grew up in Missouri, but I've no family left there. My parents are both gone. My older brother passed away just before the war, and the younger one died after he was injured by a cannonball. Since I had nothing to hold me back, I came west to satisfy my adventurous spirit." Even when she tried to keep the details minimal, the enormity of listing everyone she'd lost nearly choked her. And that last part might have been stretching truth a bit far.

An adventurous spirit was probably thirtieth on her list of reasons why she'd had to get away from Cutler. From

Missouri and the hotbed of tragedy the place had become. This territory was the first place she'd found where her spirit didn't yearn to keep pushing.

Of course, that was more likely due to the freedom of finally coming to understand God's overwhelming love for her. Of finally grieving Will's death the way she'd needed to. The death of all her family, really, although some she'd grieved long before they breathed their last.

"I'm so sorry." Nate's tender voice and the weight of his gaze broke through her swirl of deep thoughts, and she struggled to pull her mind back to the present. She worked to find a smile for him, something to show she hadn't been affected by his questions.

She couldn't quite manage it.

They rode in silence awhile longer, and she focused on enjoying the scenery without letting herself be dragged down by memories.

At last, Nate pulled back on his reins, and her own horse slowed to a halt. A glance around showed they'd arrived at the place where they usually hobbled the animals. Relief sagged her shoulders. The past was behind her, and now she could look forward to seeing their new friends and doing whatever she could to help them. The brave determination that had marked Bright Sun's young face had stuck in her memory since that first meeting.

She eased down from her saddle, careful to land only on her good leg.

Nate was by her side the moment she touched the ground. "Let me help you." He reached up to untie her walking sticks, but she caught a barely audible sucking in of his breath as he lowered his injured arm.

"I can do that." She nudged him aside. "You don't need to be reaching up with that shoulder." He stepped back and allowed her to complete the task, taking hold of the mare's reins instead.

She sent him a sideways grin. "We're quite a pair, aren't we? With your shoulder and my ankle, at least we have one able body between us."

He chuckled, too, and the vibrato sank through her, raising gooseflesh down her back with its delicious sound. She'd have to see what she could do to make him laugh like that more often.

After settling the horses, they made their painfully slow way up the rock ledge around the mountainside. Their diligence paid off, though, for they reached the cave without mishap.

"I'll go in first and light the lantern." Nate ducked through the opening before she could respond.

Probably best, for bending low to duck through would require putting weight on her sore leg. The task would be easier if he were helping from the inside.

A light flared within the cave, then lessened, then grew again as he adjusted the lantern wick. Nate's hand appeared through the opening. "Can you duck, or would you rather go down to your knees?"

"I can do it." She placed her hand in his. The rough warmth of his skin seared all the way up her arm. Maybe she should have donned gloves for this outing, but she so rarely used them that she hadn't even thought of it.

Doing her best to ignore the effect of his touch, she ducked low and hobbled through, mostly on her good leg. As she positioned the walking sticks back under her arms, Nate raised the lantern and scanned the area.

"What's that?"

The concern in his voice jerked her head up. On the side wall near the front of the cave sat a half-dozen crates, stacked as neatly as though they'd stepped into a mercantile's storeroom.

TWELVE

"Where did they come from?" Laura shifted her gaze from the crates to scan the interior of the cave, peering as far as she could into the dark depths. No movement stirred that she could see.

Nate was already walking toward the boxes, so she limped along behind him. "These are canned peaches. These are hunting knives. These are sewing notions. If the writing is correct, anyway." He turned away and raised the lantern to look around the cave as she'd done. "Think someone's in here?" His voice dropped to a whisper.

She held her breath, listening for any sound in the darkest recesses of the cavern. Nothing.

"They have left."

Bright Sun's voice nearly sent Laura's heart into her throat, and she pressed a hand to her chest to keep from squealing. The child stepped out of the shadows on the far side of the cave, near the entrance to the other cavern that held the hot springs.

"Bright Sun." Laura moved toward her, slowing as she maneuvered the downhill section with her walking sticks. Nate stayed at her side, his hand poised by her elbow, ready to catch her should she make any more foolish missteps.

"Who brought those things?" Nate motioned with his head toward the crates. "And when?"

"Two white men. They came in the dark last night." Bright Sun didn't move toward them, probably because she knew they'd want to go with her to her grandfather. And maybe she wasn't quite as eager to see them as they were to see her.

"In the dark?" When Nate repeated the words, their oddity finally penetrated Laura's thoughts.

"Who would want to hide crates of random goods in a remote cave like this? And for what purpose?" Their intentions must be nefarious. She could think of no other reason, unless . . . "Did you hike down to see what they carried the boxes in? Was their wagon damaged?"

She gave a single nod. "The wagon was full. At least it looked that way. They had blankets over everything. After they brought the crates inside, they drove away." Bright Sun's face held no smile. No light. Only a solemnity that bespoke the weight on her little shoulders. Did she ever have any times of enjoyment? Laura could still remember how heavy that crushing weight of too much responsibility could press down on small shoulders.

She forced her tone to lighten as she reached the girl. "We've come bearing gifts for you and your grandfather. How is he?"

"Sleeps a lot." Her voice held no hint of whether she thought that detail was good or bad.

Laura reached to touch the girl's upper arm, praying she wouldn't cringe away. Bright Sun stayed motionless, so Laura rested her hand gently on the child's buckskin sleeve. "Let's go see him, shall we?" She sent the girl a cheerful smile.

Bright Sun's chin bobbed a tiny bit before she turned and led the way through the tight entrance to the other chamber.

Laura edged carefully around the wall jutting into the opening between the rooms. Nate rested his hand on her elbow as she moved through. With her experiences lately, she could only be grateful for the support.

The dim glow of a small fire appeared as soon as she stepped into the humid cavern, and she moved that direction.

Eagle Soaring lay against the rock wall near the fire, but with the scant blaze flickering from the coals, he likely couldn't feel much warmth. Good thing the hot springs did much to raise the temperature in this room. The older man's gaze followed them as they approached. His face held a little more expression than before, a mixture of pleasure and exhaustion. And pain. The lines under his eyes bespoke the agony he must be suffering.

Nate knelt by the man's head. "How are you, my friend?"

As Bright Sun quietly translated his words, Nate reached out as though he planned to rest a hand on the man's shoulder draped in the buffalo robe. But a dark, wrinkled hand reached for Nate's, taking hold in a gnarled grip of friendship.

The moment stretched as Nate and the elderly Indian stared at each other, hands clasped. She could only imagine what passed between them. Gratitude? A promise to help? Perchance even respect?

Laura switched her focus to Bright Sun, who stood near her grandfather, watching the exchange. Maybe it was only the glimmer of firelight, but her eyes seem cloaked by a sheen of moisture. Did she fear for her grandfather's life? Of course she did. What young girl left in this situation wouldn't fear the worst? And in truth, her fears might still come to pass.

Nate eased the fur back to reveal the bandaged arm, and Laura hobbled closer to unwrap the bandage and apply fresh ointment, then rewrap the wound.

As though he could read her mind, Nate looked up at her, then pushed to his feet. "Let me help." He murmured the words and slipped his arm around her waist. She clutched his good shoulder as he lowered her to sit.

"There's salve and a fresh bandage in the satchel." She spoke to Nate, but sent her patient a smile as she began unwrapping the soiled cloth.

The wound underneath made her stomach churn, just as it had the last time she'd seen it. So much flesh was exposed . . . it seemed impossible the gaping wound could grow closed. Doc Micah had found an article in a medical journal that discussed how the combined effects of certain minerals with sulfur could be incompatible, possibly eating away at flesh. Poor Eagle Soaring had suffered that fate firsthand. Perhaps there would always be a dip where the muscle was missing, even if the skin grew back.

While she cleaned, salved, and rewrapped all his wounds, Nate built up the fire and brought in more wood. A good thing, since Eagle Soaring's hands were icy cold. She watched

Nate from the corner of her eye as he dumped his second load of wood in a pile. This probably wasn't what the doctor meant when he said to rest the shoulder, but she was fairly certain Nate wouldn't stop, even if she reprimanded him. His habit of putting others' needs ahead of his own seemed so deeply ingrained that he might not even realize he was doing it.

When she finished with Eagle Soaring, she pulled out the wrapped food parcels Ingrid had sent, explaining what was in each to the girl.

"Thank you." Bright Sun's voice was so quiet, so meek, as though she hated to say the words. Maybe hated to accept the gift. But this child couldn't hunt, and there weren't any berries left on the bushes now that winter had come.

"I'd like to walk to the creek." Nate's voice rumbled off the stone walls, even though he was speaking quietly. "Would you mind staying a few more minutes until I come back?"

She turned to look at him. "I want to see it, too." Did he think she had no curiosity to see the wonders of this underground marvel?

His brows lowered, the firelight casting thick shadows on his forehead. "Are you sure you can manage it? I mean . . ." He stopped, likely realizing his words would only make her rise to the occasion.

She reached for her walking sticks, then pushed up to her knees and prepared the poles to help her stand. Nate gripped her arms and lifted her, his easy strength requiring no work on her part as he set her on her feet. It was starting to feel perfectly normal, his warm touch as he assisted with whatever she might need. When her leg was healed and she no longer needed his help, she would miss the contact.

Already she missed his warmth as he pulled his hands back.

"Just tell me when you want to turn back." He gave her a pointed look she couldn't miss, even in the dim firelight.

She didn't respond, just turned to Bright Sun and offered a smile. "You can come with us if you'd like."

The girl only shook her head as she stood by her grandfather. Laura was fairly sure the girl trusted them now, at least enough to stroll with them along the length of the stream, but she probably felt she needed to stay with her grandfather, make sure he was comfortable after Laura's tending to his wounds.

Nate ambled beside Laura, carrying the lantern as she limped forward. She was probably holding him back, but when she increased her pace, he still hung back, as though he didn't want to walk any faster. She eased her speed to match his again.

After a moment, he turned to the edge of the water, paused, and peered in for a long moment, then raised the lantern high and gazed around the domed ceiling. "What do you think made this room? Maybe that spring was once a powerful geyser, shooting enough water to chip away at the rock until this room was filled. But why did the water stop?"

He didn't seem to expect an answer, and she certainly didn't have one. What he described sounded likely to create a cavern like this. Unless . . .

She spoke the only other possibility she could think of.

"Either that or God created these caves and tunnels exactly the way they are now."

He swung to look at her, his teeth flashing in a grin. "Makes you wonder how creative He really is, huh?"

A warmth eased through her chest. It'd been good to watch Nate's faith grow these past few months, to watch him at church, Bible open and leaning into every word the reverend said. A practice she was doing her best to emulate.

He swung his focus back to the river, looking first right, then left. "We've been upstream already. Shall we explore the other direction?"

She nodded and turned left. Nate held the lantern high as they walked, and she could hardly believe the beauty of the rock around them. In some areas, the stone seemed layered, with beautiful variations in coloring. A few places held more of the hanging rock formations like the front cavern, most dangling like solid icicles. Each possessed its own unique beauty, some unusual part of its makeup.

The surroundings absorbed her so fully, she tripped twice as her walking sticks snagged on stone. After she almost went down the second time, Nate touched her elbow, stilling her. "I think we've gone far enough. The last thing we need is you injuring yourself even more. I'm not sure I could carry you back with my injured shoulder." He gripped the joint, letting that side hang lower than the other as his face took on an expression of deep pain.

Feigned, all of it.

She nudged him in the side. "Worry not. There won't be a need to carry me. I'll be more careful."

His hands fell to his side as the pretense slipped from his face, but a smile played at the corners of his mouth. "We really should turn back, though."

She shook her head. "I think we're almost to the end, where Bright Sun said the water disappears into the rock. Let's go a little farther." She really had no idea if they were close to that point, but maybe that would sway him.

She hobbled forward, and after a pause, Nate's quiet boot thuds sounded behind her. "Look at that cluster of rock-cicles." She pointed to a grouping that hung from a ledge in the wall.

"What's beside it?" Nate moved to the wall and raised the lantern.

She limped toward him. "Are those carvings?" Images were pressed into the stone wall—somewhat discernible shapes that appeared to be horses with riders, then triangular forms that might be mountains, and more of the horses and riders. Or perhaps the triangles were Indian tepees. "Do you think it's a scene from an event, or just depicting the natives around here?"

Nate leaned closer to scrutinize a section of people atop animals. "Not sure. It's hard to tell which tribe they are. Maybe Blackfeet. Or perhaps Crow."

She stepped past him, but that seemed to be the only section of carvings, at least within the range of the light. "I wonder if there's more."

He came up beside her, holding the lantern in front of them as they both moved alongside the wall. For several minutes they walked, but nothing more presented itself.

At last, Nate sighed as he paused. She stopped and raised her brows at him.

The corners of his mouth dipped. "We really do need to turn back. If I keep you out here any longer, the doctor is liable to send a posse after me. I'm already risking your reputation far too much by bringing you out here alone."

She shrugged. "I've never let others' opinions rule my actions." *Mostly because I've never been allowed that luxury.*

Nate was studying her, his gaze digging deep enough to see far more than she intended. She so desperately wanted to be normal, just like the other women she'd watched from a distance living happy, fulfilled lives. She probably wouldn't have a husband and children—that felt like too much to hope for—but she could still have purpose. Still help others in the community. Still be the woman God created her to be.

That woman was who she wanted Nate to see when he looked at her. Not the shadows from her past.

"Laura." Nate's low tenor rumbled through her chest, and the way he spoke her name pressed hard. "I don't know your story, but I can tell life hasn't been easy for you." His throat worked, his Adam's apple bobbing. "I'm sorry for the part my brother and the others played in adding to your struggles." Raw pain crossed his face.

For her part, she could barely draw breath. Was he really going to bring up the kidnapping? They'd never spoken of it, not since returning to Settler's Fort.

His shoulders rose as he drew in a deep breath. "I'm more sorry than I can say. I know Aaron is, too. I only wish . . ." His voice cracked, then faded away completely.

She had to put a stop to this conversation. To his pain. She placed her hand on his arm and he stilled. "It's forgiven, Nate. I know you didn't want any part in the kidnapping. You tried to stop the others. You don't need to apologize."

"But I do need to. I know you probably don't want to talk about it." A huff slipped through his mouth. "You probably don't even want to think about it. But I needed to say that." He scrubbed a hand through his hair as he turned to look anywhere but at her.

Did he still hold so much guilt? She tugged on his arm. "Nate, look at me."

He turned his head to her, but not his body, as though he would whirl away the moment she released him.

"I've seen the man you are. A man who sacrifices himself to help those around him. A man working to grow in his faith. To be honest, I still can't reconcile who you are now with how you and the others lived. But as far as my kidnapping, I hold nothing against you. I promise."

His shoulders rose, then fell. Physical pain crossed his face, and his mouth opened like he meant to speak. But either he couldn't find the words, or he couldn't force them out.

God, help him. Show him his worth as your man. She waited, keeping her hand on his arm, a steady presence.

"And Aaron?" Nate's voice cracked, but it did nothing to diminish the blow packed into his words.

She dropped her gaze. Could she forgive his brother? Aaron *had* been part of her kidnapping. He'd been there the day Bill's mammoth grip closed over her arm, jerking her up like a cloth doll.

Eventually, Aaron had attempted to help her and little Samuel escape, but not at first. She'd tried so many times to forgive him. She'd chosen to forgive, as the reverend said to do. *"Choose with your mind first, then your heart will follow."*

But her heart still twisted every time she stepped into Aaron's room. Every time she rubbed at the scars the ropes had burned into her wrists.

A new thought slipped in, shifting the picture in her mind. She looked up to meet Nate's eyes again as the pieces resettled into a clearer image. "I've chosen to forgive Aaron. I think it's myself I'm struggling with. I didn't mean to shoot him, but if he never walks again . . ." She couldn't bring herself to speak aloud what might happen if he never walked again.

"Laura." Nate's voice took on strength, and his eyes pierced her. "What happened to Aaron wasn't your fault. It was Rex's. He raised the gun and pulled the trigger. He planned to take a life in that moment." His voice softened. "And I'm just grateful you and Aaron are both still here."

Pain sliced through her chest, raising a surge of tears to burn her eyes. "But that's exactly what I'm afraid of." Anger rose in her throat as she fought hard to hold the tears at bay. "My little brother lost his leg in the war, blown off by a cannonball. By the time he came home, the stump had healed, and he could move around with walking sticks. But he *hated* it." Her voice shook with the memories. "He hated himself. Hated his life. Hated he could never be free to walk or run or work like every other man. Hated it so much he hanged himself." She nearly shouted the last words, and the effort took everything she had left.

The tears flowed unbidden, and Nate pulled her into his arms. She let him hold her, soaking in his comfort. His strength. When would she finally stop mourning? She thought she'd let herself really grieve both Will and Robbie on her journey to Settler's Fort. She'd found peace, even.

But now that Aaron possibly faced the same fate that had been Robbie's demise . . . Robbie had been a strong, vibrant young man before that awful war robbed him of all hope. If Aaron chose that same path, Nate would lose his brother.

Would he blame her? She summoned a deep breath and pulled back.

Nate's eyes spoke of painful determination. He moved one hand from her back to cup her chin. "Laura, I need you to know something. No matter what happens with Aaron, his situation is not your fault. The shooting wasn't your fault. Whether he walks again or not isn't your fault. And whatever he chooses to do with the outcome isn't your fault."

These next weeks would be hard for Nate. She knew better than anyone just how hard. But he was right. It was high time she stop comparing the two situations. Stop living in the pain.

And the challenges ahead would be easier for Nate if he had someone by his side to support him each step of the way. She'd not had that after Will died, and maybe she would have handled things better if she had.

She met Nate's fierce gaze and, for once, it wasn't hard to summon a smile.

THIRTEEN

The first thing Nate heard when he stepped into the doctor's clinic Wednesday evening was the doctor's voice. *Thank you, Lord.*

He'd not seen the man in over a week, and he was desperate to know what Doc Bradley's thoughts were about Aaron's leg.

Nate shed his hat, scarf, and gloves and left them on the hat tree, but kept his coat on. He couldn't seem to get warm these days, although this clinic was the one place he came nearest to the feeling. In truth, this was the only actual building he entered most days.

The doctor stepped from the supply room, his own coat on and his leather medical bag in hand. "Nate." His voice sounded weary as he offered a polite nod. The doctor's shoulders hung low, as though he was exhausted.

Nate stepped out of the man's way. "You're heading out this late?" Darkness had settled a half hour ago.

"A catching fever and stomach ailment has been spreading

on the east side of town. It seems two of my patients have suffered a turn for the worse since I was there this afternoon." He glanced down the hall toward Aaron's door. "Your brother's spirits are low, even though the wound is healing fine. I've had him start doing exercises to strengthen the muscles. I think he can try to walk soon, but he has to want to." The doctor nodded to him again, turned back to the door, and stepped out.

Aaron had to *want* to walk? There wasn't anything either of them wanted more. And since Aaron had all day to do the exercises, he should make quick progress.

Nate strode to his brother's door, then gave a light knock. "It's me." He had the quip he'd use in their usual greeting banter at the ready.

"Go away." Aaron's bark was muffled, but those certainly weren't the right words. Maybe Nate hadn't heard him right.

He pushed open the door and poked his head in. Aaron lay on the bed, hands clasped over his belly, staring up at the ceiling. Clearly, the doctor was right about his spirits being low.

Nate stepped inside and closed the door behind him, then strolled around the bed to sit on the far side. "You in pain tonight?" That wasn't the line Nate was going to say, but the stony squint of Aaron's eyes made clear he wasn't up for anything lighthearted.

"I'm always in pain. My blasted bone is shattered. There's a metal rod in my flesh. How could I not be in pain?"

Nate's stomach knotted. Why did Aaron have to be the one lying there day after day, struggling through so much agony? How could God think this was the best way? If there was any chance Nate could go back in time and jump in front of that bullet—take this trial instead of his brother—he would do it without a second thought.

But there was no way to change reality. He could only help his brother work through this. He focused his gaze on Aaron, but his brother didn't meet it.

Still, Nate pressed forward. "Doc Bradley said he showed you some exercises to strengthen the leg. He said you could be up and walking soon if you do them."

Aaron snorted. "He's just trying to pacify me. Trying to hold me off a little longer so I don't tell everyone he's a fake. That all his grand learning isn't real."

Nate pulled back. It wasn't just the bitter tone Aaron used, but what in the world did he mean by his words? "You mean the surgery to add the metal plate? You have to give it more time, Aaron. It's only been two weeks, and he said now is the time to start strengthening the muscles. You've not used them in months. It's a process is all. The doctor said the wound is healing fine, so that's good. Just buck up and do the work he gave you."

"Work." The word came out as a derisive grunt. "I don't need work. I need something to stop this blasted pain. No one wants to give me anything. They don't care a lick. Not even that girl you can't stop ogling."

Nate straightened. He didn't *ogle* Laura; he respected her far too much for that. At least, he hoped he'd never given that appearance. Surely Aaron was just trying to get a rise out of him.

Forcing himself to breathe through his anger, he focused

his response on the one comment he had to address. "Be careful how you talk about these people, Aaron. You got yourself in this mess by going along with Laura's kidnapping in the beginning. They've done nothing but be kind to you ever since you got here. If you were a little nicer now, maybe they wouldn't be so reluctant to come check on you."

"I suppose putting a bullet in my leg is kind in your book? Is that what your new religion says? Turn the other cheek? More like turn the other leg."

Nate pushed up from the bed. This had to be the pain talking. Aaron knew Laura's shot hadn't been intended for him. Only a twisted accident had landed that bullet in Aaron's leg—an accident that still haunted her, if he'd gauged her reaction correctly the other day in the cave.

But was anything really an accident with God in control? How could the God who'd forgiven Nate of so many sins have intended all this pain and misery for Aaron? Was this what his brother needed to bring him to the point of repentance?

The thoughts warred in his mind like volleys of opposing gunfire. But all the questions were merely to make sense of the past. The answers would not change the fact that Aaron needed to do everything he could to walk again. He needed to pull from the melancholy and anger that seemed to be taking over.

Nate moved to the foot of the bed and turned to face his brother. "You know, you're not the only one having a hard time here. I'm working myself into the ground trying to pay back our debt. I need you to do your part and exercise if the doctor tells you to."

Not giving Aaron a chance to respond, Nate spun and walked out of the room. A few strides down the hallway, he slowed and forced his racing pulse to calm. Some days he just wanted to shake his brother by the shirtfront.

But Aaron was in pain. He should be at least a little more patient and understanding, and now he needed to see about getting his brother some relief.

The sounds of industry drifted from the family's quarters, but he didn't dare pass through the doorway into their private rooms.

"Mrs. Bradley? Laura?" The moment the name slipped from his mouth, he wanted to call it back. He should have called her Miss Hannon. She'd never actually given him permission to use her Christian name, and he wasn't certain when he'd started using it more than just in his thoughts. But in company, he needed to take more care to safeguard her reputation. People might assume there was more between them than friendship.

Soft steps sounded, walking his direction. His body tightened in anticipation. There was no denying he hoped it would be Laura. As much as he liked Mrs. Bradley, Laura had woven her way through his life and heart in a way no woman ever had. He was falling for her, although he shouldn't be. He was in no position to care for a woman. But he'd need to have that talk with himself later.

Right now, Aaron had to be his focus.

Laura's lithe form stepped through the doorway. Her smile looked a little weary as she wiped her hands on her apron, but she wasn't using the walking sticks. That was a good sign. And even though her eyes didn't shine as much as usual, she was still the prettiest thing he'd laid eyes on in months—maybe years.

His mouth stumbled over the words clogging his mind, and he worked to say something. Anything. "You're not using the walking sticks?"

Well, maybe that wasn't the smoothest opening he could have mustered, but her smile brightened. "Sometimes, but I don't need them as much. What can I help you with?"

To the point. She'd not come to stand and make awkward small talk.

He did his best to push aside his disappointment. His own weariness must be muddling his brain. "Aaron seems to be in a lot of pain. Could he have some of the medicine?"

Her brow furrowed for a moment, then she nodded. "If he needs it. The doctor said he could have it up to twice a day. I administered some this morning, so I suppose it's fine for another dose now."

She moved down the hallway. A limp slowed her stride, and he had to bite back the desire to step close and help support her.

As she passed Aaron's room, she motioned toward the door. "I'll bring it in a second."

That was probably her way of saying to go visit with his brother and stop ogling her.

Nate pulled his gaze from her pretty form and turned toward his brother's room. He needed to keep his focus on what mattered right now. He couldn't afford distractions, especially when it wasn't fair to Laura to raise any hopes—if she even was remotely interested in a courtship between them. Even if he ever reached the place where he could offer for her hand, why should she consider him?

She deserved far more than an outlaw like him.

⋅◦═◉═◦⋅

Delivering medicines to the east side of town was the least Laura could do. Doc Micah and Ingrid had done so much for her—still did so much every single day—and she struggled to find enough ways to repay them.

The doctor had been out late the night before with patients, and then the clinic had been nearly overrun that morning with people suffering all the ailments the winter season brought on. It was a good thing Doc Micah had finally allowed her to step out and help with these poor people suffering on the east side of town. He didn't speak much of the cases he treated, but apparently there was something of an epidemic happening there. Fever and stomach complaints of the worst kinds.

He'd lost one of his most elderly patients two days before, and that seemed to be weighing heavily on him. She couldn't imagine the weight of having so many people depending on him to make them well.

Lord, strengthen the doctor. Give him your healing touch. She needed to be more diligent to lift him up in prayer. Ingrid too.

She reached the first house Doc Micah had described—a small white-washed home about half the width of the buildings on either side of it. He'd left out the fact that the whitewashing had almost completely flaked off, and the boards that made up the walls looked like they would peel away next, as warped as they were.

The houses on either side weren't in much better condition, although they were indeed larger. Still, four of these structures could fit inside the building that housed the clinic and Bradley residence.

The tiny house didn't have a porch, so she stepped straight to the door and knocked. Voices sounded inside, and then the door scraped open. She couldn't help widening her eyes at the dirt floor. Even the rough cabin she'd grown up in had a puncheon wood floor, and they'd not even lived in town. How much more work she would have had keeping house if they'd been forced to live in this little shanty.

She lifted her gaze to the worn, shadowed eyes of the man who opened the door. His hair stood in awkward spikes, and his shirt looked to be a soiled mess. She extended the cloth sack that held the elderberry tonic and willow bark tincture. "Doctor Bradley sent some medicines for Mrs. Wilkinson."

The man took the bag and turned away to cough—a dry, barking sound. Then he looked back at her, whatever life his eyes had held now drained out of him. "Not many of us left, now that Ma's passed. I hope this helps Penny."

Pain twisted in her middle. This must be the home that lost the elderly woman two days before. She gripped her other delivery as she struggled for the right words. "I'm so sorry for your loss."

Such a trivial statement. Yet what could she say that

wouldn't make his sorrow even greater? "If there's anything else we can do, please don't hesitate to send someone for us." If only they would. But people didn't usually reach out to others for help. At least she never had.

But maybe they wouldn't hesitate when that help came from a doctor. She'd have to let Doc Micah know she wanted to do anything she could for these people.

Maybe helping them could be the purpose she'd been searching for. Although the thought of facing so much pain and misery again—and even death—made her stomach sour.

FOURTEEN

After bidding the man farewell, Laura walked over to her other stop, a home one street over and three doors down. A blast of heat greeted her when the door opened, and the woman holding the knob looked as lifeless as the man at the first house. A flush lit her cheeks, and the paleness of her other features proved the bright color wasn't her normal complexion.

But at least she had the benefit of a wood floor and a larger home. The paint wasn't peeling as badly on this building, and the walls seemed in better condition. Still, the weary sag weighing the woman's shoulders proved the better abode wasn't easing her distress.

Laura handed over the satchel of medicines. "The doctor sent these and bid me help in any way you need. What can I do for you?" Doc Micah hadn't exactly said that last part, but he would do the same if he were here. She should have thought to ask him exactly who was ill in each home. That way she could ask about each by name.

The woman shook her head. "There's too much sickness here to let in outsiders. Tell the doc thanks for this." She glanced behind her, giving Laura a view of the dim room. A fire crackled, and a smoky haze seemed to hover over the space, almost concealing the pile of blankets stretched out in front of the hearth. With the warmth emanating through the open door, anyone who lay that near the flame would be in danger of overheating.

A cough sounded from inside, and one of the blankets moved. People *were* lying in front of the fire.

"Thank you again." The woman moved to shut the door, but Laura placed her hand on the barrier.

She took a small step closer. "How about if I come in and do some cleaning for you? A good airing-out will probably help you all feel better."

The woman pulled her shawl up higher on her shoulders and shook her head. "Most of us have the chills. Can't keep warm. I was just going out to get more wood for the fire."

Laura nearly cringed at the thought of adding more heat to the little room. But as if to prove her words, a cold chill shook the woman's thin shoulders. The shiver made her body sway so much that the only thing that held her upright may have been her hands on the door.

"Go rest yourself." Laura motioned her into the room. "I'll bring in wood." She'd seen the stack along the side of the house.

The woman sank back with a nod and closed the door. A minute later, Laura approached that same door with an armload of dry pine. She didn't knock this time, just opened it and stepped inside. The heat pressed like a suffocating blanket, but maybe wearing her own coat inside made it worse for her.

The woman knelt between two forms stretched under blankets. Her soft murmurs were soothing, but Laura couldn't make out the words as she eased the logs down in the spot where bark and wood chips signaled that firewood had been placed there before.

She turned to the figures huddled under covers. She dropped to her knees beside one little head that poked above the blankets. Languid eyes stared up at her from the little girl's face, who was maybe about the same age as Bright Sun. Dark shadows rimmed her eyes just above flushed cheeks, the only colors in her pale skin.

When Laura reached to brush the matted brown hair from the girl's brow, her skin was almost too hot to touch. She sucked in a breath and looked up at the woman. "How long has she been this warm?"

"Two days. I'm doin' everything the doc said—wet cloths, lots of water to drink, bits of stew. I just gave her that elderberry tonic. Now we just wait for it to pass." The resignation in the woman's voice made it sound like she'd given up. But as Laura studied her, she was pretty sure this woman was simply exhausted. Maybe even ill herself.

"You need to leave now, miss." Her gaze dropped to the lad lying in front of her, his eyes closed in sleep. "These two are mine, and I'll be the one to care for them. You'd best get far away from this part of town. They say the sickness is catchin' in the air. The last thing we need is you takin' ill and makin' the doc and his wife sick, too. 'Specially with her expectin'."

She was right. Laura had to be careful not to bring this

malady home to Ingrid. But the thought of leaving these people in such a state felt just shy of heartless.

"We have the medicine now. I 'spect these two'll be perking up before the sun sets. You'd best get back to helpin' the doctor." The woman spoke the words with a firmness that seemed to take a great deal of strength.

Laura nodded. She didn't want her presence to make things harder, and this determined mother was right about needing to be mindful of Ingrid's delicate condition. After stroking the girl's hair one more time, she pushed to her feet. "Please send someone for us if you need anything at all. Either the doctor or I will be back to check on you soon."

The woman nodded and turned to pull a dripping cloth from a basin of water.

As Laura let herself out the door, the weight on her chest made it hard to breathe, even with the blast of fresh air. What could she do to help these people? The stench of sickness reminded her too much of those last days before Pa died. His illness had been brought on by the barrels of drink he consumed, but the suffocating weight of despair had been almost the same as what she'd just felt.

The sensation made her want to run far, far away. Just like she had before.

⊹⊱═──◯═──⊰⊹

Nate stepped into the mercantile just as Lanton was striding across the room, key in hand. He'd just barely arrived before closing time.

The man paused to nod at him, then turned to walk back around behind the counter. "Evening. I wasn't sure if you'd make it by tonight or not." His tone sounded light, as though whether Nate came to make his payment or not was of little consequence.

If only Nate could feel the same way. The weight of the restitution he still had to work off pressed down like a heavy yoke. He pulled out the bag of gold dust he'd just been paid at the mine and laid it on the counter. "I'll always be here on payment days if there's any way I can come before you close."

Lanton gave him a look much softer than Nate deserved. "I know you will, son. I don't worry about you." He took the bag and set it on the scale, then bent low to read the weight. "Oh, I almost forgot." Turning, he pulled a ledger from a shelf behind him and thumbed until he found the page he sought.

He laid the book on the counter and turned toward Nate. "I heard from the sheriff in Virginia City this week. Said this is all he's been able to track down so far. Here's our new total."

Nate stared at the sum, his mind doing the math of what would still be outstanding. He'd given Lanton a list of all the people and businesses they'd robbed—those he could recall, anyway—and the man sent inquiries to those people to find out how much needed to be paid in restitution. So far, the responses equaled half of what Nate knew to be their total debt. Would the others respond, too?

If they did, the sum would be staggering. Without his brother's help to work off the debt, Nate would be toiling at least half a lifetime to finish paying this restitution—and that was if he kept up his current lifestyle of living with almost no expenses. That may not be possible much longer if he didn't make more progress on a cabin.

"Just make your mark here." Lanton held a pen out to Nate and pointed beside the payment he'd just entered into the ledger. "I'll sign beside yours."

Nate took the pen and signed his name, then pushed the book back. As glad as he was to have the amount owed drop a little more, seeing the numbers in bold ink pressed hard on his chest.

He worked hard to push the melancholy aside. "One other thing."

Lanton looked up from tucking away the ledger. "Yep?"

"Do you know of anyone in town missing some crates of supplies? I saw some in a cave out past the mine. I can't imagine someone lost them, and I don't want to think they're stolen, but just thought I'd inquire." The last thing he wanted was for someone to think he'd stolen the goods.

The man studied him, then offered a slow, thoughtful nod. "I'm glad you said something. But no, I've not heard of anyone missing supplies. How many crates did you say?"

Nate scanned his memory of the stacked boxes. "At least a dozen. Marked as peaches, hunting knives, sewing notions, among others."

The grooves in Lanton's brow deepened. "I'd have heard if that much went missing. I'll keep an ear out, though."

After thanking the lawman, he stepped out on the street, then headed toward the clinic. No matter how weary he was, he had to take a few minutes to check on his brother.

And maybe, just maybe, Laura would be around, the one bright spot in a week of drudgery. Was he a terrible brother for being more excited about the prospect of seeing her than his own flesh and blood? His twin, at that.

Aaron had been so grumpy of late, almost unbearable. Probably because the exercises were painful. But they were making him stronger. Nate had seen the evidence of it the night before when Aaron had lifted his leg a handbreadth off the floor.

Thank you, God. That single feat wouldn't be possible if the leg weren't healing. A fresh surge of relief washed through him, pushing back some of his exhaustion.

He stepped onto the clinic's porch, then pulled open the door. The light and warmth inside pulled him like the star drew the wise men to Bethlehem.

"Nate. Come in where it's warm."

Laura's voice thawed his insides more than the heat drifting down the hallway. He turned to see her stepping from the examination room, a broom in one hand and a stack of cloths in the other. Her smile truly was a ray of sunshine, lighting the dim hallway and spreading even to the darkness outside. "You're later than usual tonight. Does that mean you stopped to see our friends in the cave?"

He shook his head. "I wish I could have. Had business in the mercantile."

"You look exhausted. And cold." Laura stepped nearer and reached up to press a hand to his cheek.

The warmth of her skin singed like fire on his face, yet her touch soothed in a way that made him want to reach up and hold her hand there.

She jerked back, maybe as surprised by her action as he'd been. Quickly, she turned down the hallway. "Come back to the kitchen where the fire is. I have coffee heating to warm you."

He hesitated. The Bradleys were always friendly, but he'd never invaded their personal space. The way the building was divided into separate clinic and living quarters made it seem wrong to step through the doorway at the far end of the hall.

Laura paused halfway to that door and turned back to him. "It's fine. Ingrid's back here, too. She was just saying a few minutes ago that she wanted to ask you about helping the doctor with one of his projects."

Helping the doctor. Yes, he owed the man so much for his care and patience with Aaron that he needed to seize any opportunity to repay his kindness. "All right." He stepped forward. Like a beacon in the night, she led him through the doorway and down a dimly lit corridor. The kitchen shone brightly ahead, and a silhouetted figure walked across the space beyond the doorframe.

"Ingrid, I brought Nate for some coffee to warm him." Laura spoke even before stepping into the kitchen. Probably to warn the doctor's wife they weren't alone.

He shouldn't have come back here. Shouldn't be alone with these two women. Laura didn't seem bothered by rules of propriety. Not that he really knew what those rules were, but he knew this felt like an invasion of their privacy.

But as Mrs. Bradley turned from the stove with a smile, she motioned toward the rectangular table. "That's wonderful. I've been wanting to invite you back for a decent meal, but I haven't wanted to take away from your time with your brother. Now that you're in my kitchen, we finally get to feed you."

The thought of something cooked warm and fresh made his mouth water, and his belly twisted as it tried to convince him he couldn't subsist on salted meat and corn mush.

"Sit. I'll fill a plate for you." Laura patted the table in front of one of the chairs, a spot that gave him a perfect view of the stove and work counter—although his back would be partly to the door. He shook off that long-held apprehension. Since he wasn't on the run from the law anymore, that last part shouldn't matter to him.

He eased into the chair as Laura bustled from the counter to the stove, working around Mrs. Bradley with an ease that bespoke a comfortable friendship between them. The other woman looked to be ladling some kind of soup or broth into crockery, and the slope of her shoulders made it look like she'd been at the task long enough to grow tired from her efforts.

At one point, Laura leaned close and murmured something to her friend. The two shared a smile, and Mrs. Bradley shook her head, but he didn't hear the words. He didn't mean to eavesdrop, but it was hard to keep his eyes from following Laura with every graceful movement of her willowy form.

When she turned to him, a tender smile lit her expressive eyes and tugged her full lips. His gut nearly flipped inside him. As good as that gravy-covered mass smelled, he'd rather sit and watch her for the next few hours than turn his focus to the food.

"This should warm you." She set the plate in front of him, and the scent wafting up dragged his attention downward. He had the fork in his hand and a bite stuffed in his mouth before he had enough time to register exactly what he was eating. Flavor exploded on his tongue, warm savory goodness spreading through his senses. His eyes drifted shut as the gravy-soaked venison melted in his mouth.

He had to open his eyes to load his fork again, and a glance up revealed the two women were watching him.

Staring at him. Clearly, he'd made a spectacle of himself.

"That's usually our reaction to Laura's cooking, too." Mrs. Bradley's voice held an undertone of laughter. "At least, it's Micah's. These days I'm not much for flavor. She has a way with food, though."

Those simple words didn't begin to cover Laura's talent if she'd produced this meal. No matter that he was half-starved and would appreciate anything set before him, even *he* could tell this food was superior—far and away better than the fare he'd eaten in cafes and restaurants.

Laura turned away. "That's not a bit true. Nate's just hungry. Now, Ingrid, I'll finish this. You sit and visit."

Mrs. Bradley stepped back from the stove and handed Laura the spoon handle. "Thank you."

The doctor's wife turned to him, and despite the fact he was stuffing another bite into his mouth, the pallor of her skin caught his attention. She reached for the chair back nearest her and gripped it, her fingers turning as white as her face.

"Mrs. Bradley?" He pushed up from his chair to help her. She looked like she might keel over any second.

She waved him back, but his words brought Laura around. Before she could reach her friend's side, Mrs. Bradley pressed a hand to her mouth and ran for the corridor.

FIFTEEN

Awareness soaked the air as Nate listened to the padding of Mrs. Bradley's footsteps drifting down the hallway. He and Laura were now alone in the kitchen. But as the echo of footsteps morphed into the sounds of retching, his gut clenched at the noises, and he turned away from the door.

Laura released a sigh that drew his gaze to her. "I feel so awful for her. She's just started coming back into the kitchen again, but I shouldn't have let her do so much."

Did that mean Laura managed all the cooking here? Along with helping in the clinic? No wonder she'd been cleaning the examination room so late that evening. And with her injured ankle, she must be exhausted.

He motioned toward the pots on the stove. "What can I do to work off my meal? I may not have your cooking skill, but I've made my share of campfire food. Give me a job."

She waved him away. "Your job is to eat. Don't think I didn't hear your belly growling when you came in."

He forced a chuckle. "You heard that?" His scant midday

meal had been far too long ago. He'd been trying to ration his meat to last until he could hunt tomorrow on his day off. He stepped back to the table. He would help her, but maybe he should gulp down a few bites first.

Quiet fell over them as he loaded another forkful in his mouth. With Laura's back to him, he had to force himself not to ogle her. A thought slipped in, and he swallowed his bite so he could ask. "I didn't hear what it was I can help the doctor with."

Laura turned her pretty face to him long enough to offer a smile that lit the room. "I think it was only a question, so I'm sure Ingrid will ask you later."

Yes, he certainly didn't want her to leave her sickbed on his account. He went back to his food, yet even as he ate, his mind and eyes kept wandering back to follow Laura's every action. Something about this woman had gripped him with a strength he couldn't resist. Every day, his mind played through what she might be doing, wondering if he'd see her that evening when he came to visit his brother. He'd tried to turn his thoughts into prayers for her—an effort that was definitely increasing his time spent talking with the Lord.

He scraped the last tasty bite of gravy from the plate and licked the fork clean. She turned and caught him in the act. Heat surged up his neck, but to cover his embarrassment, he sent her a wink. "Too good to waste a drop."

Her cheeks had already pinkened from working over the stove, but now her ears turned the same color. How had he never realized how fetching her ears were? Petite and perfectly tucked into her honey-colored hair.

Rising, he carried his plate, fork, and mug around to the work counter. A pot of wash water sat on the wooden surface. "This for the dishes?"

"I'll take them, Nate." She set her ladle aside and turned to reach for his dishes.

He shook his head and held tight when she tried to tug the plate from him. "I'll wash them. It's the least I can do for getting them dirty." There were a few other tin dishes in the water he could clean while he was at it. This he knew how to do.

Her brows lowered in a frown, but he eased the plate from her grip and sent her a smile. "I'll even let you inspect 'em when I'm done." He'd known more than one persnickety matron, but he could scrub hardened food with the best of them.

She turned back to her work, securing lids on the crocks she and Mrs. Bradley had filled. With him working at the same counter, they stood side-by-side, only a breath separating them. If he eased to his right, his elbow would brush hers. It took all his willpower not to close the distance between them. Did she feel his presence as strongly as every part of his body tingled with her nearness?

"I was thinking . . ." Laura's voice sounded a little breathy, or maybe that was his imagination.

She didn't continue, so he prompted. "Yes?" He used the wet cloth to wipe out his mug in the water.

She blew out a puff of air that made the tendrils of escaped hair fan around her face. "I was thinking I might go visit Bright Sun and her grandfather tomorrow after church. Make sure they have everything they need."

His heart leapt at the thought. If he woke early to hunt, he could still attend the church service he'd been missing, then spend a few minutes with Aaron before going to the cave with Laura. But . . .

He glanced down at her skirts. "What of your leg? I should rent the horses again." He'd never pay off his debt if he rented horses every Sunday, but Laura couldn't walk all the way out there.

Except . . . she hadn't exactly asked him to come along, had she? "I mean, I could rent the horse for you to take. You can't walk that far."

She stiffened. "I can walk perfectly well. I'm fully recovered."

He was almost certain that wasn't true, but before he could respond, her posture softened. "I'd be glad for your company, though, if you want to come along." She sounded so tentative, so unsure of herself.

A surge of excitement flared inside him. "Yes." He spoke almost the moment her words ceased. No need for her to wonder about his enthusiasm.

She lifted her gaze to meet his but dropped it almost immediately. For his part, he couldn't pull his eyes from the way her cheeks curved with her smile.

"If you want to come by after church, I'll be ready. But please don't worry about getting the horses." She positioned the jars in a row, then folded a towel she'd been using. "I think you have that mug clean."

He jerked his focus back to the dish in his hand. Had he been wiping this same mug the entire time? Truly, this woman distracted him more than anyone he'd ever known. He raised the mug up close to his face, peering as though looking for dirt he'd missed. "Just making sure it's clean enough to pass inspection."

She pursed her lips, and her cheeks dimpled in another grin as she took the mug from him and dried it. Did she have any idea how pretty she was? He'd be happy to wash dishes the rest of his life if she'd reward him with smiles like that.

"How's your work with the big powder? Are you enjoying learning new skills?"

He had to struggle to pull his mind to the change of topic. Maybe she realized he'd been staring at her and didn't appreciate the attention. The last thing he wanted was to make her uncomfortable.

Reaching back into the washpot, he wiped off his fork, then the other spoon clanging in the water. "The challenge is good. It's hard bearing the responsibility of knowing any error could hurt the others, but I'm careful." So careful that his shoulders always seemed tied up in knots from the constant strain.

She looked up at him, the normally smooth skin of her brow forming indentations as she studied him. He met her gaze, and her forehead eased, but she still kept those luminous brown eyes focused on him. "I don't like you in the way of so much danger, but I understand why you think you need to do it. I just wish . . ."

Her words died away, but the earnestness in her eyes turned almost haunting. His chest squeezed at the look. What had she been about to say? What did she wish for him?

He scanned her face, letting his focus roam from her long lashes over the soft curve of her cheeks, down to her lips. He'd never let himself linger on her lips before, but it was impossible not to see at a glance how perfect they were. The upper bow slightly smaller than the lower, neither too full, but just the right size for kissing.

Those perfectly shaped lips parted, and he forced his gaze back up to her eyes. Did she read his thoughts? Heaven forbid. She would hate him for such a notion.

But it wasn't hate he saw there. Her eyes had darkened, their intensity shifting to a yearning that resonated through every part of him.

Like the north star she drew him, and he slipped his hand around the back of her head. His fingers slid through the soft tendrils as he lowered his face nearer to hers. She must have stretched upward, for her breath brushed his chin.

A small space still separated them, and her eyes—so round and expressive—searched his. Seeking something.

Did she wonder if he was worth the kiss?

He wasn't. No question about it, he was nowhere near the man she deserved. But with everything in him, he wanted to be. He wanted to protect this woman, to care for her, to cherish her as God created her to be cherished.

His fingers wandered deeper in her hair, and she responded to the contact. Her eyes drifted shut, pulling him in. He closed the distance between them, brushing her lips with his. Oh sweetness.

The touch of her mouth was nothing like what he expected. Soft and supple, bending to the press of his. Returning his kiss with a giving that bespoke trust. A trust he didn't deserve, yet gratitude rose within him like a tide. She was so much more than he'd dreamed, and he deepened the kiss as her hands rose to his shoulders, sliding up his neck, fingering through his hair.

His blood heated with every touch, every delicious taste of her. He had to pull back. Had to give her space to realize he wasn't the man she should be kissing. No matter how much he wanted to be that person, she could do so much better.

With every bit of strength he had left, he eased back, putting a bit of space between them.

"Laura?" Mrs. Bradley's voice came from the doorway.

Nate stepped back as he spun, his stomach dropping to his toes. *No.*

He didn't mean to besmirch Laura's reputation. He shouldn't be in the kitchen alone with her, much less kissing her until his insides lit on fire.

"Ingrid." Laura stepped toward her friend. Her voice sounded much steadier than his would have. Maybe the kiss hadn't affected her the way it had him. Even now, his legs wobbled. He gripped the work counter for a little more stability.

"I . . ." Mrs. Bradley's gaze swung from Laura to him. "I'm sorry if I'm interrupting." Although her voice said maybe she wasn't so sorry.

He should be thankful for the interruption. He'd already stopped the kiss, but he wasn't quite ready for the moments alone with Laura to end.

Mrs. Bradley shifted back to Laura. "I only came to tell

Nate what I meant to say earlier." She looked back at him. "I know you sometimes do a bit of hunting. My husband and I are interested in buying furs from you, if you have any you'd like to part with."

He straightened. "Any particular kind?"

She shook her head. "Whatever you have. I know you can trade them at the mercantile, but Micah said he'll offer you more than you'd get there. He wants to help some of his patients on the east side of town learn to make craft goods to sell in Fort Benton. The steamship captains who make their runs up the Missouri River are looking for that kind of thing to take back to the States. He might even be able to buy the hides you haven't cured yet, if that's easier for you."

Nate's pulse leapt. "Yes, that would be a help. Certainly." He had furs rolled and stacked everywhere at his camp, just waiting to be properly worked. Not only would he be able to earn a little more than he'd hoped for them, he'd also be able to shed a bit of work in the process. *Thank you, God.*

Mrs. Bradley seemed to wilt as she turned away. "I'm going to rest awhile. I know your brother is eager for you to visit, Nate."

Her way of telling him he had no business lingering alone with Laura, no doubt. And she was exactly right.

"Yes, ma'am." He raised his voice loud enough for the doctor's wife to hear as her footsteps padded down the hall.

Then he sent Laura a smile. The last thing he wanted was awkwardness to come between them. He'd give his eye teeth for her to be more than merely a friend, but that didn't seem best for her. Not with the taint of his past and all the responsibilities he was strapped with. Even without those, she deserved someone so much better.

She turned that look on him that spoke of uncertainty, maybe even a little hope. Yet there was a guardedness in her eyes, too.

He swallowed to summon some moisture into his suddenly dry throat. He couldn't hold her gaze, but he forced himself to at least keep his eyes on her face. Her pretty, curved chin was the best he could manage as he stumbled through what he had to say. "Laura, I'm sorry. I shouldn't have done that. I shouldn't have put your reputation at risk. Please, forgive me."

He turned and strode for the door, not able to bring himself to see her reaction. To hear her agree that yes, that kiss had been an awful idea.

Better he stop this before it went any further.

SIXTEEN

*I*t's time to wake up, Aaron." Laura shook the man's shoulder harder than she probably should, but she couldn't bite back the frustration simmering in her gut toward these Long men.

First, Nate kissed her senseless the night before, then he apologized for it. Did he truly wish their kiss had never happened? That's what *I'm sorry, please forgive me* had always meant in her world. If he'd hated the kiss so much, she certainly wouldn't force him to endure any more.

Lying awake half the night mulling over his words hadn't done much for her temper this morning, and now Aaron's sluggishness added fuel to her frustrations.

"Why are you having so much trouble waking these days?" She gave him another shake.

His head jerked with her effort, and his eyes finally slitted open. "Leave me alone."

His words slurred just like Pa's used to more mornings than not. Aaron couldn't be drunk, though, nor fighting the aftereffects of excessive drink. The Bradleys didn't have a drop of strong drink in the building.

"I've brought food for you." She forced a more patient tone, even though she had to speak through clenched teeth. "It's important you keep a normal schedule with waking and sleeping, even if you don't feel like it."

He blew out a breath thick with the foul dredges of sleep.

And something else. Was that a sweetness lacing the air?

She'd not given him any baked treats the night before. Neither she nor Ingrid had the time or energy to bake much these days.

At last, his eyes opened more fully and he stared up at her. Red rimmed his whites, and the brown centers bore a glassy sheen.

Bile churned in her gut and she stepped back, pulling her hand away from his shoulder. "What have you been drinking, Aaron?"

She'd coddled her father through his drunken binges most of her life, then Robbie after he lost his leg, but those days were behind her.

She crossed her arms over her chest, wrapping her hands around her elbows to keep from gripping his neck. Or maybe to keep him from gripping hers. The flurry of unwanted emotions had her insides jumbled, and she had to brace herself to keep from backing away. She'd never wanted to feel this fear again. Had promised herself she never would. But the anger was almost as bad.

"I didn't drink nothing." His words were definitely slurred.

Get away. The thought welled in her chest, stealing her air and constricting her lungs.

She spun and lunged for the door. Thank God the doctor

was here. He would get to the bottom of this. She didn't have to face it alone. Not this time.

◦─◦ ◦─◦

Laura clamped her hands over her ears to seal out the yelling as she curled onto her bed. Maybe a childish gesture, but the words Aaron hollered were taking her right back to her childhood. This time she had her own room to hide in, but only a single wall separated her from Aaron's raging.

As soon as she told the doctor what condition she'd found Aaron in, he'd gone in to question the man. Why hadn't she left then? It had been too early for church, so she'd thought to keep herself sequestered in her room until the time came for her to accompany Ingrid and the doctor to the little chapel at the edge of town.

But now . . . she couldn't imagine sitting quietly on a wooden bench with Aaron's accusations ringing in her memory. She'd never be able to focus on the reverend's words, no matter how badly she needed to hear them.

Unbidden, the image of the mountain settled in her spirit. The mountain. She needed the peace that always came from standing on the edge of the precipice, feeling God's touch in the breeze brushing her skin. Surrounded by His creation was where she always felt the Creator nearest.

Aaron's voice rose louder as his curses rang through the clinic. Doc Micah's voice rose along with it, trying to quiet the man. The doctor probably needed help, but she couldn't be the one this time. When drunks became angry, there was nothing that could be said to silence them. You could either listen to the raging or get away from it.

This time, she could get away.

Jumping from the bed, she ignored the pain shooting through her ankle. She grabbed her coat and hat, then slipped through her door and down the hall.

Aaron's words rang even louder in this larger space, ricocheting off the hallway walls.

At the front door, she pulled on her coat and slipped outside. A blast of cold air struck her face, and she sucked in a deep breath. In two strides she crossed the porch, and if it weren't for her weak ankle, she would have leapt over the steps altogether. She needed out of here.

Needed freedom.

As she hobbled down the road toward the outskirts of town, her mind spun back to all those times she'd stepped out of their cabin, desperate for escape. So often, Will would ride out of the barn just then, reading her mind. He'd have a bridle on the old mare, but never a saddle. Even before Pa sold the saddle to pay for his wretched habit, she and Will had considered the contraption as only a bother. He'd help her climb aboard the mare, then she'd tuck herself in behind him. The mare would dance as Will held tight to the reins.

Then he'd give the ol' girl her head and a mighty kick with his scrawny legs. Those moments of flying were the best of her childhood.

If only she had a horse right now.

But she didn't, so she strode forward as fast as her ankle

would let her, soaking in the blustery wind pulling tendrils of her hair loose. Just like when she rode with Will.

God, I miss him. She let the tears fall as she walked. Let them blur her vision, and only swiped at her nose when she couldn't bear the annoyance.

Not until the long, grueling days of her journey west had she finally learned how to grieve for Will. For all her family . . . but especially him. He'd been her lifeline. Her rock through some of the hardest years of her life.

A true blessing from God, although she'd been so angry with the Lord at the time for taking Mum, she'd not been willing to ascribe anything good to Him.

Even then He'd been patient with her.

The tears fell without restraint as she walked, retracing one memory after another with Will. There had been so many good ones. With Robbie, too, especially after he'd grown old enough to be more playmate and less responsibility. A few times, they'd all three climbed aboard the mare. But the poor horse was getting older by then, and she'd not been able to manage much of a run.

And Laura had been so worried about Robbie slipping off or getting knocked by one of the branches overgrowing the trail that she'd enjoyed those outings more when it was only her and Will. Being responsible for Robbie had been her life—a hardship most times, but one she wouldn't have traded.

Had Will felt that same way about her? He'd only been two years older than her, so she'd thought of him more as a friend than a brother. Her best friend.

But maybe he'd considered her a responsibility. Someone he had to work hard to protect and cheer up when she was frustrated with Robbie or sad about Mum. A sister he had to protect against Pa's darker moments. They'd both learned early that they couldn't match their father's physical strength.

Escape was the far better option.

She reached a rocky incline and glanced around. The cave lay just ahead, although she'd not planned this mountain as her destination. Just like the last time she'd needed to get away from the clinic, something had pulled her to this place. The trail leading here wasn't very well traveled, at least not the route she took. Maybe that's why she was drawn this way when the strain of life welled up too great to manage.

She climbed partway up the mountain to the ledge and started over the narrow trail toward the cave, but her spirit was still too unsettled to face Bright Sun or her grandfather. Seeing them would require her to offer a strength and support she didn't possess at the moment.

She maneuvered the tricky spot without trouble, and at the place where the low rock required a step up, she sank down to sit. From this vantage point, she could stare out at the majestic peaks rising up to hide in the clouds above.

So much grandeur, and her such a little creature in the midst of it all. God had made every intricate detail of this vast landscape and still knew every bit that happened with any of His creation.

He even still *cared*. That was the marvel that truly stretched her mind. *Thank you, Lord.* Her emotions were too raw to summon any more than that, but God knew what she meant.

Even now, she could feel the strength of His arms wrapping around her. Tucking her under the shadow of His wing like a mother hen shelters her brood. His was the strength that had pulled her through the loss of her family, and His was the only strength that would carry her through these troubled days. Once again, He'd placed people in her life to be the good through this present trial.

Nate's easy smile swept through her mind.

Except now she wasn't sure of him. Did he want nothing to do with her since that kiss? In her mind, she'd thought never to let a man so near her, not just physically near, but so close to her heart. To her yearnings.

But Nate wasn't *any* man. He was . . . Nate. Strong and sure and good. Every part of him good.

Her chest tightened as a yearning crept through her that she had no business feeling.

She leaned back against the stone wall of the cliff behind her. This was all so exhausting. The memories. The pain. The longing. She let her eyes drift shut as weariness swept through her, stealing the strength from her bones.

⸱⟶⟞ ⟝⟵⸱

Nate stopped short when he glimpsed the form slumped against the rock ahead. *Laura.*

The blood leached from his head as he took in her lifeless form. Had she fallen and hit her head? Surely she wasn't . . . *God, no. Not dead.*

He wanted to charge forward, to shake her awake. But if

something—or someone—had hurt her, they might still be around. Maybe whoever had placed those crates in the cave.

He pulled his pistol from his waistband and held it at the ready. Maybe carrying the Colt was a holdover from his days on the run, but between dangerous animals and men out there doing what he'd once done, keeping a weapon handy seemed like a good idea.

Easing forward, he kept his senses tuned for any sudden noises. As he neared, his ears picked up the gentle sound of Laura breathing. *Thank you, Lord. She lives.* The pressure in his chest eased a little. But he still had to beware of whatever had knocked her out.

He reached her and—keeping his focus on their surroundings and his gun aimed ahead—he bent low enough to touch her shoulder. "Laura?"

She lay back against the rock wall, almost as though she'd settled herself down for a nap. But she wouldn't do that out here. Not on the edge of a precipice.

He'd returned from hunting early enough that he'd stopped by the clinic to see Aaron before heading to church. Maybe to even talk to Laura about what happened last night. To assure her he'd meant nothing untoward with that kiss, and she didn't have to fear he'd repeat it. At least, not unless she wanted him to.

But the debacle he'd found at the clinic still churned in his belly. None of what he'd seen and heard seemed as if it could be true. He couldn't believe Aaron would do what the doctor claimed.

Yes, Aaron had been struggling with melancholy, and his

temper had flared some this past week, but it was all brought on by pain. If he'd been groggy from the pain medicine he'd somehow gotten his hands on, he wouldn't have been suffering from pain that would anger him.

None of it made sense.

When the doctor said Laura had gone for a walk, Nate had known without a doubt he'd find her here. His logical side had told him he should leave her alone to work through her frustrations, especially after he'd overstepped so much the night before.

But still he'd come. At the very least, he could apologize for the words and actions of his thick-headed brother.

And now . . . thank the Lord he'd come. He rested his hand a little more firmly on her shoulder. "Laura, can you wake up?" He gave her a little shake. He'd much prefer to awaken her by stroking the hair back from her face and speaking gentle words, but he had to keep his focus on their surroundings. Had to be alert in case an enemy still lurked nearby.

He let his gaze sweep over her again. No injuries that he could see. No swipes from a mountain lion. No blows to her face from a violent ruffian.

Her eyelids fluttered open, and for a moment, she stared up at him, unfocused. Then her eyes sharpened and her entire body stiffened as she stared up at him.

SEVENTEEN

Stepping back from Laura, Nate returned his focus to a sweep of their surroundings. "What hurt you? Man or animal?" He kept his voice low so he didn't call the attacker back to them.

She sat upright and looked around. "No one. Did you see something?" She scrambled to her feet.

He backed up to give her room. Maybe she *had* been struck in the head and couldn't remember it.

He spared a longer look at her face, then her head for any sign of a bump. "You don't remember anything?"

She narrowed her eyes. "Like what? What happened?"

"You were sitting there, unconscious." He motioned toward the rock wall. "Almost like you were sleeping. I haven't seen whatever struck you. Where do you hurt?"

He glanced toward the cave. The opening couldn't be seen from this spot, but it lay just around the curve in the wall. Maybe Bright Star had seen or heard something.

"I think I *was* sleeping." Laura's voice emerged quietly, as though she wasn't sure if her words were true or not.

He darted his gaze back to her face. "Why would you be sleeping out here?" She must really have lost her memory.

But her eyes sharpened, turning a glare on him. "Because I couldn't sleep last night after a certain man visited our kitchen."

Heat flew up his neck, burning all the way to his ears. If she had to forget something, why couldn't the lost memory be *that* one? But as her words fully settled in his mind, he had to fight a smile. She'd lost sleep over their kiss? Did that mean she'd been as affected by it as he'd been?

He'd lain awake hours himself, replaying the kiss over and over. Feeling the softness of her hair, the way her hands wandered up his neck. The delicious taste of her. Even now, the thoughts stirred his body to life. Made him want to step closer for another taste.

"Don't even think about it, Nate Long."

The bark in Laura's tone brought him up short. And one more look at her glare told him she must not have lost sleep over the same thoughts and feelings he'd warred with.

Hers must have been regret.

He pressed his mouth shut as he gathered himself together. Another glance around showed no apparent threat. "You're sure you were sleeping, not attacked?"

"Fairly certain."

He'd have to take her word for it, but he'd keep his senses on the ready, just in case. "How are Bright Sun and Eagle Soaring?"

"I haven't been in to see them yet."

He raised his brows. "You haven't?" She'd just stopped here on the trail to sleep? That didn't make sense.

A hint of something—sadness? regret?—slipped into her eyes. "I just needed . . . a few minutes first."

Understanding crashed over him. *Aaron.*

A surge of anger rushed through his veins. If he could clobber his brother with a hard right hook, he would. Just enough to knock some sense in him. How could Aaron have been so harsh that Laura had to leave her own home to escape? To recover from his barbs? The doctor's tale of the morning's events must have held more truth than Nate had wanted to believe.

Then another realization washed through him. He cocked his head to study Laura. "That first day when you hurt your ankle. Had you come up here to get away from Aaron?" He'd not known her nearly as well then, so he might not have seen how caring for his brother had worn on her. Maybe Aaron said things to hurt her even back then.

She raised her chin, as though trying to appear strong. Resolution shone in her eyes. Determination not to reveal pain.

The adrenaline leaked from his limbs. "Aw, Laura." He wanted to step forward, to draw her close and take away all the misery she'd suffered, especially the pain from anyone he'd ever been connected with. Grief he'd caused, too, for he'd made his share of stupid mistakes.

But he knew better than to touch her, especially after last night. He scrubbed his hands through his hair to occupy them.

That move only made his sore shoulder ache, so he dropped his hands to his sides and looked at Laura again. "I know you said you've chosen to forgive Aaron. I also know from experience that making the choice can still mean it takes a while to finish the forgiving part. Especially when that person keeps on causing pain."

As the words tumbled from his mouth, his chest tightened like a weight was being pressed against his lungs. "Aaron is struggling. I guess no one knows that better than you."

The pain in her eyes pressed the weight even harder. "I can't dismiss his words and actions, especially the ones that hurt you." His voice cracked, and he had to swallow hard before speaking again. "But don't let his brokenness break you down. Please."

Only God could heal his brother. That truth was painfully clear all the way to his very core. But he couldn't stand by and let Laura fracture because of his brother's struggles. She was strong, and together, maybe they could help her stay that way.

She met his gaze, but her eyes had turned distant, as though her mind was drifting far away. Maybe back at the cabin where the kidnapping had ended in salvation for Laura and Samuel, but also in the end of Aaron's hope for ever breaking free from the bonds that locked him in misery?

Laura didn't move, just stood staring. Then a sob erupted from her throat. She pressed a hand to her mouth, wrapping her other arm around her middle as she dropped her face, pain riddling her features.

Dear Lord. He sent up the prayer as he stepped forward,

everything in him wanting to bring her comfort. To do something to ease the agony shaking her shoulders. She looked like her sobs might shatter her.

He touched her arm. When she didn't pull away, he gave a gentle tug and she came to him, letting him wrap his arms around her. As he cradled her, she began to relax, one breath at a time. Her sobs turned to gasps, as though she struggled to rein in a runaway horse.

He held her tight with one arm and used the other to stroke her hair. "Cry, Laura. Tears are good. Healing." Why he said that, he wasn't sure, but the words just slipped out.

The depth of her pain seared all the way through him. An overwhelming mountain of sadness and fear, almost too great to overcome. Had Aaron's words resurrected another tragedy from her past? She'd said she lost her parents and two brothers, and that was certainly enough to bring on this misery, but was there more he didn't know about? How much had this woman suffered through her life?

He'd admired her strength from the first moments he met her. He should have known that kind of calm determination in the face of danger had come from a history of facing demons. *Help her, Lord. Help me help her.*

Laura's tears finally came. Not the writhing sobs she'd fought at first, but true crying, with giant drops streaming down her face. They soaked his sleeve within moments, making him thankful he'd taken a few extra minutes that morning to change shirts after hunting. He'd certainly not expected to have this woman in his arms again, but he could only pray this helped her.

He prayed, in fact, with every other breath he took.

At last, her inner spring ebbed, and her tears turned to sniffles. For a long moment, she rested her head against his shoulder. It was his injured shoulder, but he'd gladly bear the pain of her slight weight if he could offer comfort.

She finally pushed away from him, straightening to stand on her own. She sent a hesitant glance his way as she sniffed again and wiped her cheeks with her palms. "I'm sorry."

He dropped his arms to his sides, his limbs conflicted between relief at no longer having to bearing her weight and an incredible sense of loss at no longer feeling her touch, her soft warmth.

He cleared his throat as he worked for something to say that would ease her embarrassment. "It's me who's sorry. I should carry a handkerchief, but I've gotten out of the habit."

The kind he'd carried before had been larger than the dandies used. More the size to cover a man's face while he robbed an unsuspecting stranger. He'd gladly burned all those handkerchiefs. He'd rather give her his shirt to use if she needed a cloth, but that wouldn't be acceptable, either.

She inhaled a long breath, then blew it out with a shudder. "I suppose I needed that." She turned to stare out at the mountains around them. "My father spent most of his days either drunk or sleeping off a binge. He would get angry if my brothers or I bothered him unless he needed something. I suppose what happened this morning resurrected some memories I hadn't"—she paused, seeming to search for the right words—"sorted through yet."

As she spoke, pain pressed his chest again, shortening his breath. He'd suspected there was something in her past but hadn't realized how closely Aaron's actions must have mirrored her father's. There was probably much more than she'd said, but his imagination could fill in many possibilities.

He didn't want the image that flooded his mind. Laura as a little girl, hair in twin braids and wide brown eyes filled with fear as her father raised his hand to strike her.

Anger pulsed through him, feeding through his veins with every pump of his blood. He had to force himself to push the mental pictures aside. To focus on what she needed here and now.

She was pushing the stray tendrils of hair away from her face, trying to tuck them back in her braid. Despite the red streaking her eyes and spotting her face, she looked remarkably normal. More like the strong Laura he'd come to appreciate so much.

She turned an expectant look on him. "Shall we check on our friends now?"

If he had to name the emotion blooming in his chest, he'd have called it affection. Very strong affection. He reached out and tweaked her chin. "Let's do it." He probably shouldn't have touched her that last time. If they were past her moment of need, he should go back to keeping his distance, keeping himself from tainting her prospects.

But he couldn't quite bring himself to regret any contact with her. Especially when she graced him with the hint of a smile.

EIGHTEEN

*N*ate moved to the cave opening with Laura close behind him. "I'll go in first and light the lantern." He ducked in before she could protest.

In the darkness, his fingers found the match case and lantern easily, right where he'd left them. After striking the flame, he sent a glance around before lighting the wick.

Bright Sun stood in the center of the main cavern, as still as stone. He should have expected her to be there, but the sight of her sent his heart into his throat. As he tried to regulate his pulse and his breathing, he lit the lantern, then straightened, offering the girl a smile. Had she heard Laura crying?

Before he could call for her, Laura had already ducked through the cave entrance.

"Bright Sun, how are you?" Her voice held only joy, no hint of the pain and turmoil from minutes before. "I see someone came back for those boxes. Did you see them? Did they bother you?" She strode forward to stand in front of the girl. Limped forward, actually, but her injury didn't slow her much.

He moved quickly to keep pace with her as he carried the lantern.

"I saw." The childlike tone of Bright Sun's voice reminded him once again how young she must be, despite the fact that she held herself with the proud bearing of a woman a dozen years older. "A different man this time. His wagon was empty before he carried these out."

Nate stopped beside Laura. "Did you see which way he went after leaving here?"

The girl nodded. "I followed him until he turned on the road that way." She pointed toward the south, maybe a little southwest.

"The road toward Fort Benton?" He turned to Laura. "I asked Lanton if he knew anything about anyone reporting any stolen goods. He didn't." That was something he'd meant to tell Laura the evening before, but instead, he'd kissed her and spent the night wishing there was some way he could be good enough for her.

She raised her brows at him, probably agreeing that he should have already told her that tidbit. But she turned back to the child. "He didn't see you, did he? Please be careful, Bright Sun. There's no telling how dangerous those men are. You could be hurt really badly if they found you."

Bright Sun shook her head. "He didn't see me." She spoke with certainty. Nate probably wouldn't have believed any other child her age, but this one could move with the stealth of the wiliest cougar. She probably hadn't been seen.

Laura moved to Bright Sun and placed a gentle hand on the girl's shoulder. "Let's hope so. How's your grandfather? Can we see him?"

The child didn't answer, but her solemn expression eased as Laura slid her arm around the girl's shoulders. Who wouldn't soften under Laura's sweet touch?

Bright Sun turned toward the entrance to the hot spring cavern, and they followed her into the darkness.

What must it be like to live in such a place? At least Bright Sun was able to go outside some. Her poor grandfather didn't seem to have moved much since coming to this cave.

When they reached Eagle Soaring, the girl stood by the cave wall, leaving room for them in front of her grandfather. The man was sitting upright this time.

"You're looking better." Laura dropped to her knees in front of him, and the smile in her voice lifted Nate's spirits.

The older man's eyes still had a dull, almost lifeless expression—or maybe a lack of expression was a better way to describe it. But the lines at his mouth pulled in the beginning of a smile.

"Let's see how your wounds are." Laura eased the buffalo robe off his arm and began her usual process to unwrap the bandage. "I'm afraid I don't have a clean cloth this time. Have you been applying the salve?" She raised the question to Bright Sun, who nodded.

Laura held the man's wrist with one hand as she unwrapped the cloth, and he couldn't help noticing the contrast between her young, fair skin and the wrinkled crepe-like skin of the older man's arm. The shadows in the cave made him look even tawnier than he probably was, although a lifetime under the sun would darken any man.

As she finished unrolling the bandage, Nate shifted his focus to the wound. As usual, the gruesome sight made his middle churn, but he forced himself to study it for any changes.

Maybe the gash was a little smaller. The murky sheen might be from the medicine. But at least the wound didn't have that angry, festering appearance that would make the man feverish.

Laura worked with a steady hand, never losing the gentle touch that was surely the reason she'd won the unwavering trust of this pair. Her passion to help and earnest caring shone through every action. Every word she spoke offered steady encouragement.

She'd almost finished re-dressing the man's leg by the time the thought sprang to him that he should do more than gawk. He turned to Bright Sun, who'd been doing her own staring, albeit while answering Laura's occasional questions and interpreting her words for Eagle Soaring.

The girl met his eyes, and a hint of guardedness crept over her face. If only he could break through that barrier the way Laura had.

He offered a smile. "Have you enough food? I can bring more venison in the morning. I'll leave it near the lantern at the cave entrance." He hated the way his gut clenched when he offered up his own food stores, but everything he gave away meant he'd have to take more time to hunt, instead of working on his cabin and fulfilling his responsibilities with Aaron.

"Ingrid has some food set aside, too." Laura glanced at him. "Perhaps you can get it from the clinic this evening."

Good. With the combined offering, hopefully there would be enough to see these two for another week. Hopefully.

He turned back to the girl. "Have you heard from your people? Do you know when they might come?" They could plan better if they knew how much longer it would be before these two would be reunited with their tribe.

A flash of uncertainty crossed her face. Because she didn't know the timing? Or because she wasn't sure anyone would be coming for them?

His stomach plunged. Surely the latter wasn't true. Without Laura and him continuing to provide food, these two may not survive all winter on their own.

"Do you know where your people are?" Laura's words pulled him back from his spinning thoughts. She'd focused her sweet smile on the child, and Bright Sun seemed to be struggling over how to answer.

At last, the child's voice came out in a tentative murmur. "I don't know. We fell behind when the others were seeking a winter camp. I thought someone would look for us, maybe Sees All or Three Elk. But they haven't." For the first time since he'd known her, the girl's eyes glistened with tears, and her voice cracked.

"Oh, honey." Laura pushed up to her feet and pulled Bright Sun into an embrace, much like a mother comforting her child. He couldn't ever remember feeling a hug like that, yet instinctively he knew how wonderful it must have felt. Even with her future looking so uncertain, did Bright

Sun know how fortunate she was to have Laura Hannon as a friend?

Tiny sobs hiccupped from the girl as Laura cradled her. This had to be healing for the child who worked so hard to be strong—much like Laura herself. He backed away a little to give them space. More than one female crying on him within a single hour might be more than he could handle.

Laura's soothing was clearly more effective than his had been, for only a few minutes passed before the child's sniffles faded. She backed away, wiping a sleeve across her face and straightening her shoulders. It was such a picture of Laura's own recovery a half hour earlier that he had to fight back a smile.

Staying low so she was eye level with the girl, Laura brushed hair from the child's face. "Don't worry, Bright Sun. Nate and I will make sure you and your grandfather have everything you need until your people come back. We're going to take care of you. I promise." She sent a glance to Nate and he nodded. She'd said it so much more eloquently than he could have.

But there was one more thing she wouldn't know to add. Or rather, to ask.

He stepped closer and dropped to one knee so he was a little lower than the girl. "How would you feel if I came to sleep nights here in the cave with you and your grandfather? I can help make sure you always have firewood and fresh meat, and I can protect you if anyone comes who you don't know."

The weight of Laura's stare pressed on him, but he kept his focus on the girl. The child's gaze gave away nothing as she studied him.

Then her little brow furrowed as she looked at Laura, then back to him. "You not stay with her?"

Heat surged up his neck as he realized what the girl was asking. What she must have thought. "No."

His tongue fumbled the word as he rushed to get it out. "I mean . . . Laura and I aren't . . ." He stopped long enough to gather a full, coherent sentence. "Miss Hannon and I are friends, but we don't live together." Another wave of flame seared up to burn his ears. The picture his words had painted wasn't at all what he'd meant. "I mean . . . I don't have a home. I live in the woods. In a tent."

Pistols and rifles, he'd bungled that. His gaze darted to Laura before he could stop it. If he didn't know better, he would say she was trying to cover a smile. Either that or she was doing a better job than him at hiding a blush.

He turned back to Bright Sun and took in a steadying breath. "What I mean to say is, I need a warm place to stay this winter. And if we all pitch in together, the three of us can get by easier, at least until your people come back for you. What do you think?"

Little by little, a light entered her eyes. She didn't speak but offered only a single nod.

The relief washing through his chest felt like three layers of worry fell away with that simple motion. He didn't even try to hold back his grin. "Good."

NINETEEN

Finally, the doctor was letting her actually help.

Maybe Laura shouldn't be so relieved, since the only reason Doc Micah had sent her to check on his patients on the east side of town was because Ingrid's condition had worsened.

The mother-to-be hadn't been able to keep food down all day, and Micah hadn't left her side since midmorning. Her heart ached for her friends—both of them. Ingrid insisted the sickness would pass soon, but the pallor of her skin and shadows around her eyes proved her exhaustion from the struggles.

For his part, she'd never seen Doc Micah so grieved. His gentleness with Ingrid when she'd checked on them earlier had raised a knot of emotion in her throat.

The strain around his eyes seemed more than mere exhaustion. Did he think something was wrong with Ingrid and the baby, or was this simply the worries of an expectant father? He'd said Ingrid's frequent purging didn't seem to be related to the stomach illness the patients she was about to visit now were suffering.

At least that was a relief. The doctor had been incredibly careful not to spread the illness to anyone in the clinic.

She stopped first at the tiny house where she'd delivered the medicine the week before. Instead of greeting her at the door, Mr. Wilkerson's voice drifted from inside. "Come in."

The interior of the little house was dim and smelled of putrid odors that made her want to cover her mouth and run back outside. Leaving the door open a little behind her, she took tiny breaths through her mouth and moved toward the bed beside the fire.

Mr. Wilkerson sat in a chair near the cot, and he didn't stand when she approached, just motioned toward the covers. "She seems about the same."

Laura took in the pale face lying at the end of the wad of blankets. "Doctor Bradley sent me to check on you both. I've brought more elderberry, too." She moved closer to the woman and rested a hand on her forehead. Her skin was warm, but not dangerously so. Round eyes stared up at her, circled in deep shadows. Her face was so pale, Laura couldn't tell exactly how old she was. Maybe not more than thirty.

"Have you been able to keep water down?" She brushed the woman's sweat-grimed hair away from her temples.

Mrs. Wilkerson's jaw opened with a tiny tremble, like that of a fragile older woman. "A little." Her voice quavered, too, and sounded raspy, as if she'd smoked a pipe all her life.

Laura forced a smile past the twisting in her own middle. "I'm glad. How about food? Have you tried broth?" She sent a glance to the man to see if he would offer input so the exhausted woman wouldn't have to speak again.

He nodded, his head still resting against the back of the chair. In truth, he looked as weary as she did.

Laura studied the pallor of his own face. "Have you been ill, too?"

He offered a faint lifting of his shoulders. "A little. Nothing like Penny or . . ." His voice broke, and Laura couldn't help but reach out a hand to his arm.

His mother had been one of those who passed away. The last thing she wanted was to resurrect his grief. "I'm glad you're able to be up and around. Have you both eaten anything besides broth?" She sent a look toward the pot hanging over the fire, but shadows made the contents impossible to discern.

"We've been eatin' soup. We'll get along fine. 'Preciate you bringin' the medicine." His voice held a little more energy than the woman's.

She turned back to Mrs. Wilkerson. "Make sure you both drink plenty of water. Just take sips, as much as you can keep down. Send word to the clinic if you need us for anything." She hated to leave them, but there didn't seem to be much she could do here.

At least, not in the capacity of Doc Micah's helper. She could do a lot with the place if given a broom and a tub of soapy water. But maybe she could come back another time for that.

She still had a list of patients the doctor asked her to check on. No wonder he rarely came home before dark.

But she couldn't deny the sense of purpose filling her chest as she marched to the next house and the next soul in need.

⊷⟞⟝⊶

"How could you do it, Aaron? How could you be so cruel? These people have been nothing but kind to you." Nate wanted to bite back the words the moment they slipped out.

He'd spoken truth—mostly. The doctor and his wife had been gracious beyond anything he'd expected. And Laura . . . he still couldn't fathom how she could care for his brother with such unrelenting kindness, even at the expense of her own peace. But his comment would remind Aaron that she'd shot him in the first place. Even though it had been purely an accident.

Red crept into his brother's face, a welcome change from the shiny pallor he wore most of the time. But Nate steeled himself for an explosion.

"You call destroying my leg *kind*? That—"

"Watch it, brother." Nate plunged in before Aaron could start up the tirade that had disturbed Laura so much on Sunday. Thank the Lord she wasn't in the clinic to overhear now. "You know that was an accident. You can't hold it against her. If you hadn't gone along with the kidnapping in the first place, you wouldn't be in this mess." He dropped his voice, praying with everything in him his words would break through Aaron's belligerent glare. "It's time to let it go, Aaron. You can't move forward if you hold that grudge forever."

His brother looked away, staring across the room. But this time, his brow didn't furrow with belligerence. The line of his jaw eased, almost sagging under the beard Aaron had let grow lately. Shoulders that had finally risen—albeit in anger—slumped again, just like they'd been for weeks now. "I know." The words came out as a mumble.

But at least they'd been spoken. *Thank you, Lord.* Acknowledging the need was surely a big step.

Nate leaned forward, regretting having put so much space between him in the chair and his brother on the bed. He'd thought that would keep Aaron from feeling hemmed in during this overdue confrontation. But he and Aaron were twins, brothers connected long before they'd even been born. Separation was hard on them both.

He inched a little closer to the edge of his chair. "I'm here to help you, Aaron. Whatever you need, we can do this together."

His brother turned back to him with a weary sigh, the lines around his eyes deeper than minutes before. "Then do something about this blasted pain, will ya? They won't give me anything to take the edge off. I can't stand it every minute of every hour, day and night. It's enough to push a man out of his mind, Nate."

Nate leveled a look on his brother. "They won't give you anything? Doc said he'd give you small doses of laudanum to wean you off. And he'll also give you something different to help with the pain."

But, thank the Lord, the doctor had moved the addicting stuff to some other location where Aaron couldn't find it.

That morning Laura had come upon him in such a stupor, his condition was because he'd somehow managed to get into the storeroom and find the key to the locked drawer where the doctor kept a bottle of laudanum. That couldn't happen now.

But Aaron had to have hope that he wouldn't be forced to deal with unrelenting pain day after day.

Nate released his own sigh and slumped against the chair back. "I'll see what I can do. But you have to promise you'll pull out of this slump. Do those exercises the doc showed you. He said you could even be walking with sticks now if you'd been doing them when he first said to." Although Aaron had apparently used the walking sticks to get the laudanum. Was he more capable than he let on?

Surely not. Surely if Aaron could get around without help, nothing would keep him in this room. That must have been driven by sheer desperation. He'd seen that motivation push men into much harder things.

"I will, Nate." The earnestness in Aaron's voice eased some of the tension coiled in Nate's shoulders. "I know I haven't done the exercises the way I'm supposed to. They just make my leg hurt more. And I get so tired of the pain. If you can get me something to help, I'll do better. I promise."

Nate stood and moved to his brother's bedside. He gripped Aaron's shoulder, feeling the fleshiness that had taken over where firm muscle once dominated. "I'll talk to the doctor now."

Laura squeezed her eyes shut against the lightheaded sensation. When she opened them again, the world seemed a little firmer. *Good.*

She reached into the wash bucket and pulled out another plate, but another spasm shot through her, nearly doubling her over with its intensity. She clutched the work counter.

Had there been something wrong with the beans and cornbread she'd served? Both had been cooked fresh, and she didn't usually suffer ill effects from beans like some did. But the cramping in her belly bespoke something very wrong.

Were Ingrid and Doc Micah afflicted by the same pain and clamminess? Poor Ingrid. At least she'd been feeling a little better today, but rancid food was the last thing she needed to suffer in her delicate condition.

Bile churned, rising up to her throat. She inhaled a slow, deep breath, trying to stave off what seemed determined to come. Panic swamped her as she scrambled for an empty pot. She'd barely plunged her face into it before the first heave came.

Over and over they surged, until finally she had no accounts left to cast up. A hand rested on her back, soft and gentle. Only Ingrid could manage a touch so soothing.

Laura pulled the stray tendrils of hair away from her face, then took the damp cloth Ingrid handed her. The rag cooled her face, a welcome relief after the episode.

"I suppose I'm rubbing off on you." Ingrid's voice held a gentle smile. "Although I hope your reason for being sick isn't the same as mine."

Laura took in another breath, still holding the wet cloth

to her face as she shook her head. Finally, she pulled the rag down beneath her chin and turned to Ingrid. "No, definitely not the same reason." Best to quell that idea quickly. "Maybe the beans didn't sit well with me."

Ingrid's brows lowered and worry fanned lines at the edges of her eyes. "I hope you haven't come down with the same thing Micah's been treating on the east side of town. Didn't you take medicine there yesterday?"

A sinking feeling dropped in her middle, starting up a fresh churning there. She could still see the tiny Wilkerson cottage, with Mrs. Wilkerson as pale as death itself, eyes so deep in shadows. And the mister not looking much better, even though he was trying to keep up with tending them both.

And his mother. A weight pressed hard on her chest. People had died of this. She spat a bit of the bile left in her mouth and turned from the counter. Away from Ingrid. "I'm sure that's not it. I'll just finish cleaning up, then rest for a minute."

"No, you won't." Ingrid came behind and gave her shoulders a nudge. "Go lie down. You've nursed me for weeks now. The least I can do is clean my own kitchen."

A wave of chills passed through Laura, stealing the refusal she should have given. Lying down for a few minutes wouldn't hurt. This would pass all the sooner with a short rest.

TWENTY

*S*he's been in bed for two days?" Nate wanted to spin and march back out of his brother's room, down the hall, and barge through Laura's door. He wouldn't, of course, but his entire body coiled at the thought of what might make her so ill that she couldn't get out of bed.

She hadn't even stayed in her room this long when she'd been unable to walk on her sprained ankle.

He studied his brother. "How do you know?" Maybe she simply hadn't come to wait on Aaron. He couldn't blame her for wanting to keep her distance from the man who bellowed insults about her at the top of his lungs just days ago.

Aaron shrugged. "Doc's wife told me. She's been the one bringin' meals now. Her or the doc."

A twitch started in Nate's right eye. He needed to see what was wrong with Laura. He couldn't tell if the twist in his gut was simply worry or an awful premonition.

Brushing his brother off would be rude, so he tried to

relax enough to be decent company, at least for a few more minutes. He inhaled a deep breath, then exhaled out as much tension as he could with the spent air. "How're the exercises coming?"

A snort filled the air. "Without decent pain medicine, not so well."

His muscles tightened again. "I spoke with Doc Bradley. He said he'd give you something whenever you asked for it."

"That watered-down drink he calls tea doesn't do a thing. And he's only giving me a few drops of laudanum."

The doctor must still be weaning Aaron off the laudanum. From the way Aaron tended to exaggerate when he was in a mood, the doc was probably using a little more than Aaron made it sound. And the "watered-down tea" must be the other pain remedy the doctor had spoken of. He should ask, just to be certain.

In the meantime, he focused on the other fact the doctor had shared. "He said you shouldn't be experiencing very much pain anymore. The incision site is healing the way it should. You might have some discomfort from the exercises for a few days, but once you work through it, it won't hurt as much the next time. I told him you've always been able to push through more than a little pain." Hopefully that last bit would prod Aaron's pride enough to get him started.

"That should tell you this is more than *a little* pain." His brother sent him a glare.

Nate clamped his jaw against a grunt of frustration. He wouldn't be able to hold it down much longer, so he pushed to his feet. "Buck up, Aaron. I'll talk to the doc again, but you better make sure you're doing your part, too. We *all* have to do our part."

He turned and marched out the door before his brother could respond. He had a feeling anything Aaron said would only make him angrier.

Nate stepped into the hallway and paused to listen for sounds that might tell him where the doctor was. Voices murmured from the living quarters, so Nate turned that way. He shot a look at Laura's closed door but kept himself from stopping to knock.

"Doc Bradley?" He paused before he reached the hallway to the doctor's private area.

The voices stopped, then the sound of footsteps accompanied a call of "Be right there."

The doc was in his shirtsleeves and brushing something from his hands as he stepped through the doorway. He raised his brows when he saw Nate. "How's your brother feeling tonight?"

"Says his leg's still hurting pretty bad. Before I ask about that, though, he also said that Laura's ill."

The doctor's brows rose again, an obvious question in his eyes. "It looks like the same illness we're fighting on the east side of town. From what I've seen, it's very contagious, so I've asked her to stay confined to her chamber."

Relief washed through him like an avalanche. "So she's not really that ill? She's just in there to keep from spreading the sickness?"

"Well . . . she's certainly not fine." The doctor's frown tightened all his nerves again.

"Is there any way I can see her? Talk to her from a distance, maybe?" Why did this feel so important? The doctor wouldn't allow it, surely, and if she was in her bedchamber, he shouldn't go in. Would it be less improper because of her illness? He really had no idea about such rules.

The doctor's brows lowered so his eyes were only slits. "Is there a message I can pass along?"

Nate scrubbed a hand through his hair. Was there one thing he wanted the doctor to tell her? How could he narrow it down? "I just . . . wanted to see her. To see if there's anything . . ."

With a sigh, he met the doctor's gaze. He'd have to just pass on simple well-wishes and hope Laura understood how much he meant them.

But the doctor spoke before Nate could open his mouth. "I suppose if she feels well enough for a visit, you can stand in the doorway and talk a few minutes." He leveled a firm look on Nate. "No more than a few. She's still very weak."

The breath gushed out of him as another wash of relief passed through. "Thank you, sir."

He waited like a nervous schoolboy while the doctor slipped into Laura's room to make sure she was up to a visit. He could hear Doc Bradley's deep murmur, but not Laura's response. Was she asleep, or so ill she couldn't speak?

The door opened again, this time wider. The doctor stepped out. "Don't go past this doorframe. And please don't overtire her." The man gave him a pointed look, then stepped into the hallway and headed toward his private quarters.

Nate turned his focus on the chamber, honing in on the bed where he could just see the rise of blankets that must be covering Laura's feet. He stepped almost to the doorway, and her head came into view.

The covers swallowed her up, leaving only her face framed by brown hair. Yet even her face appeared smaller than before, sinking deep into the pillow. She looked . . . tiny.

Fragile.

His heart fractured, and he stepped forward. "Laura?" Barely in time, he remembered the doctor's command not to pass the doorway. He stopped there, but every part of him wanted to close the distance between them. Run his hands over her brow and know she was still whole. And well.

Her dark eyes were only half open, as though she was so exhausted she couldn't manage anything more. She parted her lips slowly. "Nate." A flash of pain crossed her face as she spoke the faint, scratchy word. His name. The last thing he wanted was to add any more agony than what she was already experiencing.

"Don't speak, my love. Rest. I had no idea you were ill, or I would have come sooner." His chest ached so much he could barely draw breath. Could she die from this sickness? *Oh, God, no. Heal her. Please. Make her well.*

Her mouth pulled in the slightest of curves while her eyes drifted shut. As if the one act took all her strength so she could no longer keep her lids open.

"I need to let you rest, but please know I'll be praying for you to get well." With every breath he'd be praying. The thought of losing her sent another surge of fear charging through him, but he combated it with another petition heavenward.

Her eyes cracked, and she seemed to be working to speak again. He wanted to stand by her side, press a finger to her mouth, and tell her not to work so hard. To be silent and allow herself to recover.

"Stay." Again her voice emerged raspy, like she hadn't spoken in weeks. "Tell me . . . of your day." Her eyes had closed again, and her pretty features squeezed into a grimace as she spoke.

If she wanted him to stay so badly that she would make the request through so much pain, he'd gladly comply.

"I will, but you must rest. Don't speak. Just close your eyes and sleep if you can."

Her face relaxed, which was exactly the answer he wanted from her.

He struggled to force his mind back to his day, to something lighthearted he could share that would bring her pleasure in the midst of her misery. His mind couldn't summon anything especially cheerful. Perhaps just giving the details of his days would suffice.

"I moved my things to the cave Sunday eve. I knew I'd have a bit of a challenge getting used to living in the dark all the time, but in that big cavern where the stream runs, the fire gives the whole place a bit of a lighter feel. Not so stifling. And there's enough daylight coming through the connecting entrance that I can still get up early enough. It's not as smoky in there as I thought it would be, either. I think there might be a hole in the rock where the smoke is escaping, maybe where the water runs out. I haven't searched for it yet, but I plan to.

"Eagle Soaring is getting a little stronger every day. He's not walking on his own yet, but I help him to the privy when he needs it. I'm not sure it's the pain from his wounds that's keeping him down so much as just weakness from being so aged. I've tried to estimate how old he might be. Maybe seventy? He looks a whole lot older, but I'm thinking hard life in the sun and these freezing winters did that part."

He was rambling, but the words just kept coming. Laura's face had taken on a look so peaceful, her mouth curving up a little, that he must not be boring her entirely.

"I make sure Bright Sun keeps the fire going even when I'm not there, mostly for the light. That cavern stays warm enough with the hot springs, but I don't think it's good for those two to live in complete darkness. Can't be healthy. Since I'm helping bring in enough firewood, she doesn't seem to mind keeping a flame burning.

"She's such a good child. Obedient to whatever I ask and so attentive to her grandfather." A burn climbed up his throat. "She's lucky to have him." Did both of them know just how blessed they were to have each other? He suspected they did, at least in part.

"When our ma died, Aaron and I would have done anything for a grandfather or any family member to raise us until we could stand on our own. We had people who took us in, but we never stayed in one place very long."

Now that he was older, he could be thankful for each one. Even those who told them daily how much trouble they were, like the uncle who switched them for every infraction. From what he remembered, none of their sins had been so awful— not bringing in firewood each morning without being asked, not dropping on their bed pallet each night the moment they were told to. But he and Aaron must have been considerable trouble for one relation after another to send them away.

But they'd tried. God knew he and Aaron had tried to be helpful, tried not to be too much of a drain on those who were willing to keep a roof over their heads and let them sit at the family table.

Maybe if being good hadn't been so hard, Aaron wouldn't have been as eager to jump into the easier life when Isaac approached them all those years ago. If only they'd both known that life on the run, always looking over their shoulder, always smothered with a mountain of guilt, would really be the hardest existence they ever could have chosen.

He sighed. That was behind them.

Now he'd been given a chance to help someone else. He'd do everything in his power to keep Bright Sun and her grandfather together, and restore them to their own people, if possible.

He blinked, refocusing on his surroundings. Laura had asked him to talk, but how long had he been silent, wrapped in his thoughts? She still lay with her eyes shut, face serene, steady breaths barely lifting the blanket. Had she heard much of what he said?

He'd always craved the chance to watch her openly, to take in every beautiful feature with all his senses. To memorize every nuance of her.

But just now, the pallor of her skin and the darkness shadowing her beautiful eyes made his heart ache. She needed sleep—deep, restful sleep.

He'd best be on his way so he didn't wake her. He still had so much to do if he was going to help a certain girl and her grandfather live the life they deserved.

TWENTY-ONE

*E*very part of Laura ached, but at least she hadn't been doubled over a bedpan in several hours. She'd long since had nothing left inside her to cast up, but the dry heaves still came with a vengeance. This was the longest spell without vomiting she'd managed in . . . she had no idea how many days. Seemed like half a lifetime.

A soft knock sounded on her chamber door, and her heart leapt in a hopeful surge. The tap was too gentle to be Nate, but that still didn't keep her from longing for him to come again. The small bit of insight he'd given into his and Aaron's childhood made her ache for him—for him and Aaron both. If they'd had a father and mother who raised them until they were fully grown, would they have ever joined Bill's gang?

And if they hadn't, would her and Nate's paths have ever crossed? She couldn't ponder that now.

She tried to swallow before she pushed her voice over her raw throat, burned from so much bile passing through. "Enter."

The door pushed open, but it wasn't Ingrid's smile that appeared in the opening.

"Joanna." Laura tried to sit up as joy rushed over her. "What are you doing here?"

Joanna stepped inside, a tray in her hands. "We came into town for supplies, but when I heard about everything happening here, I decided to stay overnight to help out."

Laura looked to the doorway. "Isaac and Samuel are with you? And Mr. Bowen?" Joanna and Isaac were still newlyweds, and the love between them was obvious with a single glance. She had a feeling that if Joanna was staying the night in town, Isaac would be nearby, likely with little Samuel perched atop his shoulders.

Joanna's cheeks and ears turned pink. "Isaac's pa stayed at the cabin to tend the animals. My husband and son are getting settled in a room at the hotel."

If Laura didn't feel weak as a newborn pup, she would have grinned at the pleasure marked all over Joanna's face. Especially when she said the words *my husband*.

All she could manage as she sank into the pillow was a smile. "I'm happy for you, Joanna. So happy."

Joanna nodded her thanks, but then her expression changed as she studied Laura with the kind of intense scrutiny that cataloged every symptom. "I brought water and broth. How are you feeling? Ingrid said you haven't kept anything down in days."

"Better, I think. I've slept a lot today. And I haven't cast up the water she brought earlier."

The concern lines on Joanna's brow softened. "Thank

you, Lord." She placed the tray on the bedside table. "Can you drink this, or would you like me to spoon it for you?"

Laura tried for another smile. "I can do it. You shouldn't be in here. Doc Micah said this seems to be catching, and you can't afford to take sick when your husband and son need you."

Joanna gave her a half-smile that said she knew well Laura was using unfair leverage to send her away. "You need to rest, so I won't stay in here to keep you awake, but I will be nearby. I'll be back to check on you soon." She brushed a hand across Laura's brow. A gentle touch that soothed like the few memories she had of her own mother's touch.

Her eyes drifted shut against her will. Her body was still so weak.

"Rest now, my friend."

As sleep claimed her, the last thing she heard was the soft pad of Joanna's steps leaving the room.

⊰⊱◈⊰⊱

Laura awoke as sound drifted from the hallway. The front door closing, then boots thumping. Her heart leapt as it had every time she heard that sound these past days. But just like all the other times, this was likely only Doc Micah coming back from visiting patients.

But could it be Nate? A glance at the curtained window showed no light peeking through the cracks between the cloth. This should be around the time Nate came by after work.

And also the time the doctor should be returning.

Boot thuds walked past Aaron's door, but then slowed as they neared Laura's. Voices sounded in the hallway. Ingrid speaking to a man.

Her heart surged. That was Nate's voice, she was almost certain.

Her attraction to him had grown so much stronger than she'd ever expected.

Yet how could she not come to care so much for him when she saw daily examples of his goodness? His kindness. His devotion to those honored enough to be called his friends. The strength of character that must have lain deep inside, suppressed by so many years of being an outlaw.

She could understand now how loyalty to Aaron had kept him in the gang. From the outside, it didn't make sense, but when she thought back to her younger years with Will and Robbie, she could imagine herself making the same choice.

She'd raised Robbie, in almost every sense of the word. And Will . . . he had been her lifeline. Her sanity in the everyday storms. Many, many times she'd taken blows or angry words their father meant for him. Anytime she could, she took the beating meant for her brothers.

There was nothing she wouldn't have done to protect them. Nothing.

So, yes, she could understand what had driven Nate to stick with his brother, even when that required him to do what he knew was wrong. But even that had its limitations, when he'd finally taken a stand when the others kidnapped her and Samuel.

A soft knock sounded on her door, and Ingrid poked her head in. "Are you up for a visitor?" Her face held a grin that seemed half teasing.

A smile tugged at her own mouth. "Of course." That had to be Nate. She brushed the hair from her face. If only he didn't have to see her so bedraggled.

Ingrid stepped back, and another figure filled the doorway.

Nate. Her heart stuttered as joy pushed back her exhaustion.

Weariness lined his smile, and several days' worth of stubble coated his jaw, but still he looked deliciously good. If only she could call him closer. Close enough to touch him. To soak in his strength, the comfort his nearness always wove through her.

She probably shouldn't have let him become so important to her. A man hadn't been part of her plans, not yet. She'd intended to set herself well on the path to the life she craved—a life doing things that truly mattered. Then she could see how a man might fit into that work.

"You look like you're feeling better." Nate's dancing green eyes glanced over her.

She nodded. "I think I'm on the mend." *Lord, please let me be.* She couldn't remember ever feeling so near death as she had these past few days. Not even that time when she'd tried to use her father's drink to mourn Robbie's tragic choice.

"I'm glad." The weight of his two words—their depth— settled in the air between the two of them. "Is there anything I can do?" He hesitated. "Anything you need?" His brows still rested low, his forehead furrowed with worry.

Hopefully she wasn't the cause of his concern. He had enough burdens of his own without her adding to them. "Nothing." Her throat still rasped, and his brows pulled lower.

She needed a distraction. Swallowing to moisten her throat, she worked for a smile. "Tell me of your day. How are Bright Sun and Eagle Soaring?" Now that she was speaking more, her voice didn't sound as awful, although her throat still ached.

Nate's brow wrinkled even more. Definitely a scowl now, and not the effect she'd been hoping for. "They're well. Eagle Soaring seems a bit better every day. Bright Sun seems more relaxed around me, which I'm happy about."

"Of course she is." She offered an encouraging smile. "She's good at reading people."

He looked away, staring out the window. Not that he could see anything through the curtains and the darkness outside. Why wouldn't he look at her?

Maybe seeing her brought him pain. Or maybe he was regretting his choice to move into the cave with the two Indians. She'd been surprised when he suggested it, but the more she thought through the benefits, the more relieved she'd been. Why hadn't she thought of it herself?

Her weary mind ached from mulling through so many thoughts. "What is it, Nate? What's wrong?"

He was silent for a long moment, his gaze still locked on the window. "Someone brought more boxes to the cave today. While I was away at the mine."

Her stomach twisted, but not the knifing pain that signaled another round of retching. This twisting stemmed from Nate's words. Or maybe from his tone and the fact that he still didn't look at her.

But . . . why did they automatically think the men storing crates in the cave were doing something nefarious? Perhaps these were simply businessmen who'd run out of storage space.

"What was in the crates this time?"

He finally turned back to her. "Big powder. The kind we use for explosives in the mine."

All the strength fled her body with his words, muddling her mind. Only the mines would need big powder, right? And was it dangerous when stored in crates? Were Bright Sun and her grandfather in peril? Surely Nate wouldn't have left them alone if that were the case. Thinking took too much energy. And speaking . . . her mouth wouldn't move to form words, even when she told it to.

"Laura?" Nate's voice called through her fog, through the darkness. When had she closed her eyes? "Laura, what's wrong?"

The fear in his voice infused enough strength for her to force her eyes open. "I'm just tired." So very tired.

"I'll leave so you can rest. Please rest. Whatever you need to do to fight this sickness. I won't stop praying for you."

As she let herself sink into his words and his voice, her body relaxed. As though the blood had momentarily ceased flowing through her veins but now restarted, spreading life-sustaining strength everywhere she needed it.

And with that strength, the tug of sleep pulled too strong

for her to resist. The last thing she remembered was the steady thump of Nate's boots on the hallway floor.

⊶⊙⊷

Nate jerked awake as a bolt of pain shot through his shoulder. He grabbed for the hand shaking him as he struggled to make sense of his surroundings.

His gaze finally made out Bright Sun in the dim firelight, and everything flooded back. But why did she wake him? Maybe morning had come and he'd overslept. He blinked but couldn't see any daylight coming from the opening into the front cavern.

He sat up and focused on the girl, who still hovered beside him. "What is it?"

"Men." Her voice couldn't be called a whisper, but the sound barely reached across the short distance between them.

Every one of Nate's nerves leapt to alert. "Where?" He stopped breathing so he wouldn't miss the girl's response.

"Taking the boxes."

He pushed up to his feet. "Light a lantern for me." He had to catch them. Something wasn't right about the mysterious crates, especially this last group full of explosive powder. And why else would they make all their visits in the dead of night?

He'd planned to ask one of the supervisors at the mine if they knew of missing powder. Or maybe they were storing the crates here intentionally.

But if these men stole the boxes away in the middle of the night, he might be accused of scheming with them.

232

He had to know better what was happening. Then he'd decide if he needed to talk with someone at the mine.

After slipping on his coat, he reached for the rifle he always kept beside him when he slept. This chamber that held the hot springs stayed toasty warm, but the other cavern with the outside entrance was just the opposite, especially since that evening it had felt like snow would begin falling any minute.

When he turned back to the girl, she stood staring at him, the unlit lantern still on the floor where he'd placed it before going to sleep. "They'll see the light."

She was right. . . . He must be still daft from sleep.

He nodded. "Let's go."

Bright Sun led the way toward the front cavern with all the hanging rock formations. During the day, sunrays shining through the cave's main entrance gave enough light to maneuver that front chamber without a lantern, as long as his eyes had fully adjusted to the interior. But he wasn't so sure he could move quietly among the dangling rock icicles with only moonlight filtering through.

He moved in front of Bright Sun to peer into that room first. At the entrance, they both paused, and he strained to hear or see any sign of the men.

All seemed quiet. No shadows moved near the cave opening.

Maybe Bright Sun had been mistaken. And why would she have been awake and wandering the caves to see strangers in the first place? He'd have to question her later.

Bright Sun stepped around him, and before he realized what she was doing, she'd started forward and was weaving her way through the obstacles in the cavern.

He reached to grab her, but she was too far ahead. He couldn't call to her, for his voice would echo off the stone walls.

He charged forward, doing his best to focus on all the rock formations that seemed to rise up from nowhere, or drop in front of him with little warning. Yet he also had to keep an eye on the girl a half dozen strides in front of him, as well as the cave entrance where potentially dangerous men might be lurking.

His pulse thudded hard in his neck when he finally caught up with Bright Sun in the open area near the cave entrance. He dropped his hand on her shoulder and struggled to keep both his breathing and his voice quiet as he leaned close to speak. "Don't run ahead again. Please. I need to deal with these men."

He didn't have time to watch for her response, for he'd already taken in the empty wall where crates had stood when he'd come in for the night, only a few hours before. The gaping space showed no sign anything had ever been there.

Moving toward the opening, he kept his stride light. At the rock wall, he ducked low to peer outside. The thickness of the stone archway was about twice the length of his foot, and he crouched low and leaned out enough to look both ways.

The path stretched empty around the edge of the mountain, as far as he could see in the darkness. No sounds drifted to him, save the regular gusts of wind.

Should he go right or left? To the right, the mountain goat trail continued around one more turn, then ended in a small patch of evergreen shrubs. The men could be hiding in them if they'd heard Nate in the cave. But he suspected they'd not heard him. More likely, the men had finished retrieving their treasure and were even now loading the crates in a wagon or driving away.

He turned left, winding his way around the side of the mountain. He stepped over the familiar rise in the rocks, balancing carefully through the dip where the stone had broken loose and he'd ended up with a dislocated shoulder joint.

Just before he reached the place where he should be able to see a wagon parked on the dirt and rock hillside, he slowed. Then he crept forward.

But the hillside sat empty.

He strained to pick up any sound and held his breath as a distant jingling carried through the night air.

A wagon. It had to be.

TWENTY-TWO

*G*ripping his rifle tighter, Nate charged forward, moving as quietly as he could. Yet he could no longer sacrifice speed. If he didn't catch up with the wagon, he'd lose them completely. Then he'd lose any chance of finding out what these men were up to.

Maybe he should leave well enough alone. His past certainly didn't give him the right to point fingers at others. Yet he couldn't shake the feeling that something was very wrong. The urge to know—to do something about it, maybe even to right a wrong—drove him forward.

He must have run half a mile by the time the wagon appeared ahead. The rig had turned onto the wagon ruts that led toward the main road. It'd be another quarter mile before he knew whether they'd turn left toward Settler's Fort or right toward a handful of other mountain settlements, with Fort Benton lying a few weeks' travel beyond.

After ducking to the side so he could run under cover of trees lining the path, he kept a steady pace behind the vehicle. He couldn't see much from this distance, not how many men sat on the bench or what the horses pulling the conveyance looked like. He could only make out that the back was covered by a tarpaulin or blanket of some kind.

Before long, the animals swung right. Away from Settler's Fort.

Were these freighters who'd been hired to take the powder to a mine near one of the other towns? The scenario seemed unlikely, for the powder was in high demand—and hard to transport from the States. First it had to travel by steamboat to Fort Benton, then by freight wagon over weeks of bumpy roads, winding up and down steep mountains. No one would bring blasting powder all the way to Settler's Fort, then turn around and transport the dangerous material back over the same roads.

It made no sense.

He increased his speed, weaving deeper into the woods so the men wouldn't see him. He had to rely on the jingling harness and squeaking wagon to cover the rustling of the leaves under his boots.

As he closed the distance between them, two figures took shape on the bench seat. One man bent low, gripping the reins of a four-horse team. Or maybe those were mules, he couldn't tell for sure.

The other fellow sat high on the box, craning his neck from one side of the trail to the other. If Nate had to guess, he'd be fairly certain the man sat with a rifle on his lap, finger hovering over the trigger.

They expected trouble.

If he moved around in front and stopped them at gunpoint, he'd be up against two rifles. He had plenty of experience waylaying wagons on remote roads, but he wasn't part of the gang anymore.

His actions had to be above the law.

Besides, he had no proof these men were up to anything unlawful. Only his instincts told him they were trouble.

But . . . they were riding away from Settler's Fort, away from everyone under his protection, so he didn't need to intervene in their escape. He should talk to the mine supervisor tomorrow and let him know everything he saw. Lanton too.

With a sigh, Nate slowed and watched the wagon roll forward, fading into the night.

◆──◎ ◎──◆

Laura glared at Aaron's chamber door. She hated to go in there, but she had to face the man. Lord willing, Aaron's craving for laudanum had worn off while she lay near death. Now he would be sullen and depressed like before, but she could handle that version of him. Their past was behind them, and she planned to do everything she could now to help him move forward into a better life.

Forcing a smile on her face, she knocked on the door. "Aaron, it's Laura." She probably should be stricter about enforcing the use of her surname around these brothers. But she couldn't stand the thought of placing that barrier between her and Nate. She craved his nearness, not distance.

And Aaron . . . With all that lay between them—the kidnapping, the life-changing shot gone awry, and now this agonizing attempt to help him walk again—he felt too much like one of her brothers.

A brother who frustrated her. One she longed to help and encourage and nurture . . . until he sent her one of his peevish looks and she felt like dumping his meal tray in his lap.

He mumbled something unintelligible through the wooden barrier. She'd take that as a welcome. If he didn't want her to enter, he'd say so loudly and clearly enough for the entire house to hear.

Pushing open the door, she poked her head inside and sent him a smile. "Feeling well this morning?"

He glared, his lower lip poking out, just like Robbie would have done when he was five. She had to fight the urge to step closer and tweak his nose like she'd have done to her little brother. She did let her grin widen a little.

"Let's do some leg lifts and toe stretches before I head out." She stepped into the room. The stale, musky odor made her queasy, so she left the door open. Doc Micah had been surprised how quickly she recovered, but even though most of her strength had returned, she still couldn't manage to eat much. And every odor caused this same reaction in her middle.

"Thought you said the service was canceled today," Aaron grumbled as he sat up and lowered his injured leg to the floor.

She perched on the edge of the chair and leaned forward to hold her hand out, palm down, as he slowly raised his stockinged toes up to touch her palm. "The church service *is* canceled due both to the snow and because so many in town are recovering from sickness. That's why I'm going up to the cave to check on Bright Star and her grandfather." She shot a glance at the strained contortion on Aaron's face as he forced his limb up the last few inches to reach her palm.

"Good." She added a cheery note as he dropped his heel back to the floor. "Now, again."

Concentration lined his brow as he worked to perform the feat a second time. His leg was healing, little by little. While she'd lain in bed for day after miserable day, she'd realized that Aaron's personality was such that he probably wouldn't perform his best without someone goading him, or maybe even a little competition. A challenge to drive him into putting forth that extra effort he needed in order to walk again.

She hadn't decided on a challenge yet, but she could be his drillmaster for now.

"You're going to see my brother, then." Aaron didn't look at her as he spoke, just focused on lifting his leg. But something in his tone told her his statement held more import than casual conversation.

"I suspect I'll see him." She tried to keep her own voice nonchalant, despite the ache of longing in her chest as she thought of meeting Nate at the cave.

"You've fallen for him, haven't you?" Aaron's words pierced her thoughts like a needle.

She jerked her eyes back up to his face as his toe reached her hand and dropped down to the floor. "Why would you say that?"

"He's pretty smitten over you, too." Aaron didn't meet her gaze, just began the toe stretches that always came after ten leg lifts. "He'd clobber me good if he knew I told you." Then his eyes rose as he gave her an assessing squint. "I suspect he'll tell you himself soon. If he hasn't already."

Memories of their kiss flooded her entire body, warming her all the way up to her ears. She tried to cover her reaction by easing back in her chair and looking as though she were counting his stretches. In truth, her mind swam with image after image of Nate. Riding beside her on their way to the cave. His off-kilter smile that showed his dimple. That smile had the power to make her follow him like a puppy tagging along behind its favorite boy.

And maybe this walk to the cave had more to do with his smile than she'd let herself believe. She did desperately need to get out of the clinic for a few hours, especially since the sun was already setting fire to the snow crystals cloaking the ground.

This was the perfect chance for a walk, and what better place to go than to visit her friends? And Nate.

Aaron had become silent, maybe because he focused on the effort required for each stretch. Or maybe he was waiting for her to comment on what he'd said about Nate's affections.

She wouldn't. Her feelings about Nate were not his brother's concern. At least . . . not for now. If anything ever came of them, maybe.

Another wave of heat surged to her ears. She'd not really let herself think of a future with Nate.

"There." Aaron relaxed his foot, letting it rest at a slight angle. "Run along now. Tell my brother I said to enjoy himself. He deserves it after all I've put him through."

She jerked her face up to study Aaron's. Was he acknowledging how hard he'd made life for Nate these past years? His expression lacked the sullenness that usually turned down the corners of his mouth. His eyes held an alert look she'd only started seeing since she recovered from her illness. His craving for laudanum must have finally loosed its hold.

Yet the new quality his expression wore now was an earnestness that hadn't been there moments before. His brown eyes fixed on her. "I know Nate only stayed in the gang because I wanted to. Ten years ago, when Isaac quit us, Nate tried to talk me into stopping. He wanted to do something honest where we didn't have to always be on the run."

His tone never flinched, just kept its solid gravity. "He sacrificed every day after that to keep us together. Did things I know he hated. I didn't always realize it back then, but I do now. I've had a lot of time to think, lying in this bed."

Now Aaron's mouth curved in a sad look that could almost have been a smile. Almost. "I want my brother to be happy. I'm not convinced you're the one who can help him get there, but I want him to have the chance to decide."

Emotion clumped in her throat. Aaron's words weren't the most eloquent blessing, but she'd not thought he'd ever voice even this. She could only manage a nod.

He waved her off like he was shooing a pesky servant. "Go on now. We're done here, and you'd rather see him more than me anyway."

"You may be right about that." She managed a teasing tone and sent him a shaky smile, then stood and strode to the door. Somewhere deep inside a mountain was where she wanted to be just now, with the man who she could now admit had won her heart.

TWENTY-THREE

*N*ate couldn't seem to get through his list of catch-up chores. His spirit craved a trip to town. Namely to the clinic to visit Aaron and see if Laura was still recovering the way the doctor hoped she would.

He'd had to hunt to replenish food stores the night before instead of his usual Saturday night visit, and taking down the bull elk had been a blessing. But now that meant hours of preparing the meat and hide for curing. Bright Sun was helping, of course. Still, as mature as she was for a child of seven or eight years, he couldn't expect her to manage adult tasks with the experience needed to do thorough work.

She'd been roasting meat inside the cave—under her grandfather's watchful guidance—when Nate left to head back out to the grassy area to scrape the hide. As he stepped off the stone ledge onto the rock-strewn grass, a motion in the trees down the hillside caught his eye.

He stopped and honed his focus. A woman stepped from the woods onto the snowy open hillside. His heart leapt in his chest, and his feet turned to stride toward Laura before he realized he was even moving.

Since he was walking downhill—nearly running, actually—he reached her not far above the tree line. It took everything in him to stop a few steps in front of her, not to close the distance and take her in his arms, hold her tight, and breathe in the fact that she was well. Whole.

Heavy breaths raised her chest as she slowed to a stop, but he forced his gaze not to linger there. Her face still lacked color except for rosy patches at her cheeks and nose. She looked like she wasn't completely recovered, and probably shouldn't be out here. Had the doctor even allowed her to come this far? But the sight of her in all her beauty stole not just his breath but also his words.

"Hello." Laura's soft greeting tugged him from his reverie.

A silly grin pulled at his mouth. "You're better."

"Much." She offered her own smile, but her eyes lacked their normal sparkle. He needed to get her to a place where she could sit and rest.

Stepping to the side, he motioned toward the path he'd just traversed. "I was about to scrape an elk hide from last night's hunt. But you probably want to see Bright Sun and Eagle Soaring."

"I do, but then I can come back out and help with the hide." Her less-than-enthusiastic tone brought a chuckle from him as he fell into step beside her.

"After what you've been through this week, working with that mess is the last thing you need. I've plenty of time to get it done." Maybe he could talk her into sitting with him while he worked. He still couldn't believe how much he craved her presence. But not at the cost of her health.

He couldn't let her wear herself out and suffer a relapse.

As they retraced his many tracks through the snow, Laura seemed to slow and her breathing grew thick, probably from the steepness of the hill. He moved closer and offered his elbow. She might decline, but he couldn't watch her suffer without trying to help.

She took his arm without a word, and the pressure of her touch—even through her gloves and his coat—sent a flood of heat up his arm.

He led her past the hide he should be working on, then stayed close behind her as they navigated the stone ledge. "I cleared a path through the ice so it's not too slippery for Bright Sun."

"That's good for you, too. We can't have you dislocating that shoulder joint again."

He grimaced. "That too."

When they reached the cave opening, he touched her arm. "Let me light the lantern first."

He was half surprised when she obliged without argument. Clearly, she wasn't her usual independent self.

When they'd both ducked into the cavern and paused to adjust their vision to the darkness inside, Laura's gaze wandered to the place where the crates had sat against the wall. "Any sign of the men with the boxes?"

"Not since the two took the big powder in the middle of the night. I asked Bright Sun more about the men who delivered them, and from her descriptions, I think those were different men than those who picked them up. It seems like this cave is being used as a holding place for freight, maybe goods that are being sold."

She turned to study him, and he soaked in the way her luminous brown eyes glimmered in the lantern light. "You think they're being sold unlawfully?"

He shrugged. "That's what my instinct says, but I can't prove it."

She was so pretty, even with shadows cloaking part of her features. Her sickness this week had shaken him, especially when Doc Bradley admitted three people had died from the illness. *Thank you, God, for saving her.*

Maybe he should feel more sorrow for the other families who mourned lost loved ones, and he did feel badly for them. But relief eclipsed every other thought as he stood here with Laura.

She was still watching him, and the softness in her expression drew him. He reached out for her before he could stop himself, taking her arm and drawing her near.

She came to him, nestling into his chest as though she craved his touch as much as his body needed to hold her. To feel for himself that she was whole and very much alive.

He wrapped his arms around her, careful not to let the lantern bump against her. Raising his free hand to cup the back of her head, he pressed his face into her hair and breathed in her softness. The sweet essence of her.

This woman brought him alive like nothing ever had. He could fill himself with her every day for the rest of his life and still not get enough.

Too soon, she shifted in his arms. He had to let her go, had to put some distance between them. He certainly couldn't kiss her again, no matter how much his body craved that deeper connection.

He forced himself to loosen his grip and slide his hands to her upper arms so she could pull back if she wanted to.

She did, though only enough to look up into his face. Her eyes shimmered with a glaze that almost looked like the sheen of tears. Her lips parted and her mouth turned up the tiniest bit. "I've missed you."

He focused on her words, tearing his attention from her mouth back up to her eyes. "I'm just glad to see you well. You have no idea what a scare you gave us." He should have said *me* instead of *us*. He'd meant to say *me*, but lost his courage at the last minute.

Stroking his thumb over her coat as he still held her upper arms, he offered a sheepish smile. "You probably scared the others, too, but I'm really talking about me. When the doctor said three people had already died from what you had, I nearly lost my meal then and there. I can't imagine what I'd do if something happened to you." He frowned as one of his earlier thoughts slipped back. "Don't you think it would be better for you to give a wider berth to patients who are so sick?"

Her mouth flattened a little and she shook her head. "If I hadn't gone, who would have? Ingrid's health is already so fragile with the coming baby. And the last thing she needs is for Doc Micah to bring an illness back to her, although he goes out to help the sick every time they come, regardless. I suppose he's learned how to be more careful than I have."

Then her eyes grew round and a little pleading. "I want to help people, Nate. More than just organizing the doctor's supplies and cleaning up the clinic. I want to do something important with my life."

The delicate lines in her neck worked. "My growing-up days were always such a struggle. Hard and frightening, and worry always hung over me like a smothering blanket. That's behind me now, and I don't want to waste time. Surely God has something meaningful for me. Work that will actually help others. I need to find that, even if it involves risking a bit of sickness."

His gut churned, both at the thought of Laura putting herself in the path of even greater risk, but also with pride and love for this woman.

Did she even know how remarkable she was? From her beauty to her passion for helping others, no matter the cost to herself. From the very first time he saw her during the kidnapping, when she'd done everything she could to protect little Samuel, putting herself in harm's way so he would be safe, it'd been impossible not to admire her. The more he came to know her, the more certain he was that he couldn't imagine a life without her.

At least not a happy life.

As the thoughts spun inside him, the sudden urge to tell her what he'd finally allowed himself to realize nearly burst inside him.

Before he could speak, she pulled away. Disappointment washed through him as she turned her back to him. "Bright Sun?"

The girl stood only a few paces behind them. Laura must have heard her, but he'd been so focused on his thoughts, he'd missed all other sounds. Not only was he losing his finely honed instincts, he must be losing his mind to let a woman—even this woman—affect him so.

Laura moved to the girl's side and hugged her. When she pulled back, the child's face shone in a smile. A real grin that flashed white teeth, the first he'd seen from Bright Sun.

He couldn't help a matching grin. No one would be able to resist that sweet smile. And no wonder a hug from Laura had been the cause. She'd had that same effect on him only moments before.

"Tell me, how is your grandfather?" Laura brushed the black strands that hung in front of the girl's eyes.

"He's better. Right now he's watching the meat cook so I could come see you."

"I'm glad to hear it." Laura's voice was rich and warm, so motherly that the sweet sound tightened something in his chest. "Shall we go visit with him, too?"

Laura sent a smile over her shoulder as she turned Bright Sun toward the cave's interior.

He nodded and motioned for her to go ahead. As he followed near enough that light from his lantern would guide their way, he couldn't help the thought that his chance for happiness strode just ahead of him, almost within his grasp.

If he didn't step forward and claim it soon, his opportunity might disappear forever.

Nate crouched in front of the hole he'd hacked in the stone, smoothing the explosive powder so it filled each crack. His heart pulsed hard in his chest as he rose to his feet and studied his work. Was he missing anything?

Setting a blast without Barlow or one of the others to oversee still made his palms clammy, but this was only a small charge. And he'd gone through all the steps they'd taught him.

"You down here, Long?"

Nate spun at the voice calling from the other end of the tunnel. "I'm here." That was Marson, if he wasn't mistaken.

"I'm comin' through. Don't blow me up."

The words pulled a half-smile from him as boot thuds echoed off the mine walls. Yep, that was Marson's measured drawl. He brushed his sleeve over his face to wipe away any powder that might be smudged there. The act might only make him look worse, depending on how much black powder clung to his shirt and how grimy his face was.

At least he looked the same as everyone else working in the place.

The glow of a candle bobbed in the distance, illuminating a felt hat, then the craggy face of the man wearing it. "Propst said you wanted to see me."

"I do." Nate's throat went dry as he thought through what he needed to share. Better to be straightforward. Just state the facts. "I saw something I think you should know about. This might not be my place—might not be anything at all—but it's bothered me enough I need to tell you. After that, you can do with it what you think best."

Marson studied him, his expression not giving a hint of his thoughts.

"There's a cave in the mountain about five minutes' walk north of here. The cave's not easy to find, but I go there a good bit." He wouldn't say he slept there unless the man asked questions. "Twice now, crates have been dropped off there and stacked against the cave wall. Then, a few days later, they disappear. It's almost always at night when they come and when they're taken. The boxes have always been nailed shut, but the first time they were marked as different things—peaches, notions, knives. The second time, they were marked as blasting powder."

Marson blinked at that. Just a single quick reaction, and nothing else in his expression changed. But Nate had caught his full attention.

"When was this?" His voice held the rasp of a man who'd worked many years amidst the dust of a mine.

"They took the second load away two nights ago."

A line in Marson's brow deepened. "And they brought that load when?"

"Three nights before that."

"Who's bringing these boxes?" His tone didn't change, just stayed matter of fact.

"I haven't seen them, but my . . . friend said there have always been two men." He'd not meant to mention Bright Sun, and Marson's brows rose at the word. "You and your friend spend a lot of time in this cave?" The man's interest was definitely piqued—and probably his suspicion, too.

No matter what, Nate had to prove his innocence in this.

And to do that, he'd need to tell all. If Marson suspected he was holding back, he'd assume a devious motive.

Nate straightened. "I've been living in there for a while now. Before that, I was staying in a tent on the southwest side of town, but nights have gotten colder. There's a hot spring in a back chamber of the cave that keeps it pretty warm. An Indian girl and her injured grandfather showed up in the cave a few weeks ago. Doc Bradley treated the man's injuries, and I make sure they have enough food and firewood. The girl is the one who's seen the men come and go with the crates. She's not made herself known to them, but she could describe them for you if you want more details."

His voice faded into the stillness of the tunnel as Marson studied him. Did he read truth in Nate's words? The man had always been fair. Even kind at times, like when Nate had suffered his shoulder injury. But he'd also seen Marson rail into a worker who cut corners or slacked off. He showed little tolerance for those who spun tales to get out of work. Just the week before, he'd sent Danvers home without pay for two days because of ongoing tardiness in the mornings. Would he think Nate had come up with this story for some kind of personal gain?

The man still regarded him. "How many crates of powder did you say?"

"Twelve or thirteen. I didn't take an exact count. I have no specific reason for thinking they were stolen. It just seems . . . strange. Thought I'd mention it in case anything's come up missing." Nate turned back to the charge of powder he'd set.

"I appreciate you telling me. If anything more shows up,

come get me straightaway at the widow's boardinghouse, will you?"

Nate turned back and nodded as he met Marson's gaze. "Yes, sir."

⊰⊱⊶⊷

Aaron was walking again.

Nate's breath blew white in the dim light of the quarter moon as he traipsed back to the cave after spending the evening at the clinic. Even his pleasure with Aaron's progress and time spent with Laura didn't ward off the frigid wind buffeting his body and slipping its icy fingers through the cracks between his coat and scarf.

He still couldn't believe Aaron had finally accomplished this milestone, but he was fairly certain they owed the excellent turn of events to Laura. Apparently, in the week since she'd finally recovered from her illness, she'd been an unrelenting taskmaster, ensuring Aaron did the leg exercises many times each day.

Nate still couldn't fathom why his brother didn't take initiative to do them himself, since they were clearly what strengthened the leg enough to finally hold his weight.

Lord, help my brother. Aaron seemed to be on the mend in his body, especially with Laura nearby to goad him into the necessary effort. But his spirits were still so low. So often, despair seemed to settle over him.

Nate reached the edge of the trees and paused, staring up at the lofty peak that concealed the cave he now called home. God had provided shelter for him through the winter, although certainly not what he'd expected. Surely the Almighty could also heal his brother and bring him back to the man the Lord made him to be.

Nate raised his eyes to the stars that peeked out around the clouds. "What do I do, Lord? How can I help him? Show me." He waited, the pounding of his heart and the whistle of the wind the only sounds in the still night.

He was still learning how to hear God's leading. Reverend Vendor said the Lord's voice often came so quiet that the message settled more like a feeling, like certainty and intuition, but he'd know it was God because of the peace that came with the thought.

Nothing slipped into his mind that fit that description, but he kept his face upturned to the heavens. "When you're ready, Lord, show me what to do." He breathed in a lungful of frigid air, letting the burn saturate his chest. Then he exhaled, surrounding himself with a white haze.

He'd best get inside now. Bright Sun would be waiting up for him. Eagle Soaring still slept a good deal most days, although during his waking hours, he seemed to be getting stronger. Nate wasn't sure whether he should worry about all the sleep the man seemed to need, or if that was typical for a fellow of his years. He should ask the doctor the next time he saw him.

After trudging up the rocky hillside, Nate gained the ledge and stepped carefully over the icy rock around the side of the cliff. As many times as he'd traipsed this path lately, he knew better than to get too confident about even one step.

Each time he'd let himself believe he'd mastered the same skill as a mountain goat, he'd slip and add another bruise to his backside.

This time, he managed to make it to the cave without incident and ducked inside. Thick darkness settled around him as he crouched down to where he kept the lantern just beside the entrance.

A scuffing sounded behind him, and he turned to look for Bright Sun among the shadows.

A blow slammed hard into his head, knocking him sideways. His breath jerked out of him as light exploded in his vision. Another blow to his back threw him forward. His head smashed into the rock wall.

Pain radiated through his skull, even after the darkness closed in.

TWENTY-FOUR

*S*omething wasn't right.

The thought had niggled at Laura throughout the night, waking her more than once with an overwhelming sense of dread. She'd even risen from bed and walked through the house and clinic, just to make sure someone else wasn't up and suffering.

All seemed quiet, except the gentle snoring drifting from the Bradleys' chamber. The common areas were empty. But now as she stood outside Aaron's chamber, no sounds came from within.

Not Aaron's steady snore that always murmured from inside when he slept. Was he up and searching for laudanum again? *Lord, no. I thought we were through this.*

But addiction's cruel claws gripped its targets with a relentless hold, rarely letting go with only one bout.

She tapped on his door. "Aaron?" If he was skulking through the house, seeking Doc Micah's new hiding place for the medicine, he wouldn't answer.

"What?" The voice from inside didn't sound drowsy, as if she'd awakened him. Nor slurred, like it would if he'd found the laudanum.

Relief eased through her, and she pushed open the door enough to poke her head in. He sat on the edge of the bed, fully dressed and the coverlet straightened. "Are you all right?"

His brow wrinkled. "Yeah." But his expression bespoke the lie.

She pushed the door wider and leaned against the frame. "You're up early." Was he hurting again? Maybe he was after walking for the first time last night. She didn't dare ask him, though. She still wasn't sure how much of his supposed pain was real and how much was his attempt to get laudanum.

His brows sank lower. "Can't sleep." Then he looked at her, as if finally seeing her. "You're up early, too."

She wrapped her hands around her elbows. "I couldn't sleep either. Something doesn't feel right." And saying it out loud gave urgency to the knot in her stomach. "All seems well in the house, though. I wonder if something's wrong at the cave?" The thought tumbled out of her mouth before she stopped to examine it.

He studied her. "I was thinking the same thing. Not that I can do anything about it."

Purpose sluiced through her. She pushed away from the wall. "I'm going up there. Just to make sure they're all right. If you hear the doctor or Ingrid stirring, will you let them know where I've gone?"

His mouth pinched. "Maybe I can go with you."

She barely bit back a snort. "You took your first steps last night. There's no way you can walk all the way to the cave, even with walking sticks." She pulled the door behind her as she went for her coat and her possibles bag. "I'll just check on them and be right back."

The wind gusted around her as she stepped off the porch and set off in long strides toward the mountain. Snowflakes began falling before she left the outskirts of town.

Would Nate be working in the mine yet? He said he started just after sunrise, so maybe he was only now entering the darkness of the tunnel. Would he be warm enough in there? She'd heard that mines dug down below ground grew excessively hot inside. But the place where he worked had been hacked sideways into a mountain cliff, which probably wasn't nearly as warm. She should ask if he needed any extra clothing sewn. Maybe a scarf, too.

She was halfway to the cave when movement ahead caught her focus. Through the falling snow, Laura could make out a dark figure. She tensed, but then she made out the form of someone too small to be a man. Bright Sun?

She plunged forward to close the distance between them, her heart racing. What had happened? She'd never seen the girl outside of the cave.

"What is it?" Upon reaching the child, Laura took hold of her shoulders and pulled her into a quick hug, just to assure herself the girl was real.

Then she pulled back and studied Bright Sun's face. "What's wrong? Is it Nate? Your grandfather?"

Bright Sun usually guarded her expressions so they could

be impossible to read at times, but this wasn't one of those times.

Fear swam in her dark eyes. "They took him."

Nate wriggled his wrists, trying to loosen the cord strapping them behind his back. He had to be careful not to let his efforts show to the three men tucked with him in this tiny burrow dug into the mountainside.

After a long, miserable night on the cave's hard floor, his head pounding, Sloane and Danvers had moved him here just before first light. Hiram Mathers had been sitting here waiting for them, the quiet mine freighter who'd given him rides to town. Nate had never imagined the man would be part of a crime like this.

And from the commands he was giving, it sounded like Hiram was more than just a freighter who transported the stolen goods away from this part of the country. He was also the mastermind behind the whole scheme, probably paying Sloane and Danvers for whatever they could steal for him, or maybe giving them a cut of the profits.

Now Sloane and Hiram were facing off like two bulls in the springtime. Even with the dugout open on one side, the place was way too small for this much tension in the air.

"I thought you said the cave was empty. No one knew about it." Hiram's gravelly voice was low as he narrowed his dark eyes. The weathered lines on his face deepened.

"It was empty when we first checked it out. There's only

the two rooms, and not a soul was in either one. Not even an animal." Sloane spat his response. "He can't have been livin' there long." He shot a glare at Nate.

They'd not questioned him once, just bound his hands and feet and tied a foul-tasting piece of leather around his mouth. For the walk from the cave to the hideout, they'd had to untie his legs, but securing them again was the first thing Danvers did after pushing him down to sit in a back corner of the dugout.

Now the big man leaned against an opposite wall, rifle pointed loosely in Nate's direction. He kept his focus mostly on Nate, but an occasional glance at Hiram or Sloane proved he was keeping up with the conversation.

Hiram turned back to glare at Sloane. "What about the Indian man and girl? Are they still there?"

Nate steeled himself not to cringe at the words. How had these two men overheard him tell Marson his story at the mine? The tunnel he'd been working in was plenty long enough that his voice wouldn't have carried to the main shaft. One of these two must have crept close enough to hear the conversation. But why? Had they suspected something? Or had they simply been in the right place at the wrong time?

His chest squeezed. Nothing was outside of God's control, and surely God wanted these thieves to be brought to justice. From what he could gather, Hiram had a whole chain of thieves working for him, stealing supplies from mines all through these mountains. He went from one to the next with his freight wagon, picking up blasting powder and any other supplies they tucked away for him in hiding places. How long had Sloane and Danvers been working for him?

"We didn't see 'em when we were there just a bit ago." Sloane's voice came out almost a whine.

"Did you look?" Hiram was losing patience. That couldn't be good.

Sloane darted a glance at Danvers. "We didn't go back in the room with the spring in it, but we'd have heard 'em."

Hiram spat an oath as he spun away to stare out through the thickly falling snow at the wagon. The poor mules were covered in a tall crust of ice.

The man straightened, apparently having made a decision. "We'll have to kill them." He jerked a glance at Nate. "All three of them. I want it done before I leave so I can make sure you don't turn yellow." This time he sent a pointed look to Danvers.

The man paled at the words, his jowls hanging lower than before. He eyed Sloane, then Nate, not meeting his eyes.

Sloane shifted his feet. "That's the other thing. There's no way we can keep takin' from the mine here now that Marson knows. We wanna ride out with you. Thought maybe we can get on with another outfit down the trail and keep workin' for ya."

Hiram's breaths came hard as his stare slid between the two lackeys, and a vein on his temple rose high enough for Nate to see, even in the dim light. At last, he seemed to regain control of himself. "Fine. But we take care of these three first. I won't leave behind someone who can identify me."

Danvers straightened. "If we just put out this fire, he'll

freeze to death in a couple hours. It's cold enough." He motioned the gun toward Nate.

"Tryin' for the easy way out again, are ya?" Hiram puffed out another hard breath. "Let's go. Put out the fire and be quick about it. You won't get off so easy with the Indians, though."

As his words echoed through Nate's core, Hiram stalked out into the snow.

Sloane motioned toward Nate. "Make sure he's tied good and tight. I'll put snow on the fire."

Nate had to rein in his anger as Danvers's big paws jerked at the leather binding him. His heart raced as the men grabbed the last of their belongings and stomped out toward the wagon. He had to get to the cave before they did. Bright Sun and Eagle Soaring would be no match for these three and their rifles. They wouldn't know to leave before the men came, not unless he could warn them.

It took every bit of his control to stay still until the wagon rumbled out of sight through the curtain of snow. But he used the time to scan the area for something sharp enough to cut his ties. Nothing presented itself, but surely he could find a sharp edge once he was up and moving.

The moment the dark form of the wagon disappeared through the falling white, he attempted to get to his feet. He had to twist to get himself upright with his hands and feet bound, and the numbness in his legs made him totter sideways. He braced himself against the wall until he found his balance. The stinging in his feet and legs brought his entire body to life.

But he didn't have time to waste coddling himself. He scanned the area once more for something sharp, then hopped toward the fire, straining to see anything other than coals and ashes and the snow they'd used to douse the flame. Was there enough heat left in the coals to sear through the leather bindings?

He turned and bent low to feel with his hands tied behind him, but he was able to touch the embers with no problem. Sloane had kicked so much snow on them that they were barely warm. He let out a frustrated groan.

"Give me wisdom, Lord." He'd been silently praying those words with every other breath, but now he mumbled them around the binding still covering his mouth.

One more hard look around the dugout showed nothing that could help free him. He couldn't spare any more time looking.

He had to get to the cave.

After hopping out into the snow, he paused to get his bearings. The men had taken him northwest of the cave, farther away from town. He could just barely see the peak of the mountain containing the cave, rising up through the falling snow, which was finally beginning to lighten.

He started hopping that way. Hopefully, whatever road the men were driving would be roundabout, and he could reach the cave faster moving in a straight line through the woods.

But he wouldn't make much time hopping like a rabbit. His legs burned with the effort, and his sore shoulder throbbed from having his arms strapped behind him for so long. Would all this activity knock the joint out of place again? *God, no.* He couldn't get to Bright Sun and Eagle Soaring in time if he had to fight through that pain, too.

Maybe he could find a rock to scrape the leather bindings against. He'd have to find a sharp one—and quickly. *Help me, Lord.*

Every part of his body ached as more strength drained out of him with every jump. Would he be faster crawling? But he couldn't crawl with his ankles tied and his hands bound behind him. Maybe he could roll? No, he'd be soaked from the snow and he'd have to maneuver around trees.

The burning in his thighs and hips felt like a fire raged inside him. He barely had the strength to stand upright any longer, much less keep driving himself forward.

Maybe if he rested, just for a minute, he could keep going.

He dropped to his knees, but his traitorous body refused to stop him there. He tottered forward and landed nose first in the snow. Frigid ice stung his face, but the pain brought a blessed distraction, cooling the flames leaping through his lower body.

"God, please. Help." He'd never be able to do this.

He was too weak. Too impotent.

An innocent man and child would die, and there was nothing he could do to save them. *Help them, Lord. Use someone else. Whatever it takes.*

TWENTY-FIVE

$\mathcal{L}$aura clutched Bright Sun's hand as they ran, weaving around trees, ducking under limbs, and leaping over fallen logs. The story the girl had told, in quick frantic bursts, intensified every fear she'd harbored all morning. Now instead of vague wonderings, images filled her mind—Nate struck by two men, bound and gagged on the cave floor all night while captors took turns sleeping and standing guard.

Bright Sun and Eagle Soaring had watched it all from the entrance to the other cavern. How the poor girl must have worried, not just for Nate's life, but for her own and her grandfather's as well. No child should be subjected to such fear and violence.

At least they'd not tried to rescue Nate on their own, with only a bow and arrows for protection. When the men took Nate to another hideout at daybreak this morning, Bright Sun had left her grandfather at the cave and followed the men at a distance to see where they took him, then she'd come for Laura.

God, don't let us be too late. Help us.

The fear she'd been fighting pressed in, nearly stealing her breath. She couldn't lose Nate. Not when she was just realizing how much he meant to her. Life without him would be . . . She couldn't think of it.

They had to get to him in time.

Bright Sun pulled her forward at a breathless pace, leading the way. Branches scraped against Laura's face, and her chest burned from drawing in the cold. Were they almost there? They'd passed the cave at least ten minutes ago. How much farther had the men taken him?

Suddenly, the girl jerked to a halt, yanking hard on Laura's arm as she skidded to a stop. "Look." Bright Sun's whisper was frantic as she pointed ahead of them.

Had she spotted the men? Laura stepped in front of the girl as her eyes strained to see what had stopped her.

A dark lump lay in the snow about twenty strides ahead, not the right shape or color to be a downed tree. And it lay on top of fresh snow. An animal?

The form moved, and an arm became visible, wrapped in a dark sleeve.

Laura's heart lurched as she surged forward. "Nate!"

He raised his head higher as she closed the distance between them. She had almost reached him by the time she realized his hands were tied behind his back and a strip of buckskin covered his mouth.

But he was alive. *Oh, God.* "Nate. Oh, God, thank you." She dropped beside him and reached for the cord at his wrists. Even after yanking her mittens off, the knot was pulled too tight for her cold-numbed fingers to work it loose.

"Here." Bright Sun held out a hunting knife, large enough to be the kind warriors carried.

Laura took it and made quick work of slicing through the leather rope around his wrists, even though her hands trembled.

As soon as his arms were free, he rolled over and sat up, fumbling with the tie at the back of his head. Muffled sounds spilled from his mouth, but she couldn't understand anything. His green eyes were frantic about something, though.

She moved behind him. "Be still and let me cut this." Bright Sun's knife pierced through the leather with only a few saws.

Nate jerked the gag away and sucked in a hard, raspy breath, as though he hadn't inhaled for hours. His chest heaved as he spun back to them, his eyes even wider. "Eagle Soaring. Is he still at the cave?" He reached for the knife, but his manner was so desperate, Laura almost pulled the weapon away. But she gave it to him.

"I left him watching from the room where we sleep." Bright Sun's usual mannered cadence tipped high with worry.

"No." Nate slashed through the tie at his ankles with a single vicious swipe. "They've gone to the cave for him. I have to get there." He stumbled to his feet. "Stay here. I'll come back for you."

Without another word, he charged forward, knife still in his grip as he flew over the snowy ground.

Laura's heart hammered as she pushed to her feet. Bright Sun had already started after Nate, despite his command. Laura couldn't heed his words, either, not with both halves of her heart sprinting toward danger. Neither had a gun, and the knife Nate held would be poor protection against the two armed men Bright Sun had spoken of.

Laura patted the satchel holding her pistol, then gripped the bag to keep it from hitting her side as she took off toward the cave.

⊰⊱═◉ ◉═⊰⊱

Nate's heart had never pumped so hard in his chest, not even the moment he'd watched his brother jump in front of Laura's gunshot all those months ago.

He ran with every bit of strength and speed he possessed. In truth, the power surging through his body couldn't be his own. Only minutes before, he'd been lying facedown in the snow, nothing left in his spent body.

But God had given him another chance.

Through Laura and Bright Sun, maybe the Lord would help him reach the cave in time to save Eagle Soaring yet. With every leaping stride he ran, his ears strained to hear a gunshot. Any sign he was too late.

The trees ahead thinned enough to see a clear view of the mountain housing the cave. He slowed to move more quietly. He was approaching from the opposite side from how he usually came, so he would have to run around the base of the mountain—just below the ledge—to get to the rocky section where he could access the trail onto the ledge.

Too bad he couldn't climb straight up like the mountain goats did.

He moved in close to hug the cliff's base as he ran, as light on his toes as he could manage. There was nothing he could do to quiet his heaving breaths, though.

Don't let them hear me, God.

He finally came in sight of the sloped base of the mountain where he could climb onto the ledge path. The view before him made him jerk back, his stomach sinking to his toes.

A freight wagon sat at the edge of the woods.

Fear clamored through his chest, swirling with the anger already there. If those blackguards had killed that innocent old man . . .

He crept forward until he could peer around the edge of rock at the wagon. Was one of the men standing guard? If only Nate had a gun—anything that could take down a man at a distance.

But no outline of a man sat atop the wagon bench. No shadows shifted around the body of the rig. No movement at all except one of the mules stomping an impatient hoof.

Did he dare risk exposing himself to a bullet? He had to.

If all three of the men were inside the cave, who knew how much abuse Eagle Soaring was suffering. Would they torture the man to death?

Just as he was about to dart forward and sprint to the path leading to the ledge, the sound of sharp breathing and running feet pricked his awareness.

He spun, raising the knife to strike.

Bright Sun slipped from the trees to tuck herself close to the base of the cliff as he'd done. A fresh wash of fear and anger sluiced through him. Why hadn't she listened? There was too much danger here. Too much risk that she would be hurt—or killed.

As the girl darted toward him, the noises he'd heard grew louder, but not from the Indian child.

Laura's gray skirt appeared through the trees.

God, no. He fisted his hand around the knife handle, trying to hold in the fear surging through him. Not Laura. What was she doing putting herself in such danger? If something happened to her—if these men hurt her in any way—he would never be able to live with it.

As he waited for them both to catch up to him, he tried to take in slow, steady breaths—anything to quell the panic threatening to undo his focus. He couldn't lose his senses. So much was riding on his ability to take out those three would-be murderers.

It's not on your ability.

The thought crashed over him like a bucket of icy water. Hadn't he just been thinking how only God's strength could have propelled him to the cave at the speed he'd managed?

God had brought them this far. *He* was the only one who could keep them all safe.

Especially Eagle Soaring.

Bright Sun reached him first, and he couldn't fight the urge to reach out and touch her, to rest a hand on her shoulder.

She raised her dark eyes to him, fear churning in their depths.

His heart ached for her. When this was all over, he would take her in his arms and promise to do his best to make sure nothing like this would happen to her or her grandfather again.

If only he could keep that promise.

Lord . . . The ache in his chest made it hard to find words to express what he wanted to say. Why did God allow things like this to happen to people he loved? Why couldn't they just live calm, happy lives without all the pain?

My grace is sufficient. Words he'd planted in his memory during a recent Bible reading. And they brought back another passage. *But we glory in tribulations also: knowing that tribulation worketh patience; and patience, experience; and experience, hope.*

Experience they had in droves. And maybe that did make them stronger when they reached the other side of each struggle.

As for hope . . . His gaze slid to Laura as she puffed to a stop in front of them.

Her eyes held the same churning worry Bright Sun's did. He opened his arms, and she stepped into them. He clung to her, breathing in the rich scent of the woman he loved with every part of his being. If he'd been afraid to acknowledge it before, he'd willingly shout the truth now.

She was too precious for him to keep silent about his love for her.

Did he dare hope she would come to return the feeling? When they finally made it through this tribulation—God *would* bring them through, he had to hold onto that hope—he wouldn't be able to pretend she didn't hold his heart in her strong, competent hands. Whether he deserved her or not, he had to tell her how special she was to him.

With one final inhale of her sweet strength, he pulled back and looked into her beautiful face. A face he wanted to see every day for the rest of his life.

"Laura." Her name slipped out in his raspy voice, not at all the beautiful sound she deserved.

He needed to leave, to get into the cave. He might be too late, but if there was any chance he could help Eagle Soaring, he had to take it. But what if something happened to Nate while he was in there? What if he never had the chance to tell Laura he loved her?

He stared intensely into her beautiful brown eyes. "I love you. I need you to know that."

Her eyes gleamed as she nodded. "Me too." A tiny laugh slipped from her lips. "I mean I love you, too."

Joy soared through him, driving him forward to press a quick, fierce kiss to her mouth. He pulled back after only a second, using every bit of self-control he had. "I have to go. Don't come after me." He slid a pointed look between Laura and Bright Sun. "Please."

Nate pulled away, but Laura clutched his arm. "Wait."

When he turned back, she pressed a pistol into his hand. Fear shone in her eyes again, but she nodded.

He squeezed her fingers. "I'll be careful." Inhaling a strengthening breath, he turned to Bright Sun. "I'll be back with your grandfather."

She nodded, and a sniff slipped out, but she held her jaw clamped tight.

Laura came up beside the girl and wrapped her in a sideways hug. Her eyes had turned glassy again, but her expression spoke of determination.

Protect them, Lord.

Eagle Soaring had to be his focus now. *God, give me strength.*

TWENTY-SIX

Nate had only run three strides when an explosion thundered from the cave entrance. Just like the blast of big powder in a mine shaft.

It had to be a gunshot.

He looked up, but his position wouldn't let him see anything on the ledge above.

More shots ripped through the air.

He had to get in there. As he sprinted forward again, a clattering sounded above, like boots on stone.

He paused again and aimed the gun to the source of the sound. Just above him now.

A loose stone skittered off the ledge, dropping down to the ground on his right. He still couldn't see the man, but he was running over the dangerous path above. A shout sounded.

"Run!"

That growling bark had to be Hiram.

The footsteps clambered along the ledge, loud enough that there must be at least two men running full tilt.

Finally, Sloane appeared ahead, leaping from the rock ledge onto the grassy, boulder-strewn slope. He ran toward the wagon, and Hiram jumped down behind him. His longer legs outran Sloane in four strides, passing the miner in a fluid motion as he kept running toward his rig.

Nate aimed the pistol. The little gun wouldn't have much power or accuracy at this distance. They looked to be leaving. Where was Danvers? Maybe he should save the shot to face off with him.

The indecision swirling in his mind made him hesitate too long. The men were out of range, almost to the wagon. They leapt aboard, Sloane in the bed and Hiram on the bench.

The man hollered a vicious obscenity at the mules, slapping the reins hard. The animals jolted, pushing into their harness. He raised a whip and struck the near team. "Git on!" His bark echoed across the distance.

Nate didn't have time to waste watching. If they were leaving Danvers behind, what had happened in the cave? Nate had to get to Eagle Soaring.

He didn't worry about stealth any longer, just charged forward toward the entrance to the ledge path. When he'd almost reached it, he glanced sideways toward the large freight wagon. The mules pulling the rig had been whipped into a lope, and the conveyance seemed to be rushing toward the road through the woods.

A crack split the air. Not loud enough to be a gunshot, but . . . the wagon tipped toward its front left corner. A wheel must have broken off.

Nate's chest clutched as the left side of the wagon teetered, bouncing as the force of the mules' efforts dragged the axle over the ground. The animals fought to push forward, but the wagon's weight pressed the axle hard into the snow, jerking the rig in an uneven line. The left side struck a thick oak, and an awful crunch of shattering wood filled the air, mixed with the yells of men.

A heartbeat later, flame exploded from the rig, engulfing it in a cloud almost as high as the trees. The ground shook like a violent earthquake, rattling him all the way to his core.

Nate's entire body tensed for danger, but he couldn't take his eyes off the cloud of fire. Within seconds, the puff of flame settled into a smaller blaze.

Frantic, fear-filled shrieks filled the air. Those poor animals. The wagon must have been loaded with crates of blasting powder. He turned toward the ledge, a cloak of sadness weighing his limbs. No matter how heinous the crimes committed, death of God's creation was no small thing.

His body stilled as his eyes took in a figure standing on the ledge. It couldn't be.

Nate blinked, trying to focus his blurry vision. His nerves must have finally snapped.

Surely that wasn't Aaron standing on the ledge. Another figure stood behind him. Doc Micah.

Aaron stepped forward. . . . No, he hobbled forward, swinging on walking sticks. Now a third man appeared behind the doctor . . . could that bent, shuffling form be Eagle Soaring?

Nate took a step back. God could do anything, sure, but

this? Why was Aaron out here? And could Eagle Soaring really be alive?

They were drawing close to Nate now, and Aaron's face tipped into an off-kilter grin. The kind of grin Nate hadn't seen in so many months.

His heart soared. It was all he could do not to stride forward and wrap his brother in a hug.

But the ledge was too narrow for more than one person at a time. Better to wait until they reached the grass. He propped his hands at his waist as he drank in the sight of his brother hobbling toward him.

A hand slipped around his arm, and Nate looked down into Laura's face as she tucked herself beside him. Just exactly where she belonged.

Her expression held the same wonder stirring in his chest. He wrapped his arm around her waist, pulling her closer.

Whatever had transpired here at the cave, only God could have orchestrated this outcome. With the woman he loved nestled beside him, his brother walking toward them, and their two Indian friends safe and whole, he could only imagine what else God would accomplish in their future.

TWENTY-SEVEN

*L*aura stepped through the doorway that separated the Bradleys' residence from the clinic, her heart full from the gathering she'd just left in the kitchen. It'd been two days since the awful ordeal at the cave, and Bright Sun and her grandfather had settled in well at the clinic.

Now, Isaac and Joanna were visiting with little Samuel, and the boy hadn't stopped talking to Bright Sun for the last hour. It turned out Isaac knew a bit of Eagle Soaring's language, too, and he seemed to be gathering details about where their people had gone.

The older man hadn't been hurt by those thieves from the mine—thanks to Aaron, who'd been so worried about Nate, he'd insisted the doctor let him come along to help. They'd arrived just in time to meet Eagle Soaring and defend him from the three men who thought they'd have an easy time with a weak old man and young girl.

When Danvers fell with a single well-placed bullet, the

others decided two Indians weren't worth their lives and freedom.

Thank the Lord for Doc Micah and Aaron.

She paused at the sight of the man standing by the hall window, staring at the white world outside. Aaron.

He turned from looking through the glass to regard her. He held a walking stick under each arm but didn't lean against them for balance. It was remarkable how much he'd improved in the mere two days since he'd become mobile again.

"Good morning." She smiled a greeting, but something about the solemn expression on his face made her pause.

The look wasn't his usual sullen melancholy. More like . . . a soberness.

Had something happened? Her heart stuttered, then scrambled forward. "Is Nate . . . ?" She couldn't finish the question.

"Sleeping." Aaron glanced toward his bedchamber door, the room the brothers had shared these past two nights. "But he was stirring when I left the room, so he'll be underfoot soon." The corners of his mouth curved in what could pass for a smile, but the seriousness didn't leave his eyes as he returned his focus to her.

"What's wrong, then? What is it?"

Aaron turned back to the window and stared through the glass. His jaw flexed, an action she could see clearly since he'd shaved the day before. She'd not had the nerve to ask if the act came from Nate's prompting or if Aaron was taking steps to improve himself on his own. Either way, the change had to be a good sign.

"I need to tell you . . ." Tension laced Aaron's voice, and when he paused, his Adam's apple bobbed. "I need to apologize." He turned toward her again, and pain swirled in his eyes. "For the way I've acted. For blaming you for my troubles. I knew it wasn't right, but I just couldn't face . . ." A sigh leaked out. "I knew what happened was payback for everything I'd done. All those years. I just couldn't make myself face it." Red rimmed his eyes. "None of that was fair to you, and I'm sorry."

Laura's thoughts had frozen at the word *apologize*, and her numb mind struggled to keep up with each comment after that. She eased out a breath. "Thank you for saying that. You can't imagine how many times I've regretted that day."

A corner of his mouth tipped in a sardonic half-grin. "That makes both of us."

The tightness in her chest eased a bit with a little chuckle. "I'll bet so."

Then his face straightened, his eyes showing that soberness again. And an earnestness. "I also wanted to say thank you."

Again, his words stole her breath. He was thanking her? For shattering his leg?

"For not giving up on me. For not showing how much you hate me." His gaze shifted back to the window. "I know you must, at least a little, for everything I was part of. But you've never once made me feel that way."

"I don't hate you." The pressure in her chest finally eased.

He turned back, and it wasn't surprise shimmering in his

eyes so much as doubt. "I'm glad." After a pause, he added, "Even though I'm not sure I believe you."

Part of her wanted to smile at his attempt at light words, but his pain was still so fresh. He was finally facing it—the first step. Yet if she could make the path to healing easier for him, she would in a heartbeat.

"I know I'm not the man I should be—I'm certainly not the man my brother wants me to be—but I need you to know I'm trying to do better." His eyes shone with that earnestness again. His throat worked in a swallow.

"I'm glad to hear it." She gathered her courage. "God can help you if you ask Him." Sharing her faith was still so new, but that hadn't been as hard as she'd expected.

Aaron's mouth tipped up again, and this time real humor touched his eyes. "You and Nate really are a good fit." He held the look for a moment, then nodded, as though he'd confirmed something inside himself. "I'm trying. Let's just leave it at that. Me and God are talking finally, so we'll see if anything comes out of it."

For the first time since she'd come into Aaron's presence, the knot in her middle finally unclenched, and the last of the weight lifted from her shoulders. She couldn't have stopped her smile if she'd wanted to. "I'm glad."

A sound from down the hall drew her attention as Nate stepped through the bedroom door. He paused, standing in the hallway, strong and tall.

Her heart surged with a love she no longer tried to deny.

He sent her one of those off-kilter smiles that made her stomach flip, and she jerked her focus away from him to stop the heat from surging up her neck. Especially with his brother watching. "I, um, came to tell you both the morning meal is ready in the kitchen. You're welcome to eat any time."

The scuffle of footsteps sounded from the corridor leading to the kitchen. She turned to see Samuel pulling Bright Sun by the arm as he rambled on to her. "C'mon. My daddy and I play it all the time. It's so fun."

Laura stepped aside to allow them passage, and Samuel paused long enough to send her a grin. "I'm gonna show Bright Sun the new game me an' Daddy Isaac made up. She's gonna love it."

Bright Sun's grin was sheepish, but she let Samuel pull her toward the front door. They made an incongruous pair—the barely-six-year-old boy with his red hair and energy enough for three lads, and the staid Indian girl who stood at least a head taller than him.

But the picture soaked through Laura's chest like warm tea and honey soothe an aching throat. The girl needed the chance just to be a child. And no one could pull her into childish abandon like Samuel Watson Bowen.

"Guess I'll head to the kitchen, then." Aaron's voice pulled her back to the present.

She nodded as he walked past, then she turned her focus to the one remaining person in the hallway.

A smile quirked Nate's lips as he strode toward her, and when he stopped in front of her, his nearness seemed to magnify his presence. He settled those warm green eyes on her, roaming her face with a look radiating so much love that her heart squeezed with the intensity of that exact emotion welling inside her.

He reached out a hand, and she slipped hers into his, allowing him to pull her a step nearer, so that only a hand-breadth separated them. His gaze never left her face. His eyes never stopped their caress. "I need to tell you something, Laura Hannon, and I don't want to wait another minute to do it."

She could barely breathe as she soaked in every word. The sweetness in his look.

"I love you. I know I don't deserve you, but I promise there's not another man alive who could love you more. You can take as long as you want to get used to the idea. I can be patient if I have to, but I want you in my life. I want to be the one who makes you laugh, the one there when you need a sidekick on your next adventure." His hand tightened the tiniest bit around hers, and his voice grew hoarse. "I want to protect you and never let you forget how special you are. How much you're loved."

Oh, dear God, you're good to me. Tears of overwhelming happiness welled in her eyes, cutting off both her breath and words. She could only release a strangled laugh as joy surged through her.

She stepped into his waiting arms, releasing his hand and wrapping her arms around him as the tears spilled down her cheeks. He wrapped his arms around her, locking her tight against him. She wouldn't have left his embrace for anything in the world.

"So . . . does that mean I'll need to be patient awhile?"

Nate's deep voice rumbled in her ear, not covering up the humor in his tone.

She chuckled a shaky laugh as she pulled back enough to look into his handsome face. He raised his eyebrows and cocked his sideways grin. "No need for patience on my account, although I'd be happy to wait awhile before we have any more adventures. At least the kind that involves men with guns."

His face sobered, and his arms around her tightened. "I plan to do my very best to make sure you never have to face another gun pointed your way. You can be sure that'll be in every one of my prayers, too."

With that, he sealed his promise with a kiss so achingly tender, she couldn't imagine ever loving him more than she did now. The rest of her life with this man may not be long enough.

Epilogue

$\mathcal{A}$re you sure you know where we're going?" Nate couldn't help asking once more, if only to see the sassy smile Laura sent his way. He'd never seen her so happy—almost giddy—as she was today.

"Be patient. The surprise will be worth it, I promise." She sent him that gleeful smile, but her attention quickly turned back to the trail ahead of her as she guided her horse through the woods. She'd taken a wandering route through the land-scape, maybe to keep him from recognizing the scenery, but he was fairly certain they were somewhere near his old camp. A pair of perfectly spaced aspens they'd passed a few minutes back were ones he'd used to stretch hides.

The ring of an ax blade sounded from ahead, then a man's shout. Nate's body coiled. Was there a threat ahead? Perhaps someone in trouble?

"Stop, Laura." He nudged his horse up alongside hers. "Wait here while I see who that is."

"No." She grabbed his arm, pulling him backward. "That's part of the surprise."

He glanced at her as he halted his horse beside hers. His pulse pounded, all his instincts on alert. He couldn't let her ride into danger. He'd made a promise—to her, to God, and even to himself—he'd never let that happen again. "Who is it?"

Her lips pressed in frustration. "They're not a threat."

Could he trust that statement? He had to know for sure. He couldn't leave Laura's safety to chance. *Not to chance. To God.*

He eased out a frustrated breath as the thought pounded through him. *Lord?*

Hadn't he learned this lesson already? That God was the only one truly in charge? Yet how could he let her ride forward without knowing for sure what lay ahead?

God knew. He'd have to trust in the Lord's protection.

"I promise, Nate. This is a good surprise. It's like that verse in Jeremiah. God has plans for peace and not evil. Plans to give us hope for the future. I think you'll be amazed at what He has planned this time."

Peace slid through him as he lost himself in the fathomless brown eyes of the woman he loved with every part of his being. He reached out, letting her hand slide down his arm and into his palm, taking her gloved fingers in his own.

"I'm amazed at a lot of things these days." A ball of emotion lodged in his throat, and he swallowed to clear it.

Her smile turned impish. "Let's get moving, then."

He let her take the lead again, and this time he did his best to enjoy the scenery. Yet as they progressed, the ax blows grew louder. Not just one man cutting—at least two or three. Occasional calls and shouts mixed with the blows, but the trees muffled the words so he couldn't make them out.

The scenery around them looked as familiar as his left hand, but he couldn't quite place it. Someone had been cutting trees through here, leaving stumps scattered all around.

At last, the trees ahead thinned, showing people moving around the half-built frame of a cabin.

His stomach dropped with realization. *His* cabin.

Laura had led him around to enter from behind, instead of the trail he usually took. And where he'd managed to lay a single foundation, the logs now rose up almost to the height of a man.

Three men were hoisting a log up a pole ramp, settling it in place to form the start of another layer.

Emotion warred within his chest. Had someone else taken over his claim? Built on what he'd started? But Laura said this was a surprise for him. How could all these men working here have anything to do with him?

He sent a quick glance her way to see if her expression would give him answers.

She nearly bounced in the saddle, her face glowing with unfettered joy. "Isaac and Doc Micah mentioned to a few men from the mine that you hadn't been able to finish your cabin. They all wanted to pitch in and help."

His mind struggled to make sense of what he was hearing and seeing. The words she spoke formed complete sentences, but they couldn't be right. Isaac and the doc? And other men from the mine? Why would they do this?

He turned back to the scene before them. Isaac strolled across the open area, an ax over his shoulder. When he saw the two of them, he waved and shifted his direction toward them.

Nate's gut clenched as the man approached. Isaac had been one of the founding members of their gang of thieves, but he'd had the good sense to get out after the first year.

Now, a full decade later, Isaac had finally pushed away the chains of the past and made a new life with Joanna and Samuel. An example Nate wanted to follow with everything in him.

Isaac saluted when he reached their horses. "Come on in and see the progress we've made."

His words blew the last of the fog from Nate's mind, thrusting him into action. He leaned forward and swung off his rented gelding, helping Laura down a moment later. They tied the animals to a tree, then fell into step beside Isaac as he moved toward the log frame.

So many questions spun in his chest that he had to work to separate them into logical thoughts. "How did you get so much done this morning?" According to the sun, they'd not even reached midmorning. Even with the half-dozen men he saw working, they couldn't have completed this much since sunrise.

"We worked last Sunday afternoon, too."

Nate spun to his friend. "You're jesting. I would have helped. I didn't know."

Isaac shrugged. "We wanted to have a bit of it done before we let you in on the secret." He slid Nate a half-grin. "Didn't want you to find a way to stop us."

He would have tried, too. These men shouldn't be doing all this for him.

He looked over at Laura. It was for her, too, though. He'd not officially asked for her hand, but he'd made it clear he planned to as soon as he had a decent place for her to live. Now that Aaron was starting to help pay their debt, this would allow them to take that next step.

His focus shifted toward the cabin. This home would be far more than decent. Had he really laid the foundation so big? He'd only been planning for a single room, at least for now. Maybe adding on later.

Isaac cleared his throat. "We, uh, took the liberty of adding a few rooms off the back, and we're going high enough for a loft. Thought that might come in handy."

The words pressed into Nate with a new weight. A couple of rooms? That would be enough for . . .

He looked back at Laura. Her shining brown eyes met his, and the hopeful joy made him want to pull her into his arms, twirl her around, and never let her go.

She slipped her hand into his, and he gripped it as hard as he dared.

This woman. She must have had a part in coordinating this work. As unworthy as he was, he couldn't help the joy that slipped into his own chest.

With a solid hold on Laura's hand, he turned back to Isaac. "Thank you. I had no idea. Thank you isn't near enough, but—"

Isaac reached out and gripped Nate's upper arm. "It's what friends do for each other."

Friends. Did he dare let himself believe? Dare accept the help these men offered? He wasn't worthy, but maybe that didn't matter so much. He'd happily repay the kindness any time he saw opportunity.

He locked his gaze solidly on Isaac's and nodded. "It's what friends do."

Nate's body ached in the very best way. The last of the men were packing up their axes and building supplies, but he had to take a minute to revel in the sight before him.

A cabin. Almost fully completed.

They'd built up the sides and part of the roof, and the men all promised to return next week to finish the shingles and the interior. How was it possible his cabin would be finished within seven more days?

Not only *his* cabin.

A swish of skirts sounded beside him, and Laura slipped herself under his arm, where she fit perfectly. She rested her head on his shoulder and pressed a hand to his chest, the warmth of her palm increasing the beat of his heart.

For a moment, he let himself linger there, simply enjoying her touch, the sweet scent of her hair, the softness of her melding against him.

He brushed a kiss to her hair. "Does two weeks give you enough time?" He wasn't sure he could stand waiting two more weeks before marrying this woman, but he'd need that time to finish a few pieces of furniture.

She pulled back enough to look up at him. "Sunday two weeks from now?"

He looked down at her, almost falling into the rich brown of her eyes. "The reverend should be back by then. We can have a ceremony after church, if you'd like. Or another time. Whatever you want." He'd take her to the top of the tallest mountain to marry her if that's what she asked.

She laid her head back on his shoulder, and he tucked her in close. She let out a sigh. "I suppose. If we have to wait that long."

His blood surged, and he gripped her waist tighter. "I'll take you to Lanton's now, if you prefer. He's been deputized to serve as a justice of the peace. We can be man and wife before the sun sets." He was only half-teasing, but he pressed his lips in to nibble the side of her neck with a little growl.

She ducked away with a giggle, pulling loose from his arms. He grabbed at her, capturing her hand so she couldn't go far.

She raised her brows at him. "I think waiting a couple weeks would be good for you. Maybe make you a little more eager." Her eyes sparkled, and he had to force steady breaths to rein in what his body really wanted to do.

She didn't seem to notice her effect on him, just slipped back into his arms in the same position, resting her head on his shoulder. He soaked her in, working to calm the excitement inside him. Working to simply relax and enjoy her presence.

This woman.

After a few minutes of quiet, her voice surfaced with no

hint of teasing. "Have you thought about what we should do with the extra room?"

The question gave his mind something to latch onto other than Laura's nearness. "Not yet. I'm still taking in the fact that there'll be a wood floor. That's more than I thought I'd be able to manage."

Her chuckle bubbled against him. "It's going to be so nice. All of it."

Then she looked up at him again, her expression taking on a hesitant look. "What do you think about asking Eagle Soaring and Bright Sun to come stay with us?"

The words settled in his chest with a sense of rightness. "Really? You'd like that?" Much of their care would fall to Laura while he worked. He couldn't lay that on her lightly.

She nodded. "Eagle Soaring told Isaac their people should come back through here in the spring. We can help get them back to their family. Or if we're not able to find the tribe . . ." The same hope burgeoning in his chest also shone in her eyes.

He reached his hand up to cradle her jaw, holding his other arm around her waist. "Eagle Soaring may not have many years left." The man had regained some strength while he stayed at the clinic, but he still walked in a stooped shuffle with the help of a cane, and often slept much of the day. "That means if we don't find their family, Bright Sun would stay with us?"

She nodded again. "It would be up to her, but maybe we could . . . raise her? As our own? But only if we can't find her real family." Laura didn't seem to breathe as she waited for him to respond.

For his own part, the love swelling in his chest made it hard to take in air. This remarkable woman God had placed in his life. His throat wouldn't work to form words, so he drew her closer to show his agreement another way.

Her kiss sank through him, weaving together strands of hope and purpose that he'd never thought he'd be allowed to possess.

Together they could join in with this community of people who'd accepted them. Together they could make a difference, one person at a time. Giving back in the abundant measure God used to pour so much grace into their own lives.

Together.

USA Today bestselling author **Misty M. Beller** writes romantic mountain stories set on the 1800s frontier and woven with the truth of God's love. She was raised on a farm in South Carolina, so her Southern roots run deep. Growing up, her family was close, and they continue to maintain those ties today. Her husband and children now add another dimension to her life, keeping her both grounded and crazy. God has placed a desire in Misty's heart to combine her love for Christian fiction and the simpler ranch life, writing historical novels that display God's abundant love through the twists and turns in the lives of her characters. Learn more and see Misty's other books at www.MistyMBeller.com.

Sign Up for Misty's Newsletter

Keep up to date with Misty's news on book releases and events by signing up for her email list at mistymbeller.com.

More from Misty M. Beller

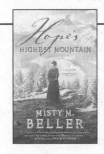

On her way to deliver vaccines to a mining town in the Montana Territory, Ingrid Chastain never anticipated a terrible accident would leave her alone and badly injured in the wilderness. When rescue comes in the form of a mysterious mountain man, she's hesitant to trust him, but the journey ahead will change their lives more than they could have known.

Hope's Highest Mountain
HEARTS OF MONTANA #1

You May Also Like . . .

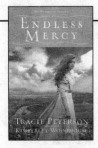

When Madysen Powell's supposedly dead father shows up, her gift for forgiveness is tested and she's left searching for answers. Daniel Beaufort arrives in Nome, longing to start fresh after the gold rush leaves him with only empty pockets, and finds employment at the Powell dairy. Will deceptions from the past tear apart their hopes for a better future?

Endless Mercy by Tracie Peterson and Kimberley Woodhouse
THE TREASURES OF NOME #2
traciepeterson.com; kimberleywoodhouse.com

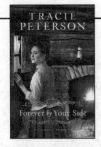

Accompanied by her best friend, Thomas Lowell, Constance Browning returns from studying in the East to catalog the native peoples of Oregon—and to prove that her missionary parents aren't involved in a secret conspiracy to goad the oppressed tribes to war. As tensions rise amid shocking revelations, Constance may also have a revelation of the heart.

Forever by Your Side by Tracie Peterson
WILLAMETTE BRIDES #3
traciepeterson.com

After receiving word that her sweetheart has been lost during a raid on a Yankee vessel, Cordelia Owens clings to hope. But Phineas Dunn finds nothing redemptive in the horrors of war, and when he returns, sure that he is not the hero Cordelia sees, they both must decide where the dreams of a new America will take them, and if they will go there together.

Dreams of Savannah by Roseanna M. White
roseannamwhite.com

◈ BETHANYHOUSE

More from Bethany House

Troubled by painful memories, Olivia Rosetti is singularly focused on running her maternity home for troubled women. Darius Reed is determined to protect his daughter from the prejudice that killed his wife by marrying a society darling. But when he's suddenly drawn to Olivia, they will learn if love can prove stronger than the secrets and hurts of the past.

A Haven for Her Heart by Susan Anne Mason
REDEMPTION'S LIGHT #1
susanannemason.net

In this epistolary novel from the WWII home front, Johanna Berglund is forced to return to her small Midwestern town to become a translator at a German prisoner of war camp. There, amid old secrets and prejudice, she finds that the POWs have hidden depths. When the lines between compassion and treason are blurred, she must decide where her heart truly lies.

Things We Didn't Say by Amy Lynn Green
amygreenbooks.com

After being robbed on her trip west to save her ailing sister, Greta Nilsson is left homeless and penniless. Struggling to get his new ranch running, Wyatt McQuaid is offered a bargain—the mayor will invest in a herd of cattle if Wyatt agrees to help the town become more respectable by marrying...and the mayor has the perfect woman in mind.

A Cowboy for Keeps by Jody Hedlund
COLORADO COWBOYS #1
jodyhedlund.com

BETHANYHOUSE